The Little Exile

Jeanette S. Arakawa

Stone Bridge Press • *Berkeley, California*

Published by
Stone Bridge Press
P. O. Box 8208, Berkeley, CA 94707
sbp@stonebridge.com • www.stonebridge.com

Front cover inset: Photograph of the author as a child, courtesy Jeanette S. Arakawa. Front cover background and frontispiece photograph: "Camp entrance, Jerome concentration camp, Arkansas, June 18, 1944," Densho Encyclopedia, http://encyclopedia.densho.org/sources/en-denshopd-i37-00798-1/.

Book design and layout by Linda Ronan.

Printed in the United States of America.

Library of Congress Cataloging-in-Publication data on file.

P-ISBN: 978-1-61172-036-5
E-ISBN: 978-1-61172-923-8

To Mama and Papa

Note to the Reader

Although the characters in this story are fictional, the story itself is not. It is based on my childhood just prior to and just after World War II. It is a collection of recollections, over seventy years passed. From this vantage point, what I vividly recall are incidents devoid of much detail. The mundane of that period is missing from the store of my aging memory. As a result, the details I have provided to accompany the incidents are as I imagined they might have been. I have changed the names of the people in the story to protect their privacy, as well as their innocence in the event the details of my memory deviate significantly from theirs.

The songs and singers noted at the beginning of each chapter are intended to provide the ambiance of the period—music I recall hearing on the radio at the time.

Japanese was the language spoken in my home. That is to say, my parents spoke in Japanese with a sprinkling of English, and I responded in English sprinkled with Japanese. For expediency, and because of my inability to do dialects well, I have written most of the dialogue in my version of standard English.

Writing has caused me to retrace a journey long passed: occasionally joyful, occasionally painful. I believe that underlying everyone's experience are threads that weave us all together into one large tapestry. It is my hope that you are able to find a common thread in my story as you read it.

JSA

The Little Exile

CHAPTER 1

"Polly Wolly Doodle (All the Day)"
SHIRLEY TEMPLE

There was a Murphy bed in the apartment in back of a dry cleaning shop in the Polk district in San Francisco, California. It stood concealed behind a revolving panel door during the day and revealed itself every evening as it emerged from its hiding place and descended into the space where a dining table had previously stood. *born*

On October 6, 1932, the dining table remained shoved into the corner, and the bed lay in the middle of the room, although it was mid-day. That's because something very important was about to happen.

At exactly one o'clock, a stork magically appeared and plunked down its delivery in the middle of the bed. Me.

The stork got the time and place all wrong, but my mother said it wasn't the stork's fault. It was I who was so eager to join the family that I insisted on arriving a week early. According to Japanese custom, it was the year of the monkey. People born under this sign are supposed to be intelligent and clever, but mischievous. My parents named me "Shizuye" (Japanese for "quiet blessing"), in hopes that I would live up to my name, and not my sign. We were in the middle of "the Great Depression," and my older brother, Brian, was just beginning to toddle. They didn't need another challenge.

As I grew older, I loved standing at the front door of our dry cleaning shop, which was home to my parents, Brian, and me. By day the wood-framed glass door was a portal to the outside world. I watched people in passing cars and streetcars return my wave and saw tiny beads of water dance on the sidewalk when it rained. When I was lucky, I saw kids skating down the hill making sparks by dragging one skate as a brake. Or I saw a horse struggling to get its footing on the brick pavement and slippery streetcar tracks, as it pulled the junk-man's wagon. Or I made faces at the organ grinder's dancing monkey as he pressed his face on the glass.

Against the darkness of night, the door was magically transformed into a full-length mirror. Then I, Shizuye Mitsui, became the view. I, with my short, straight black hair with bangs cut in a line just above eyes shaped like quarter moons, floating on a face the color of plain Ovaltine. Walking, skipping, dancing, or just twisting my face into funny shapes.

One evening I came running from the back and headed straight for the closed door. I had just put on the new striped seersucker dress with matching white bolero Mama had sewn me. As I stood examining Mama's handiwork and looking at my skinny arms jutting out of the broad sleeves, I caught a glimpse of Mrs. Terrace, our customer, out of the corner of my eye. I hadn't noticed before that she was at the counter talking to my mother. I knew it was Mrs. Terrace, because she was wearing her brown coat with the dead red fox attached to the collar. Suddenly, the sickly smell of damp fur and stale perfume struck my nose. Too late to escape. I turned and looked up.

"You look just like Shirley Temple . . . ," she said through puckered red lips as she bent down. She grabbed my cheeks in her gloved hands and lifted my face up. She drew it close to the glass-eyed fox that dangled from her neck. I didn't like her, and I didn't like her fox. I definitely didn't look like Shirley Temple! Did I have blonde sausage curls that stuck out of the top of my head? Were my eyes round, and light brown, sitting deep in a dimpled and peach-colored face? My friend, Beverly Jensen, the Norwegian princess, looked like Shirley Temple. Maybe. But, not me. I wanted to pull away and run, but I had been taught to be polite. I said what I thought I should say.

"Thank you, Mrs. Fox."

"Mrs. Terrace," Mama corrected.

★ ★ ★

Beverly Jensen wasn't really a Norwegian princess. We just pretended. I once wore a costume for a Buddhist church parade that included a delicate gold crown which sat perched on a little pillow on top of my head. I imagined I was a Japanese princess. I told Beverly about it, and that's how the "princess" game got its start.

There was a box in the corner of the Helen Wills Playground clubhouse, where we often played. It brimmed with dresses, skirts, robes, scarves, and hats of every kind, shape, and color. My friends and I would find what we needed from the box to transport us to our parents' native countries. I became a Japanese princess—Gina, an Italian princess—and Estella, a Mexican Princess. All our parents were immigrants, here to become Americans. It was fun to pretend we were in their countries.

In my case, many said that Papa resembled the emperor of Japan. They were both short, had mustaches and heavy curved eyebrows arched over dark round eyes. Although Madame Chiang Kai-shek was Chinese, some said that my mother, with high cheekbones, round hairline, and angular face, resembled her. That didn't exactly make me look like the princess of Japan. Actually, it didn't make me anything. But I thought it was kind of interesting. Anyway, when my friends and I were together at the Helen Wills Playground clubhouse, the dress-up corner overflowed with "royalty."

Beverly Jensen was my best friend. She lived in an apartment down Polk and around the corner on Broadway. We were the same age, but when we started school, she went to Sherman on Green Street across Van Ness Avenue, while I went to Spring Valley on Jackson on the other side of Larkin Street. We played together a lot because we could go to each other's houses without crossing a street.

I had lunch at her house once.

"We're having rice, Shizuye!" Beverly said. "You like rice, don't you? You have to come over!"

She was right. I did like rice. Actually, I didn't feel as though I had really eaten, unless the meal included rice. It was very nice of Beverly to invite me. I had never had lunch at a friend's house before, so I could hardly wait until Saturday.

I was at her apartment shortly before twelve. Beverly met me at the door and led me to their breakfast nook in the kitchen. Mrs. Jensen was busy at the stove. She was heavyset and had very short "bobbed" hair, parted on the side and pushed into waves. She wore a pink apron splashed with different colored daisies, and ruffles that traveled along all the edges, including the straps. It belonged on a slender lady with long hair, I thought. But I didn't say anything.

She looked up from the pot she was stirring and welcomed me.

"I'm so glad you're having lunch with us," she said. "Why don't you take the seat next to the window."

There were four matching white chairs around a matching white table. The chairs had tall backs that tapered to rounded pieces of flat wood decorated with flowers. They were supported by five rods that rose out of the backs of the seats. The rods were also handles for moving the chairs. I grabbed the rods in the chair closest to the window and dragged the chair back from the table and scooted into the seat. The table was set for two people. Beverly sat down across from me.

At my place, there was a large spoon placed on a red-and-white checkered napkin on one side of a bowl with a broad rim, and a knife, on the other. There was a small plate above the spoon and a glass above the knife. Rolls peeked out from under a napkin placed in a basket in the middle of the table.

"Thank you for inviting me," I said as I sat down.

As soon as I was seated, Mrs. Jensen came to the table with her pot and started to spoon out little bits of white stuff into the unusually shaped plate. The rice I was accustomed to stuck together and was served in a bowl that I could pick up and put to my mouth. As I sat there wondering if I would be able to do that with this strangely shaped dish-bowl and move the rice across the brim without spilling it, she leaned in between my eyes and the rice. In her right hand, she held a spoon brimming with sugar and moved it like a wand over the rice and sprinkled the white dust all over it. Then came the milk. As soon as her right hand finished its job, her left emptied the contents of a small pitcher over the sugared rice. I watched as the little grains of rice struggled to stay afloat in the sea of milk. Soon the mound flattened and sank out of sight. She repeated the sugar and milk thing on Beverly's rice.

As soon as Beverly was served she sat up in her chair and rubbed her hands together. "Hmmm," she said. "Rice is my favorite thing to eat!" Then she stirred and spooned it to her mouth. She closed her eyes and smiled as she chewed and swallowed.

I watched her in amazement. Well, she seems to be enjoying it, it probably isn't as bad as it looks, I thought.

Then she looked up and said, "Why aren't you eating?"

I smiled and picked up the spoon. I stirred and scooped a little and put it in my mouth.

I loved rice, I loved sugar, and I loved milk. So, how could all the things I loved so much taste so bad when they were all put together?

Then to my surprise, Mrs. Jensen said, "You don't have to eat it, if you don't want to, Shizuye." That's amazing, I thought. She was able to read my mind! I put down my spoon and filled up on rolls.

★ ★ ★

What I liked best was skating with Beverly on the sidewalks around our block. It was our goal to be able to skate down Van Ness Avenue all the way from Pacific to Broadway. But we weren't able to control our speed down the steep and slick hill. We had conquered Polk Street, though, which was as steep as Van Ness, but older and slower. Parts of the sidewalk, broken down over the years, had been replaced by a hodge-podge of rough squares of cement, which slowed us down. There were also lamp posts on the right edge of the sidewalk that we could grab if we were going too fast or trying to avoid pedestrians emptying out of the stores or apartments along the way. But, of all the streets, flat, smooth, broad Pacific Avenue was the most fun. We had only driveways to the auto repair shop and garage to contend with. We could do fancy stops and turns and pretend we were the ice-skating movie star Sonja Henie. Sonja Henie was from Norway, just like Beverly's grandmother.

"When I was in Los Angeles visiting my cousin, I was able to jump off high curbs with my skates, because there was almost no traffic," Beverly said.

That sounded exciting. I hoped that I would be able to go there someday and see for myself.

Beverly also played violin. When I went over to her apartment one morning, she opened the door, and to my surprise, she had a violin sticking straight out of her neck through a folded hanky. Tears were streaming down her face. It must be as painful as it looks, I thought. But it turned out it wasn't the violin that was making her cry. It was her mother.

"Beverly!" she screamed from the kitchen. "You know you can't go out until you finish practicing your violin! I told you not to answer the door!"

Beverly told me later that her mother wanted her to play violin, because she was a great fan of Yahoody.

"What's a 'Yahoody'?" I asked.

"You've never heard of Yehudi Menuhin?" she said dropping her jaw.

"He's a famous violinist! The most famous in the whole world! And you haven't heard of him?" She went on, "And he started playing when he was three."

"Oh. So you're going to be a famous violinist like Yahoody."

"My mother would like that."

"Well, I'm going to be a famous singer some day. And I would like that. I don't know about my mother."

"I've heard you sing, Marie," said Beverly. "And you need to practice more if you want to be famous."

When we weren't playing at Beverly's, we were at the playground. Actually, that's where we first met. The playground was on Broadway, but across Polk Street. It was down the hill, across the street, and around the corner from the cleaners. Brian, who was two years older, took me most of the time. When he didn't, Mama watched for traffic as I dashed across Polk Street to the furniture store with the enormous "ufolstreer" sign stretched across the top of the building. Going home, I looked for the nice lady with dark wavy hair and thin milky skin in the store to get me back across safely. Thin blue lines traced paths on the side of her forehead. Mama said those were blood vessels that could be seen through her thin skin. She was tall and skinny. Mrs. Jensen's daisy-covered apron would have been perfect on her.

"Thank you, ufolstreer lady," I would say. She would just smile.

One of the proudest moments of my life was when I figured out what that sign above the entrance to the store actually read.

Brian was disgusted with me for calling her the "ufolstreer" lady. He wouldn't say the word properly for me, but he helped me figure it out.

"Try to break the word down into syllables," he said. "You're making the word more complicated than it is."

"Up-hol-ster-er. Upholsterer!" I shouted.

"About time . . . ," said Brian. I was six.

I could hardly wait to use it. The next day, after playground, I told Brian to go home without me, so I could get help crossing Polk.

"Upholsterer Lady! Upholsterer Lady!" I shouted into the store.

She ran from the back with outstretched arms and scooped me up.

"You've finally figured out how to pronounce 'upholsterer'!" she said as she held me tight. "You're all grown up now! Let me show you what it means." She took my hand and led me to the back of the store.

"From now on, please call me Mrs. Pringle," she continued. We walked through the neat, orderly showroom to the back of the store. There in the large work space were skeletons of chairs and sofas stripped bare of their stuffing and covering. It was as messy as the front area was neat. On one side of the room cluttered with bits of fabric, white puffs of cotton, and scraps of wood, a woman was hunched over a sewing machine stitching together oddly shaped pieces of material. A short distance away, a skinny man in dirty white coveralls and straggly brown hair on the edges of his balding head and upper lip tugged and pulled on a beautiful blue cover and stretched it over a padded chair. Then he pulled the nails that stuck out like stiff whiskers from under his mustache and hammered them into place to hold the cloth.

"Does he ever swallow a nail holding them in his mouth like that?" I whispered to Mrs. Pringle.

"No. But don't you try that at home," she said and then continued, "When a chair or sofa gets worn out, many people choose to have it reupholstered rather than throwing it out. That's another way of saying we replace the stuffing and cover it with new fabric."

As she spoke I thought about our sofa at home. It had a nasty stain on it from the time Brian cracked a raw egg on my head. He said he thought it was hard-boiled. Because of the lump on my head he created, Mama's attention was then focused on me and my gummy hair, and she didn't get around to the sofa until much later. By that time, the stains were set.

"We have a sofa at home that could use upholstering." I told Mrs. Pringle.

"I can come over sometime and take a look," she said as we walked out of the store.

When I got home, I told Mama about my visit with Mrs. Pringle and her offer.

"The sofa is fine just the way it is," Mama said, "And I don't want you going in the back of their store like that anymore."

"Why not? Mrs. Pringle invited me . . ."

"It's just not a place for little girls."

"Why not?"

"You just do what I say!"

★ ★ ★

The rings at Helen Wills Playground were my favorite. There was a ramp for little people like me who couldn't reach them from the ground. I would make my way around the circle of rings, which dangled like limp branches on a metal tree. My goal was to be able to skip the closest ring and lunge for the second one.

Although I rubbed tan bark on my hands, I developed blisters, which soon became hard yellow ridges on my palms at the roots of my fingers. I was proud of them. That's how you could tell who played on the rings. I liked to compare mine with Beverly's.

On Saturday mornings at Helen Wills, there was an amateur hour contest at the clubhouse, and kids of all ages entered. Beverly played her violin, and I sang, though not together. I often forgot the words and had to make them up as I went along. I guess that's what Beverly meant when she said I needed to practice more. But I had a lot of fun and a lot of fans. Since the one who got the most applause won, I won often. The playground director would pin a short piece of colored satin ribbon on my dress with a tiny brass safety pin.

★ ★ ★

Mr. Goldberg, a short, stout, Jewish man from Russia with reddish hair combed straight back, ran the coffee shop next door to our cleaners. He was also a fan of mine. He had no children and no family except for a sister who lived far away. He had large, droopy brown eyes on a sad face, which brightened whenever he saw me at the door.

One foggy Monday morning in July, I went to watch the doughnut machine.

"Good morning, Marie," he said as I entered his shop.

"Good morning, Mr. Goldberg. Do you notice something different about me today?" I asked as I climbed up on the stool.

"Umm. Let me see now. New sweater?"

"No."

"New shoes?" he asked peering over the counter and down at my feet.

"No. I'll give you a hint. It's not new clothes."

"Hmm. Is that a new blue ribbon that is shining so brightly I can hardly see?" He said shielding his eyes with his arm.

"Yes! You're so . . . good!"

"Observant?"

"So observant!"

"You won again at the playground amateur hour! Maybe, one day you can sing on the Major Bowes Amateur Hour."

"Maybe."

"Did you sing a Japanese song again?"

"This time I sang a song Stella taught me. I'm sure you know it. It's on the radio all the time. 'El Rancho Grande.'"

"It's one of my favorites. Are you going to sing it for me?"

"Well, not right now. I'm anxious to watch the doughnuts."

"Okay."

The doughnut machine occupied most of the show-window area and could be viewed from the outside.

"I feel so . . . good to be sitting inside," I said looking at the little boy standing on the other side of the window with his mother.

"Privileged?"

"Yes."

The oil was hot and ready to go. He pressed some buttons and pulled some levers, and the chugging and churning started. A thick blob began oozing out of the doughnut shaper thing and finally dropped a well-formed blob into the hot oil. It sizzled as it fell to the bottom of the vat. Then it slowly rose to the top, brown and crisp, releasing its delicious aroma. Every so often a new blob fell into the oil and up rose a beautifully formed doughnut.

"Mr. Goldberg! One doughnut done. Two doughnuts done . . . ," I said, and continued until he came over and scooped them out with a wire basket.

"I wish I could give you free samples, but business is bad . . ." The sadness returned to his face. "We have to wait until business gets better."

"That's all right, Mr. Goldberg. I don't need a sample. It was a priblege just watching them cook."

I was there when the utility company turned off Mr. Goldberg's electricity because he couldn't pay his bill. Mr. Goldberg watched as the electricity man climbed up the pole and did something. His doughnut machine stopped and his lights went out.

After the man left, Mr. Goldberg took a ladder outside and leaned it against the pole. Still in his apron, he climbed up the ladder and stretched for the foot rests mounted barely within his reach and pulled and shinnied his short, stout body up the pole. He did something up by the wires and the lights went back on in the store and the doughnut machine began to chug.

"Without electricity I can't run my restaurant and I won't be able to pay my bills," he said. "Including the electricity bill."

★ ★ ★

When I was five and a half, I started kindergarten at Spring Valley School on Jackson Street. Papa took me the first day.

The teacher, Miss Czenchowski, looked at my name, Shizuye, on my birth certificate and said that it was too difficult to pronounce.

"She'll have an easier time in school if her friends don't have to struggle with her name," she said. "I think you should give her an English name."

Mary Pickford was one of Papa's favorite actresses, so he said, "Mary is good name." My father had a heavy Japanese accent. The teacher thought he said "Marie." And that's what she wrote on my records. That's how I came to be called "Marie."

CHAPTER 2

"When You Wish Upon a Star"
JIMINY CRICKET, FROM *PINOCCHIO*

I loved going to the movies. Occasionally we went as a family and it was then we saw pictures like *Pinocchio, Snow White and the Seven Dwarfs,* and *The Wizard of Oz.* My father also took us to see another kind of movie. The one I remember most clearly was *The Eagle and the Hawk.* It was playing at the Temple Theater on Fillmore Street. It was named after Shirley Temple. But the movie turned out not to be about birds or anything cute like Shirley Temple. It was about war and a crazy man. Halfway through, I insisted on going home because the movie was too scary. I made such a fuss, the usher shined his flashlight in my face and told me to be quiet. Papa had no choice but to take us home. This made him very angry, and Papa didn't take us to the movies for a long time after that.

Those were special movies. The ones we saw as a family. They were more expensive, and we saw them at night. On Saturdays, Brian and I went to matinees by ourselves. Mama would give us each a dime from the cash register, and we would spend the afternoon at the Alhambra Theater, three blocks down Polk Street. For ten cents, we were treated to the news, cartoons, two features and a serial—and more.

When I stepped into the lobby of the theater, it was as though I had entered a different world. Ticket takers and ushers were dressed in dark red uniforms and hats trimmed with gold string and brass buttons, much like the costume the organ grinder's monkey wore. They looked as silly as the monkey. At the same time, they looked important. The ticket taker welcomed me as he tore my ticket in half and motioned me in. I stepped onto the beautiful maroon-patterned carpet with my shoes on. Our family friends, the Nakatas, had floors that weren't nearly as nice, and they made us all—Papa and Mama included—remove our shoes before setting foot in their house. So I felt a little guilty walking on the Alhambra's carpet. My feet sank deep into what felt like a bed of marshmallows as I moved uphill toward the auditorium. The walls soared up to a place I couldn't see without throwing my head way back. The ceiling was covered with windows that allowed sunlight to pour down on me. The lower part of the walls was covered with beautiful designs and decorated with posters of coming attractions. These were placed in deep, wide, gold frames with swirls like so much gold whipped cream. That was just the lobby.

The auditorium was even more wonderful. The plush carpet now sloped downhill into the enormous half-darkened room. If we were late and the room was in total darkness, the usher lit a path for us with his flashlight. When I unfolded a seat, I sank into the soft, padded, mohair seats that matched the maroon carpet. Even sitting on the edge of the thick spring-filled folded seat was comfortable. I often did that when a large person sat in front of me. The stage was draped in heavy maroon velvet and was outlined with an arch of fancy gold shapes. Overhead were millions of pieces of colored glass glued together like a kaleidoscope in a giant upside-down cup. There were fake sitting areas, too small for anyone to sit, along the wall covered in wallpaper speckled with gold designs.

I could raise my voice at Brian in the theater, but the sound would be sucked out of the air by some mysterious force. The voices of other children, shouting as they entered the theater, were also no more than muffled mumbles.

At exactly one o'clock, the theater lights dimmed. The thick curtains were suddenly covered by a picture projected on its folds. Then they slowly parted, and the wavy image was transformed into a perfect, flat picture. It was "coming attractions," a preview of next week's features.

Then—"Tan-ta-ra-ran . . . ta-ta-ta-ta-ran . . ." The familiar sound of the musical theme introduced the newsreel.

"This is Movietone news . . . ," a man announced in a rather frantic voice. He always sounded like he was on the edge of tears. Every week there was ordinary news, and then there was news of the war in Europe. We saw pictures of small children and their mothers with head scarves tied under their chins framing thin faces with large frightened eyes waiting to board trains. German soldiers kick-marched across the screen, accompanied by reports that they were invading different countries in Europe. I was glad I was safe in a theater and not there.

A short feature of some sort and a cartoon like "Porky Pig" followed that. The main feature was next and finally the serial, my favorite. There were different feature films and cartoons every week, but the serial was always the same. They were short, action-packed episodes about a superhero.

"The weed of crime bears bitter fruit. Who knows what evil lurks in the hearts of men. The Shadow knows . . . he, he, he, ha, Ha, HA!"

The Shadow was my very favorite. He was an enemy of evil. In everyday life, he was Lamont Cranston. When he was a young man living in the Orient, he had acquired the ability to cloud people's minds so they couldn't see him. I felt a connection with him, because my parents were also from the Orient. The Shadow was in constant pursuit of the Black Tiger, also invisible. He spoke through the head of a shiny black cat surrounded by a wispy mist and with eyes that flashed green with each word he spoke. Every episode would end with the Shadow about to be captured or killed. I could hardly wait from one Saturday to the next to see how the Shadow would get out of his predicaments. They were cliffhangers.

Brian and I also listened to cliffhangers on the radio every weekday evening at six. The deep, round tone of an enormous bell sounded, followed by the roar of a diving plane. "Captain Midnight . . ." shouted the announcer. "Brought to you by Ovaltine . . ."

Captain Midnight was all about an airplane pilot and his sidekick, Chuck Ramsey, who were in endless pursuit of the evil Ivan Shark.

Brian and I had a collection of decoder badges, rings, and mugs, all through the courtesy of Ovaltine. We carefully removed the freshness-seal foil from new cans of Ovaltine and sent them along with nickels for a decoder ring, or whatever else they were selling. At the end of each episode the announcer read us a scramble of letters and numbers. It was a message in secret code. This we deciphered with our decoder. It was hints about what lay ahead for our heroes in the next episode.

Sometimes we dropped by the playground on our way home from the movies. One such afternoon, Brian decided he wanted to practice a little handball. Brian's pocket always bulged with the tennis ball he kept stuffed in it. When his friends came over, he greeted them by squeezing the bottom of his pocket so the tennis ball squirted out. He would snatch it in midair.

"Wanna play catch?' he'd ask.

"Not in the store," Mama would say.

At Helen Wills Playground there was a wall that kept the hill above it from sliding into the tennis court. On this wall, about the level of Brian's chest, there was a broad white line. Brian's goal was to hit his tennis ball above the line with his open hand. He had to keep the ball in motion when it bounced back. When he played with his friends, they would take turns hitting the ball. Most often, he played against David.

"Haven't been able to beat David, huh? Is that why you want to go in?" I asked.

"You wanna go in or not?" he asked. "If you don't, you can just go home by yourself. Mrs. Pringle can help you cross." I shouldn't have made the remark about David. Actually, since I had just learned to jump to the second ring, I wanted to see if I could still do it.

"I want to go in," I said.

"Okay, then. Let's go," said Brian.

All too soon the sun was dropping behind the clubhouse.

"It's getting dark. Take one more turn. Then we have to go," Brian said looking up at me as I swung past him. "Mama will be worried if we aren't home soon."

The sand crackled under our feet as we hurried down the sandy stone steps into the short tunnel to the exit of the playground. It was always dark and damp in the passage to the door and had the sweet smell of wet dirt. Our footsteps and voices echoed on the concrete that surrounded us. I loved this part of the playground. I imagined I was leaving a castle. When we reached the door, Brian slipped his hand through the metal handle and pressed his thumb on the latch. He tugged at the heavy wooden door made of thick planks. Its hinges creaked and the bottom scraped the sandy concrete.

As the door opened, bright daylight bounced off the sidewalk flooding the "castle." I closed my eyes against the brilliance. I gradually opened them a slit at a time. When they adjusted, I was surprised to see a girl, around twelve or maybe even sixteen years old, next to a car parked at the sidewalk. Her dark wavy hair dripped water on her otherwise dry wrinkled plaid shirt and overalls. She had a large spoon in her hand. The car door was open and there was a dented pail, bruised with rust, next to it on the ground.

"Let's see what she's doing," I said.

"It's late, Marie, I think we should head home."

"I just wanna see what she's doing," I insisted.

"Okay. But just for a minute."

I walked over, squatted next to her, and peered into the water-filled bucket. She used her elbow to gently move my face, so she could reach into the water. She came up with slimy, slithering jellyfish that kept gliding over her spoon.

"What d'ya gonna do with that?" I asked.

"Just watch," she said. After another unsuccessful attempt to scoop up the slippery creatures, she tipped the bucket so that most of the water escaped. Then she carefully poured the drained jellyfish onto the seat of the car! The furry mohair upholstery slurped the remaining water like a thirsty sponge. Sandy mounds of live jellyfish remained. I was amazed at how calmly and deliberately she did it. Like placing a cushion on the seat. It was as though she thought there was nothing wrong with what she was doing.

But it was definitely wrong. We'd heard about kids getting into mischief at the playground but had never seen it ourselves. And Brian and I soon discovered that we were wrong just being there. The playground director happened by at just the right moment. Or wrong moment. It was her car and she thought we were helping the girl!

Papa thought the worst.

"You've ruined the director's car seat and disgraced the family!" he said.

"But we were just watching," I said.

"You should have tried to stop her or told someone what was going on!" Papa said, glaring at Brian.

"Well, I tried to make Marie go, but she wouldn't listen!" Brian said.

"You're her older brother. It was your responsibility!" I had never seen Papa so angry.

CHAPTER 3

"The Way You Look Tonight"
THEME FROM *MR. AND MRS. NORTH*

Soon after the jellyfish incident my parents announced we were moving. That was in the summer of 1940. I was almost eight and Brian, almost ten. My best friend Beverly Jensen had moved earlier when her parents bought a house in Millbrae. I had asked Mama then what "moving" meant, because I couldn't understand. How is that done, I had wondered. If we were to move, how could the Murphy bed, stuck on the dark, shiny, revolving door, and the beige walls with tiny yellow and blue flowers move with us? Would our upstairs bedroom that looked out onto the store move with us? And my favorite front door. And the streetcars. How would we be able to move them? What about my friends?

"Only the furniture and things like that can be moved," Mama had said. How awful that must be, I thought. Poor Beverly. I watched as the Jensens' shelves were stripped bare and curtains came down and boxes were packed. Then they were loaded along with tables and chairs into a large truck until all that was left was naked rooms.

"I wish we could take you with us," Beverly sobbed as she climbed into her packed car after the moving van had left. Tears streaming down her face, she waved to me. I hope it never happens to me, I had thought. But, now it *was* happening to me. And I was older now, so it was easier for me to understand what could and could not be moved. I still cried when I thought about it.

★ ★ ★

It was the fall of 1940. Papa found a place on Lawton Street in the Sunset district and took all of us to see it. I guess he thought it would be easier for us to move if we were involved in the decision. The empty store was located near the corner of a one-block shopping area in the middle of a quiet neighborhood of houses. They were all the same size and stood in a line, shoulder to shoulder, with large windows that stared out at the street. Unlike the Polk district, there were no apartments or flats.

All my friends in the Polk district had lived in apartments. We would play "secret passage." From Maria's apartment on the third floor, we would skip down the stairs that zigzagged the back to a small yard. Dodging sheets, shirts, and socks flapping on clotheslines, we climbed the fences that had ledges we could walk on. We followed the fence trail to Theresa's apartment that faced the next street. From there we would drop into her yard, go up her zigzag back stairs to her apartment on the top floor. We'd enter her kitchen and stop for a snack her mother prepared for us. Then it was out her front door, down the stairs, and out to the street. It was my "long-cut," home.

Since Maria and Theresa shared their secret passages, they, of course, wanted me to show them mine. But it didn't work at my house, because if we went in through the front door of the store and out the back, we would end up trapped in our backyard. The fence was well guarded by petunias, stock, and morning glory.

Then one day, I had a great idea! Beverly's grandmother lived in the apartment house a couple of doors up the street. I played there often. I would often go with Beverly to visit her, because Grandma Jensen was sick with goldstones. I wasn't sure what that meant. But I knew it was serious.

My plan was to enter her building through the service alley, go up the back stairs, through her apartment, and come out front. That would work! I told Maria and Theresa my great plan. I hadn't had a chance to discuss it with Beverly. But I was sure she wouldn't mind, because we were best friends.

Theresa came over one evening after dinner. Her black sausage curls were tied with ribbons and stayed rigid while she bounced like a spring as she ran toward me. I was with Red and Irene. They were brother and sister like Brian and me, except they were twins. Red had bright orange hair that was always combed neatly to one side, while Irene had short straight brown hair held away from her face with a small barrette. Brian had a look about him that seemed to say, "I'm smart."

"The look of intelligence," was the way Mr. Goldberg described it.

We had planned a game of hide-and-go-seek and were waiting for Brian. He had gone to get his friend David.

"I wanted you to see my Shirley Temple doll!" Theresa said. Her broad smile glistened white against her dark skin. She held her doll out to me. It was a tall, rigid stand-up doll with flexible arms and legs and eyes that rolled shut when she lay down. Silky, yellow curls circled her dimpled smiling face. She was dressed in a thin, blue, ruffled dress and white laced-trimmed socks with buttoned Mary Janes.

"She's beautiful!" I said as I took the doll from her. "Thank you for bringing her over so I could see her!"

It was the first time I had seen Theresa on my street, although I had been over to her house many times.

"Wanna play hide-and-go-seek with us?" I asked.

"No, I better not. My mother said that I could come

over to show you my new doll. Then I'm supposed to go home."

But I felt a need to do something for her to repay her for coming all the way over to share her doll . . .

"Theresa!" I said. "Would you like to see my secret passage? It'll only take a minute!"

"Are we going through your cleaners? I thought that didn't work," said Theresa.

"Don't you remember? My friend Beverly Jensen's grandmother's apartment?"

"Oh, yeah. Is that far?

"We're standing right in front of it!"

"What about hide-and-go-seek?" Red asked.

I had forgotten all about that. "You can just play without me. Theresa and I are going to my secret passage."

"I don't think you should do that," said Red. "It's not right."

What's not right about it, I thought. Beverly's my best friend and I'm over there all the time.

"He's mad, because I won't let him come with us," I said to Theresa as I glared at Red.

"Don't pay any attention to him. He's just jealous. Let's go."

I opened the door to the service alley and led Theresa down the dark narrow passage past the garbage cans. Then we climbed up the zigzag stairs to Grandma Jensen's kitchen door. It was unlocked. As we entered the empty, lightless kitchen, I felt a strange sense of relief. Grandma Jensen is out, I thought. Good. We continued through the apartment with the front door as our goal. I pushed through the swinging door into the living room. And there on the sofa lay Grandma Jensen, pale with sunken cheeks and half-closed eyes, encircled by Beverly and her parents! They all looked up at us with wide eyes and gaping mouths. No one said a word.

Everything got a little blurry for a moment. Maybe I was becoming blurry to them as well, and maybe I would disappear, like the Shadow, I thought. But I wasn't disappearing. Even through the blurriness I could still see those eyes fixed on me. Then I did the only thing I could do. Without saying a word, I grabbed Theresa's arm and ran out the front door.

When we got outside, Brian stood waiting for us, below the marble stairs on the sidewalk, surrounded by the others.

"Boy, are you in trouble!" he said. "I'm telling!"

Soon after that, Grandma Jensen died, and Beverly and her family moved away.

* * *

We were told that there was once a gas station on the empty corner lot on Lawton Street next to our new store. But all that remained were chunks of concrete scattered about, looking like toppled headstones in a messy cemetery. On the other side of the new store and across the street were a variety of shops. But there were no doughnut-cafes or upholsterers. Two blocks up the street was a huge sandbox with slides and swings without a clubhouse, pretending to be a playground. Lawton, the school we would be attending, was two blocks beyond that. Between the store and the playground lay sand dunes, like beaches that got lost on their way to the ocean. When the wind blew, loose sand escaped the embrace of the sidewalks and swirled onto the street.

Papa's store was a cavernous white room with the fresh smell of new paint and linoleum. There were show windows in the front and regular kitchen windows in the back. In the windowless area between, light streamed in through windows in the ceiling. The rear of the store narrowed a bit to accommodate storage rooms and the bathroom.

The walls chattered with our footsteps as we walked the

length of the building to the door leading outside. There lay sand that might have stretched out to the ocean, had it not been interrupted by a wooden fence, houses, and streets. Back inside, Papa's eyes sparkled as they scanned the room. But I could not think of anything nice to say about the store. Mama and Brian were also quiet. Then I noticed the walls in the middle of the room were studded with a series of electrical outlets. There were ten of them placed about five feet apart on each side. I pointed to them.

"Why are there so many?"

"This was designed to be a beauty shop," Papa said. He seemed pleased I'd asked. "That's also why the store's so deep. So there would be room for many chairs. But because it's so big, I can make this into a cleaning shop and a place for us to live." He made a wide circle with his arms. He paused as his eyes seemed to measure the room from corner to corner.

"The kitchen will extend to here. And this is where our bedrooms will be, between the store and the kitchen." he paced out the space with even strides. "Your bedroom," he said looking at Brian and me, "will be to the left. We'll build a wall here in the middle and Mama and I will sleep over there. What do you think?"

We're going to live back here? We lived in an apartment on Polk Street. It had the warmth of wood and windows and wallpaper. Here, I thought, the blank walls and high ceiling make me feel like I'm standing in the bottom of a deep well. It feels so cold.

Then Brian asked, "Why don't we just live somewhere else?"

"Yes. Why not one of the houses around here?" I added.

Papa's face quickly tightened from a smile to a scowl that made the veins in his forehead bulge. Then words just exploded from his mouth.

"The real estate man said that houses in this neighborhood have racial covenants!"

"They have 'what'?" Brian asked. I didn't understand the words Papa spoke, but the message was clear enough to me. Those houses were not for us. But Brian's desire to hear exactly what Papa said seemed to make him oblivious to the storm that was raging inside Papa. He glared at Brian. Now, fire seemed to shoot from his eyes. The storm could not be contained.

"The houses have racial covenants!" his voice thundered. "That means we can't live in a house in this neighborhood!"

The room became filled with his loud words as they crashed against the walls and floors and ceiling and bounced and bounced until the sound died. No one dared say a word. Not even Brian. Then Papa continued, barely a whisper.

"That's enough. We have to live here. That's all there is to it. We're just going to have to do the best we can."

"Okay, okay," said Brian. "But is there really enough space for two beds and desks in our room?"

"You'll get bunk beds," said Papa in a soft voice without looking at Brian. "Marie will get the top, because you're a restless sleeper and you'll probably fall off!"

I turned away from Brian, so he wouldn't see that I was pleased. I knew he would have liked the top. I felt so lucky I would get the best bed.

★ ★ ★

In December, the store was complete. The part I liked best was the customer area. It was beautiful. There was the show window. It was an alcove that started about two feet above the floor. On the window an electric neon sign, twisted glass tubing containing colored gas, formed the words "Safe Cleaners." Stand-up advertisement posters were placed on the alcove, but there was room for me to sit in the sun or watch the rain. A waiting customer could also sit there, if the two chairs in the area next to the counter were occupied. The counter was a soft pink with a gleaming white top. It was flush with the wall on one end and nicely rounded at the opening on the other. A narrow strip of chrome traced a path about four inches below the top. It was matched by the same trim on the partition behind it, which separated the customer area from the work area in the back. But there was another partition four feet from the opening, which blocked the view of the work area behind it. It also blocked the view of customers entering the store. Fortunately, when customers stepped on the mat at the entrance, a bell rang in the back announcing their arrival.

Papa's pride and joy, the pressing machine at which he was so skilled, dominated the work area. I often sat on the floor just to watch him as he smoothed a pant leg and positioned it perfectly on the cloth-covered anvil and pressed the vacuum pedal with his left foot to hold it in place. Then he would pull down the matching pressing iron using his right leg on the broad pedal and his right arm on the iron handle. With his left hand he would smooth any ripples the vacuum may have created. Then, barely escaping the closing jaw of the descending iron, his hand would slip away. Just as the iron met the anvil, he would deftly slide his left foot to the steam pedal below and his index finger to the steam lever above, and the two bursts of steam collided on the pant leg. Sometimes he would stand on the pressing iron pedal and gently bounce up and down. Then he would step off and raise the iron. It was like watching an elegant dance.

"The mark of a well-dressed man is the sharpness of his creases. A good presser can always press on the original crease. Some pressers create new ones, making double creases. "I never make double creases," he said. I was very proud of Papa.

Papa was also an actor and loved to sing. Although I had never seen him in a play, he was active in a Japanese theater group. My uncle Jiro was a very famous actor in Japan, so acting was in Papa's blood. At least that was what Papa always said. Uncle Jiro came to the U.S. for a theater tour Papa had arranged for him about the time Brian was due to be born. Actually, Papa was on tour with Uncle Jiro when Brian was born. I knew this, because Mama mentioned it whenever she argued with Papa.

Once Papa brought home a Japanese stage make-up kit to practice on Mama. He painted her face white and lined her eyes with black and red makeup. Then he had her press her upper and lower lips on the inner surface of a bowl covered with a brilliant red substance.

"That's how lipstick is applied by Japanese theater people," Papa said. When Papa finished, Mama looked pretty grotesque.

"You're not supposed to look at her close-up," he said. "Pretend she's on stage. You have to view her from a distance." I couldn't get far enough away to appreciate the effect.

Papa had also been a part time Japanese-language announcer for the San Francisco radio station KPO before he married Mama. He worked at many other jobs as well after his arrival in the U.S. in 1917.

That was also the year Mama made the journey across the Pacific alone to the U.S., but they didn't know each other at the time. She was twelve and Papa was sixteen. Mama had left Osaka, Japan, to join her parents in Stockton, California, after a seven-year separation. Her father had come to the U.S. shortly after she was born. When she was five, her mother left with a promise to send for her as soon as she was settled. When at last they were reunited seven years later, Mama was given the responsibility of babysitting her toddler brother.

Papa had come from Hiroshima, Japan, as a

sixteen-year-old to work at a chicken ranch in Sebastapol, just north of San Francisco, in order to fulfill his father's financial obligation.

After completing the contract, he followed the job opportunity road wherever it took him. He joined a railroad gang repairing track, and eventually settled in Alaska to can salmon. The trail then led him back to California to settle in San Francisco. There he bussed dishes in a restaurant until he found work in a laundry and dry cleaning shop. Here he learned a trade. He eventually opened his own dry cleaning shop. And it was then he married Mama. He was twenty-seven and she was twenty-three. That was June 29, 1929, four months before the stock market crashed, plunging the nation into the Great Depression.

★ ★ ★

Mama finished silks in the back of the store beyond the pressing machine. Most of the gross pressing was done by Papa, and she would smooth out wrinkles around collars and sleeves with the steam iron. Mama also waited on customers and did minor repairs and alterations. In her spare time she sewed our clothes. She could draft patterns from clothes brought in by customers. If I saw a dress I liked, she could make one just like it. But that also meant she could make several dresses in the same style with different fabrics. I had many of those.

Behind the work area, there was a cozy spot for company. A hot plate to boil water for tea sat on a cabinet against the left wall, although Papa's friends mostly drank beer or sake when they came to visit. A sofa against a wall that separated the work area from the bedrooms formed an angle with an armchair. A coffee table was nestled in the crook of the angle. To the left of the sofa, there was a door that led to our bedrooms and kitchen.

When we first moved, it seemed there was no floor space for our beloved free-standing Gilfillan radio, and we thought it would not make it to our new home. But Papa thought to build a cabinet over some equipment, creating a perch for it. No floor space required. He was so smart!

The beautiful brown mahogany radio, with its rounded corners and dial that glowed green, filled our space with its magical sounds.

The deep tones from the large speaker made the "I Love a Mystery" theme song soothingly scary and the roar of the plane that heralded "Captain Midnight" sounded like it would come crashing into our home. We could also get all the stations in the world, including Japan. My parents could listen to the radio in Japanese. The broadcast from Japan had the rhythm of the ebb and flow of waves as it traveled the distance from halfway around the world. I guessed that was why it was called "short wave."

★ ★ ★

Brian and I transferred from Spring Valley in our old neighborhood to Lawton School as soon as we moved in December of 1940. Lawton was newer than Spring Valley and had "bungalows" for some of its grades. These were temporary buildings that sat on the playground until they could add onto the main building. My class was in a bungalow. Brian's was in the main building.

He was in fifth grade and I was only in third, so we weren't dismissed at the same time. His school day was forty-five minutes longer than mine. Although it hadn't been a problem at Spring Valley, when we started at Lawton, Papa and Mama made me walk with Brian to school and wait for him, so we could walk home together. I pounded erasers and cleaned the blackboard for Miss O'Brien, my teacher, until Brian was dismissed.

After a few days, I decided I would ask permission to walk home by myself.

"Why do I have to wait for Brian after school? It's not as though I'd get lost walking the four blocks straight down Lawton."

"Okay. Why don't we see if that works," Papa said to Mama. Then he turned to me. "Just be sure you come straight home. And if you want to go somewhere to play, come home first and let us know."

"Okay!" I said.

After school the next day, as the rest of the class was leaving, I waited to speak to Miss O'Brien to tell her I wouldn't have to wait for my brother anymore.

"Wonderful, Marie. Just be sure you go straight home."

"I will," I said and rushed into the cloakroom to gather my things. It was empty. I was the last one out. That's okay, I thought. It isn't as though I needed someone to show me how to get home.

I was feeling pretty good about my new-found independence and was trudging up the steep hill that led away from the school, when I heard what sounded like chanting.

"Monkey! Monkey! You look like a monkey!"

I looked around and realized there was no one but me and the chanters. They were chanting at me! They were a group of six kids. I turned quickly and continued walking up the hill. I didn't say anything, but walked faster.

"Sticks and stones will break my bones, but names will never hurt me," I thought. Besides, I know what I look like, and I know what monkeys look like. I definitely don't look like a monkey. Stupid kids.

"You belong in a zoo!" A raspy voice bellowed behind me.

"Who let you out?" a strained squeaky voice added. They were getting closer. I walked faster. Then I could hear someone say, "She's a Jap. My dad told me. She doesn't belong here. She should go back to Japan!" Then it was, "Jap! Jap! Go back to Japan!"

Now, *that* made me angry. What's wrong with these idiots, I wondered. This never happened in the Polk district. What a strange place. Is this why Papa and Mama didn't want me to walk home by myself?

* * *

Actually we had come very close to not being able to attend Lawton School. When Papa had brought us to Lawton to register, the principal, Miss Baker, stated that the school was overcrowded.

"Your children will have to go to Jefferson School on 19th Avenue," she had told my father.

"But Lawton close to our home and Jefferson far away. Crossing 19th Avenue dangerous," Papa said. "No make sense."

"I don't make the rules, Mr. Mitsui."

"Who make rules?"

"The superintendent."

"You ask him, then!"

"I can. But I know what the answer is going to be."

"And what happens Brian and Marie? Against the law not to be in school."

"Alright. They can stay until we straighten this out," said Miss Baker.

But that first day at Lawton, Brian revealed his talent as a poet. As a class assignment he wrote a clever poem about Lawton. His teacher was so impressed she posted it in the main corridor, so everyone could read it. Including Miss Baker.

When we got home that afternoon Papa said that Miss

Baker had called to say that we could stay at Lawton. There was no doubt in Papa's mind that Brian was responsible for our good fortune.

"The principal must have thought that because I couldn't speak English very well, that I was stupid; therefore, she no doubt thought that you children were also stupid. She was probably afraid that you two would require a lot of extra attention. Brian, you showed her!" Papa was proud of him.

★ ★ ★

I reached the top of the hill. I turned and looked down at them. Then I shouted, "I'm an American just like you! I've never been to Japan, so how could I go back?" Stupid, stupid kids. Don't they know that Americans don't all look alike and can look like me?

They all stopped. Although I was very short, I towered over them from the top of the hill.

"She can talk," a dark-haired girl with a chalky white face whispered loudly.

"I'm an American just like you. I was born here. I've never been to Japan, so how can I go back?" I shouted again.

"So which Jap zoo did you say you were born in?" said a skinny boy with straggly brown hair. He laughed and made faces.

"Yeah," the rest chimed in, laughing.

"I wasn't born in any zoo. And I wasn't born in Japan. I was born here. San Francisco. Do you understand? Do you need me to spell it for you?"

"Yeah. Spell it!" said the skinny one.

"S-a-n F-r-a-n-c-i-s-c-o. San Francisco!"

"Did she spell it right?" he asked in a whisper to his friend with short blond hair that stuck up in the back.

"I think so. Ask her to spell California."

Before the skinny one could ask, I shouted, "C-a-l-i-f-o-r-n-i-a, California!"

Then a strange thing happened. Once I started spelling, all the hurtful words seemed to disappear from their feeble minds and were replaced by requests to spell words! Weird. They caught up with me and began spitting out words for me to spell. Fortunately, they were simple words, which weren't difficult to spell. Actually, I could have misspelled them, but they probably wouldn't have known the difference. They weren't very smart. Once I started spelling they must have gotten confused and forgotten they were teasing me. Thank goodness for that!

As we continued down Lawton Street, they gradually dropped away like clumps of dirt off a muddy shoe, and each went in their own direction toward home. After what seemed like forever, the last of the idiots, the girl with the chalky face, left. Her parting words were "How do you spell Lawton?" and she walked off before I could answer. I was finally alone and within sight of the cleaners. I ran down the hill the rest of the way home.

"How was your walk home?" asked Mama.

"Fine," I said, "I made some new friends," and quickly walked to the back to my room. I didn't want to tell them what had happened. They would make me wait for Brian if I did.

I climbed up to my bed and stretched out. I thought about what had happened and realized how lucky I was to have gotten home safely. It could have gotten ugly if I hadn't started spelling. I could have gotten beaten up. I shook off the chill that suddenly surged through me.

From now on, I would be smarter about walking home. I decided that I would never leave school alone. I would make certain to leave with the rest of the class. Jean Ireland, one of my classmates, lived on 25th Avenue, a block from the cleaners. I would walk home with her. She was about a head taller than me, and she commanded a lot of respect. Her father was also a high-ranking police officer.

Fortunately, most of the other kids at Lawton were not like the "chanting idiots," although a couple of the idiots continued asking me to spell things for a while after that. But that was better than having them tease me or beat me up. And from time to time one of them, Nancy, a rather quiet girl who always smelled like Ivory Snow, would walk with me when I wasn't with Jean. We tried to be friends, but our friendship never extended beyond walking home from school together. Perhaps it was because she lived on the other side of the sand dunes.

But Jean Ireland and I became best friends. We were inseparable. She was as tall as I was short and had curly brown hair with light-colored eyes that were set deep in her face, against my straight black hair, dark eyes, and flat face. Jean's teeth were covered with wires and chunks of metal. When we dropped by Mrs. Bagley's variety store across the street from the cleaners, she said that Jean and I were "a study in contrasts."

We tried to do everything together. Even the bus that took Brian and me across town to a Japanese-language school could not separate us. Jean persuaded her parents to let her learn Japanese along with Brian and me. Japanese school was held after regular school every Monday, Wednesday, and Friday in the Buddhist Temple in Japanese Town on the other side of the city. We didn't learn much Japanese, but we had a great time on the long bus ride to and from school.

When we weren't at school of one kind or another, we were at Jean's house. I never invited her to my house, because I was embarrassed about the makeshift nature of our living quarters behind the cleaners. Hers, particularly her room, was gorgeous. Pale violets bloomed in profusion on her curtains and bedspreads, and her soft-pink walls were lined with shelves decorated with dolls from every country in Europe.

"Your room and house are really very beautiful, Jean. I wish that someday I could live in a house like this. But I know I can't."

Why not?"

"Because all the houses around here have rayshulcubnants, and my father doesn't like them."

"All the houses have what?

"My father says he doesn't like the rayshulcubnants. He says all these houses in the Sunset have them. So you must have them, too."

"What's it called again? A Rachel Cubnant? That almost sounds like a person's name. But I've never heard of it. Must be a fancy word for something simple. I'll ask my mother when she gets home. She'll know," said Jean.

Jean's mother was a school teacher. She knew everything.

★ ★ ★

As a neighborhood, there wasn't as much to do on Lawton Street as there was on Polk Street, since the playground didn't have a recreation program and Lawton was very quiet, even with the shops. The cleaners was open almost every evening until seven, though most of the other stores were closed. By then, there was almost no traffic on Lawton. Though closed, the shops stayed bright with their show windows and neon signs, and children often gathered on the well-lit street after dinner. Jean was never allowed to come out in the evening. Most of the kids who did went to St. Anne's or were in junior high. Often, we played kick the can, a form of hide-and-go-seek in the street. Thankfully, neither the can nor we children ever got run over while playing kick the can.

★ ★ ★

Cinnamon toothpicks were a favorite treat of mine. The drugstore on the corner of Lawton and 25th sold tiny bottles of liquid cinnamon. They cost a dime and were just large enough to soak toothpicks. After a good soaking, I would lay them out on wax paper to dry. They became sucker sticks that would release their spicy cinnamon flavor when I placed them in my mouth.

I shared my toothpicks with Joey, a skinny boy with dark brown hair and enormous eyes, who lived on 25th Avenue near Kirkham. He always wore short pants and shirts with "Peter Pan" collars.

"I go to a private school and this is my uniform," he said. He not only dressed differently, he had to follow very strict rules. For example, although he was nine years old, he wasn't allowed to cross the street by himself.

One day, Joey wanted some of my cinnamon sticks, but I had only a few left, and I wanted to keep them for myself.

"I'm sorry, Joey, I'm all out," I said. "I spent my allowance on something else, and I can't buy any cinnamon right now. I'll have some next week."

"But I want some now!" he said. "If you don't have any, I guess I'll just have to make my own."

"Good. Do that."

"How do you make them?"

I told him what to do, and he sounded confident he could do it.

But the drugstore was "off-limits" for him, because it was across the street. He had to be taken by his mother or nanny. I wondered if they would approve. I wondered what he would do.

The following day shortly after I got home from school, I heard the screech of brakes and ran outside. I could see a crowd forming around a white pickup stopped by the corner. I ran over and pushed my way through the people clustered at the front of the truck. On the ground lay Joey! I suddenly felt very ill. I felt like vomiting. I ran from the crowd and managed to reach the gutter storm drain in time.

Joey had dashed across the street by himself and got hit by the truck. And it was all my fault. If only I had shared my cinnamon sticks, it would never have happened. If only I had even offered to buy the cinnamon for him, it would never have happened.

Fortunately, my selfishness didn't kill him. It only broke his ankle. A few days later, I heard from the other kids on the block that Joey was home from the hospital. So I went to visit him. His nanny, a chubby lady in a black dress with white lace collar, opened the door. I had seen her before, when she brought clothes to our cleaning shop. That was how I had met Joey. She had brought him into the store with her.

"I'm here to visit Joey," I said.

"You a friend of his?"

"Yes."

"Wait a minute . . . I know you!" said the nanny as she looked down at me with narrowed eyes. "You're the girl from the cleaners, aren't you?"

"Yes. Can I see Joey? I'd like to see Joey." A heavy feeling of sadness started to fill my entire body, bringing tears to the edge of my eyes.

The nanny's glare began to soften.

"Okay, you can come in, but only for a couple of minutes. He's been injured, you know. He can't play. You can only talk to him." She led me down the hall to his room.

I had never been in a boy's room before. I was immediately struck by the oily sweetness that greeted me as I entered. The smell of a broken ankle, I thought. I was further surprised by the gloom of Joey's room, compared to the cheery brightness of Jean's room. Dolls and flowers were replaced by heavily framed pictures of clowns on a dark wallpaper and dark brown furniture. Joey lay propped up in his bed reading. There was an outline of a box under the brown covers that matched his wallpaper. His injured ankle lay under that, I thought. Poor Joey. Because of me, he has to endure the pain of a broken ankle and its accompanying smell in this dark, gloomy room.

"I'm really sorry, Joey," I said. "It's a little late, but I brought you some cinnamon sticks."

"Wow. Thanks, Marie," he said, as he pulled himself upright. He took them and tucked them under his pillow with a grin.

"Hey, do you want to see my ankle?" he said as he began to throw off his blanket.

"No, no. It's okay," I said. "I've got to get going. I'll see you outside when you're well."

But I never saw him again. Kids said he moved away.

CHAPTER 4

"God Bless America"
KATE SMITH

As far back as I could remember, Mama's lap was my seat in the car whenever we traveled together as a family. But as time wore on, it was getting increasingly uncomfortable. For me as well as Mama. Her lap wasn't as soft as it used to be, and she complained that I made her legs go numb. I particularly dreaded the long trips to Stockton when we visited Grandma and Grandpa. We made the three-hour trip about four or five times a year.

Our sedan delivery had a bench seat only in the front, and it had to accommodate all four of us. Papa in the driver's seat, Brian in the middle straddling the gear shift post, and Mama on the end with me perched high up on her lap. The area in the back was flat with a rod running above it near the ceiling. That was Papa's delivery rack. During the day, when he wasn't out on deliveries, our car was parked in front of the store. At night, he parked at the Mobil gas station on the corner of Lawton and 25th Avenue. It was against the law to leave a car parked at the curb at night.

One day I returned home from school to see a beautiful gray car parked in front of the cleaners, instead of our green Chevrolet. Papa's out, I thought.

"*Tadaima, kaerimashita,*" I shouted as I walked into the cleaners. That meant "I'm home" in Japanese.

"*Okaeri,*" was the response. That meant "Welcome home." It was Papa's voice. Papa's home?

"Someone's parked in your space, Papa," I said as I walked in.

"That's our car," Papa replied.

"No, Papa, there's a gray Dodge sedan out there."

Papa appeared from the back. He had a large grin on his face.

"I just bought it."

"That car is ours? What happened to our sedan delivery?"

"I traded it in."

"It's really ours? That beautiful car with two rows of seats is ours? But, how will you make your deliveries?"

He took my hand and led me outside to the car. We stood and looked at it for a moment. Its sleek silvery body was one sloping unbroken line from the windshield to the rear fender. It looked like a torpedo that could go as fast as the wind. Papa finally stepped up to it and opened the rear door.

"See the bar that goes to the other side?" he said pointing to the rod that was fastened on either side just above the doors. "That's where the clothes go. And it's removable, so you won't bump your head on it when you sit back here."

"I'll have my very own place to sit! Thank you, thank you, Papa!" I said and hugged him.

★ ★ ★

One chilly Friday evening we closed our dry cleaning shop early. Business was good, so we were going clothes shopping for Brian and me. A new jacket for Brian and a coat for me.

Beams of light sliced through the clear night sky as we

drove across town. Soon we neared the origin of the light. We had been following their beckoning in our car, since we spotted the hide–and–go–seek lights a few blocks earlier.

"There it is, on the right!" I shouted when I spotted the monster searchlights. The huge, burning, mirrored beacons made the surrounding area in front of the Sears Roebuck department store bright as day. The lights also illuminated a group of ragtag men who marched in a tight circle in front of the store. They wore zippered jackets and wrinkled, uncreased pants.

"UNfair! UNfair! Sears Roebuck and Company is UNfair!" they chanted, holding signs that echoed their message. People scurried in and out of the store trying to avoid the picketers, paying them little attention. The spectacle of all the people, the chanting, and the brilliant lights was exciting. At the same time, I felt afraid.

"What's happening, Papa?" I asked.

"The sign carriers are pickets and they're saying that Sears Roebuck isn't paying them enough. The searchlights are Sears Roebuck's way of announcing they are opening a new store."

"Something like the Batman Bat–signal . . ." Brian whispered in my ear. "Instead of the Gotham police commissioner calling for Batman, Sears is calling for customers."

"I know!" I whispered back in his face.

"Just stay close to me, Marie," Papa continued. "And don't look at the pickets. We're going in."

I clutched his hand and could feel his pants brush against my leg as we walked. I looked down at a jumble of feet going every which way. I didn't know where to go, but it didn't matter. I felt safe glued to Papa. He decided. Brian and Mama were somewhere behind us.

I was relieved to finally enter the store and leave the confusion behind. I looked up from the ground and into a huge brightly lit store with rows of showcases that glittered far into the distance. Sears Roebuck and Co. occupied an entire city block.

Now, how were we going to find the clothing section, I wondered. Before I could ask, Papa suddenly began walking briskly toward a wall, dragging me behind him. He had located the elevators and the store directory as well.

Brian ran past us to the directory. When we caught up, he announced proudly, "The children's department is on the fourth floor." We boarded the waiting elevator and gave the elevator operator our floor. When the door opened at the fourth floor my eyes feasted on a room with racks and racks of dresses, blouses, skirts, and coats as far as the eye could see. Even as a dry cleaner's daughter, I had never seen so much clothing in one place before. Every color in a jumbo box of crayolas could be found on those racks. I made a dash for the coats. The beige one with the reversible dark brown velvet hood immediately caught my eye. It was love at first sight!

The same velvet was used to trim the collar and two rows of dark brown buttons. I pulled off the light, thin, blue coat Mama had made me and handed it to her. I then removed the heavy wool beige off the hanger and carefully put one arm, then the other, through the slippery satin sleeves. I flipped the hood up over my head, although I wasn't sure if it was allowed. As I adjusted the hood and pulled it tight around my face, the velvet lining felt like a soft kitten against my cheek.

Someone once told me that I resembled the Japanese emperor's daughter. I imagined that she would wear a coat like this. As I looked in the mirror my long black hair blended into the dark chestnut of the velvet hood and framed my pale round face. The princess line of the coat flowed gracefully below my waist into ever so gentle broad ripples. My knees peeked just below the hem. I was pleased with what I saw. Perfect. There stands a princess, I thought.

"I don't have to try on any more coats. This is the one I want."

"Are you sure? What about this navy one? I think darker would be better." Mama said. "Stains are harder to remove from light colors." Mama liked practical, comfortable clothes. You could tell by the way she dressed. She sewed most of her plain, straight-line dresses herself, which she wore with comfortable lace-up shoes with cuban heels. She had pretty dresses that Papa bought her, but they just hung in the closet. Her long hair was rolled up along her neck around a "rat." Makeup for special occasions was a hint of lipstick applied with her pinky and a puff of powder on her nose to remove the shine.

Papa, on the other hand, was known as a "dandy." That's what I heard people call him. He sported a well-trimmed mustache and always wore a three-piece suit and hat, perfectly matched. Dressing down for him was removing his coat and rolling up his sleeves. At the beach, that meant also removing his shoes and socks and rolling up his pants. He never wore zippered jackets or uncreased pants, because he didn't own any. At night he wore a cotton yukata, which was a Japanese nightgown. When he was in his yukata, he sat cross-legged on chairs. He never did that in his suits.

★ ★ ★

"I want this beige one." I insisted.

"I think it looks great on her," said Brian.

"I don't know. . . . What do you think, Papa?" Mama asked.

"I like it, too. Let her have it. We're in the dry cleaning business. Remember? If she gets it dirty, we can clean it."

"Okay . . . ," Mama said reluctantly, "but you have to be very careful when you wear it. I hate to see light clothes covered with spots. Sometimes they don't come out."

"Thank you! I promise to be careful!"

It was the most beautiful coat in the whole world and it was mine! Then my mother returned to the rack and began flipping through the coats. What is she doing, I wondered. I thought we had decided.

"Here," she said. "Put this one on." She handed me an identical coat in a size 10 as she took my perfect size 6 from me. Although I had just turned nine, I was very short for my age. My mother was confusing my age with my size. But I did what she said and pulled the large heavy coat over my shoulder and slipped my arms through the openings. My hands disappeared in the sleeves that hung down to the tips of my fingers. The hem skimmed the top edge of my socks. I looked back in the mirror. From princess to clown.

"Don't worry. I can shorten it." Mama assured me as she knelt down at my feet to fold the hem up. "About four inches, I think. You can get more wear from it this way."

CHAPTER 5

"Let's Remember Pearl Harbor"
SAMMY KAYE

12-7-41

Two days later, on Sunday morning, December 7, 1941, we were at home at our cleaners. Brian was reading *White Fang* at the kitchen table. Papa was changing the cover to the pressing machine. And I watched as Mama shortened my new coat. Finally. She didn't have time on Saturday, because that was a workday. She had me put the coat on and I twirled like a ballerina in slow motion, as she placed a trail of pins above the hem at the level of my knees. After I took it off, she unraveled the old hem and ironed a fold along the line she created with tailor's chalk to make a new six-inch hem. She was basting it with long stitches when the phone rang out front.

"Who could be calling on Sunday morning?" said Papa as he walked through the archway into the customer area.

"Hello?" I could hear him answer with a slight edge to his voice. Then, "What?" I could hear him shouting. "No! . . ."

Brian ran in from the kitchen. "What's Papa shouting about?"

"Are you sure? Maybe it's one of those radio tricks! Like Orson Welles and that Mars invasion thing." Papa continued loudly. "Okay, okay. I'll call you back."

Papa came running toward us, his large eyes wide and wild. It frightened me. What could anyone have said to cause such a reaction in Papa?

"That was Uncle Ray on the phone. I have to turn on the radio!" Papa said as he ran toward the bedroom. Brian was already there. He had turned the radio on and was waiting for the thirteen tubes to warm up.

"Which station, Papa?" asked Brian.

"Any station!" He pushed Brian aside and turned the dial until the hum turned into words. ". . . So, for those of you just tuning in, Japan has attacked Pearl Harbor in Hawaii. U.S. battleships anchored there have been hit . . . thousands of sailors have been killed!" He tried different stations and the news was the same. Papa crumpled into a heap on the bedroom sofa, eyes closed.

"All that killing and destruction . . ." Papa said as he slowly leaned forward. He put his head between his hands, covered his ears, and stared at the floor, "Why did they do that? Why? Why?" Then he sat up. "That means war!"

"What's happening, Papa?" asked Brian.

"Japan has done a terrible thing. They bombed American battleships. This means war."

"War between us and Japan?" I asked.

"War between us and Japan . . ." Papa echoed. "That's right . . . war between us and Japan."

"Where is Pearl Harbor? I'm scared. Are they going to bomb us, too?" I asked. I ran to Mama who had sat down in the large green armchair. I flung myself into her protective arms.

"Pearl Harbor is a long way from here. I don't think planes can fly this far. So I don't think we have to worry about that for the moment. We have other problems," Papa said.

"What do you mean 'other problems'?" Brian asked.

"This could mean trouble for us. . . ." Papa said. No one said anything. The shrill ring of the phone broke the silence again. Papa got up once more. This time it was Uncle Kazuo who lived in "Japanese Town."

"It's very frightening out there," Papa said when he returned. "Uncle Kazuo says people are throwing eggs and tomatoes at stores and people on the street. We're definitely not going over there for dinner tonight. He says it's too dangerous. Everyone's staying inside."

My grown-up cousin, Brent, called later to say that he had been stopped at the Bay Bridge toll plaza on his way back from Marysville with his new bride. He had to prove that his home was in San Francisco before they would let him pass. He also said the FBI had picked up a Buddhist minister.

"That was probably Rev. Nakamura, our Japanese-school teacher," said Brian. No one knew where they were taking him. Not even his family.

Police Captain Ireland, Jean's father, also called to see if we were all right. Papa said he sounded relieved that no one had bothered us. He left his number in case we needed help. Jean's mother also offered to drive us to school the next day.

By evening, a knot had developed in my stomach that grew into a rock that rubbed against my stomach wall and left me with an upset stomach and no room for food. Mama was worried because I was not eating.

"You must eat or you'll get sick!" she scolded as she held a spoonful of rice to my mouth. I turned my head.

I had never told my parents about the kids who followed me home from school when we first moved here to the Sunset. Now with all that was happening to people in Japanese Town, I felt afraid about what might happen when I returned to school. That night I slept fitfully as I dreamt about dodging bombs that looked like huge pearls exploding as they dropped on my new coat.

The following day, Papa said, "I think it'll be all right for us to open the store, today. No one has bothered us. I think it'll be all right. You both should go to school, too." Brian and I didn't say anything. Papa didn't really want to discuss this anyway. It was an order.

"Mrs. Ireland will be here soon to pick you up. I want you to be ready when she gets here," Papa said. Then, suddenly, his shoulders rose and the muscles in his jaw became tight. It was a signal that he was about to say something very important. He made certain that we were looking at him as he said very slowly, "I want you both to know that Mama and I are very angry with Japan for their sneak attack on Pearl Harbor. Mama and I hate Japan! Isn't that right, Mama?"

Mama nodded.

Why are you telling us this, I wanted to ask. Of course, you hate Japan. Who doesn't? Instead I said, "I think it's better if I don't wear my new coat today. Is that O.K.? I don't want anyone to be jealous of it. I don't want to do anything that would make people notice me."

"That's a good idea." Papa said, "Hurry and change. Mrs. Ireland should be here any moment."

I was so relieved that she drove us that morning. Jean and I didn't talk very much. It was hard to know what to say. She just held my hand tight in hers. I knew then that she was the best friend a person could ever have. She was my best friend forever, I thought.

She stayed close to me as we entered the school grounds. I was relieved that the bell rang shortly after our arrival and we didn't have to spend any time on the playground.

We started the morning as usual with the Pledge of Allegiance. I probably recited it louder than anyone else in the class. I thought Papa would have wanted me to. This was followed by sharing time.

Kay was the first to raise his hand.

"Miss O'Brien! Miss O'Brien!" he shouted. He was a runt of a kid. He was about my height. Very short. And had a large head with hair that grew out of it in straight lines.

He stretched his short body as tall as he could as he waved his hand wildly. He brushed his stiff red hair out of his eyes and started to bob up and down in his seat. Miss O'Brien finally called on him.

"My Dad and I went to Japtown last night," he said, barely able to get the words out as he panted like an excited dog. "You should have seen all the cars with people throwing tomatoes at those Japs and Jap stores, and they were all running around . . . they deserved it! Bombing Pearl Harbor and everything . . . it was really exciting being there!"

I sat frozen in my seat. Here I was in the same room and he was talking about "Japs." I wanted to hide. Then I thought, he must not notice me. Actually, I didn't think I'd ever talked to him. I knew who he was. He was one of the popular kids. But he probably didn't even know I was in the class. Or maybe he thinks I'm different from those other "Japs" in Japanese Town. Whatever, it's best to stay away from him. I sat very quietly hoping he wouldn't turn my way. I didn't hear what Miss O'Brien or anyone else said after that. All I heard were my thoughts.

When I returned home from school that day, our Gilfillan radio was gone.

"Where's our radio?" I asked Papa.

"Captain Ireland called to say that the police had received orders to collect our radios, cameras, binoculars, and things like that. So we took it with the rest of the things to his station."

"And what are they going to do with it? When will we get it back?"

"He said he would take care of it for us. I feel it's in safe hands with him, rather than a stranger. We're so fortunate to have him as a friend."

"That's true. I guess we are lucky to be able to turn it over to someone we can trust."

★ ★ ★

Jean and I remained best of friends, but gradually, I saw less and less of her after school. She started taking French lessons, since Japanese school was discontinued.

A few weeks later at school, a student monitor brought a note to Miss O'Brien during class. She looked at it, stood up, and came over to me, while he waited. It was just before recess and I had flipped the top of my desk open to put my things away. She leaned over to bring her face close to mine. We both had our heads behind the lid to my desk.

"Marie, the principal would like to speak to you," she whispered as she cupped her hand as if she were telling me a secret.

"Would you please go with Robert? And take your coat." Since our class was in a portable, and it was cold outside, Miss O'Brien was concerned that I might get chilled, I thought.

When we arrived at the principal's office, I was surprised to see that Brian was sitting in a chair next to her desk.

She looked up when I entered. Miss Baker was a short, chubby woman with black hair parted in the middle and plastered in uniform waves on her very round head. She had a softer look on her face than at our first meeting.

"Marie, please take a seat next to Brian," she said without looking at me. She fingered the papers on her desk for a moment. Then while continuing to fix her eyes on the paper before her, she said, "The reason I've asked you to my office is I received a call from your father, and he wants you to go home immediately. He didn't give a reason, but he did say that he and your mother are not sick or injured. You have my permission to leave."

"What about my books and homework?" asked Brian.

"Don't worry about that. I'll take care of it. You really need to go home right now," Miss Baker said, as she walked us out the door.

"I wonder what's going on?" said Brian as we headed home.

"Brian, do you think it has anything to do with the war?"

"Like what? Miss Baker said that Papa had called. That means he's still around. Nobody's taken him away. I overheard Papa saying that men were just snatched off the street by the FBI. They didn't have a chance to say goodbye to their families or anything. So we know that didn't happen to him."

"That's true," I said. Then it occurred to me that they could have taken Mama!

"Do you think they took Mama? Miss Baker didn't say anything about Mama!"

"Calm down, Marie. Remember? Miss Baker said that Papa AND Mama were okay. Anyhow, I don't think they would take women or children."

"Why not?"

"I don't know. Maybe they think only men do bad things? And women and children don't? I don't know. Anyway, I haven't heard of any women being taken away by the FBI."

When we reached the cleaners there was a "CLOSED" sign on the door.

"Great!" Said Brian. "How're we supposed to get in?" He jiggled the door to confirm it was locked. To our surprise, it opened with ease. The bell rang in the back when we stepped on the mat. Mama came running out to greet us. I was so happy to see her that I burst into tears. We stood there a moment while she held me.

Brian pulled us apart and asked, "What's going on, Mama? Is Papa okay? Why did we get called out of school?"

"Are these your children?" a deep unfamiliar voice shouted from the back.

"Yes."

"Bring them back here, please." Two strangers were sitting on the sofa in the work area. As we approached they stood up, stretching to the ceiling like two towers. One man was well dressed with smiling eyes and dark, shiny hair, while the other had tousled light brown hair and looked like he slept in his clothes. Papa was sitting in the armchair next to the sofa. He was staring at the floor.

"You must be Brian and Marie. I don't want you to be afraid," said the handsome man. He paused for a moment. "We're from the FBI."

"Are you here to take my father away like you took Rev. Nakamura? You can't take my father!" Brian blurted as he moved toward the stranger.

"Brian!" Papa shouted, as he leaped out of his chair and placed himself between Brian and the FBI agent. "You don't talk that way to him! Apologize! I'm sorry, Mr. Scott."

"It's okay, Mr. Mitsui. Calm down, Brian. Nobody's taking your father away." Then he continued. "Brian. And Marie. I'm Mr. Scott and this is Mr. Allen." He shook our hands. "Our boss at the FBI asked us to stay with you and your family for a while. That means that your parents will not be able to leave the store without one of us. And I'm sorry, but you children won't be able to go to outside or see your friends.

"I guess that means we can't go to school," I said.

"I guess not," said Brian with a smile.

I wasn't sure staying home from school was such a great thing. I wouldn't be able to see Jean. What would we do, if we didn't go to school, I wondered. It wasn't like a weekend or a school holiday, where we were free to play outside and be with our friends.

"Why can't we go to school? Why can't we go out to play? What did we do wrong?" I asked.

Mr. Scott took hold of the sharp creases on his pants and hiked them up as he lowered his tall frame to my level. He looked at me with his smiling hazel eyes and put his hand on my shoulder.

"That's what we're here to find out. But don't worry. I'm sure everything will be all right," he said. "Mr. Allen and I will be staying here day and night. We'll take turns sleeping on the sofa out here. Most of the time we'll be here together, but at least one of us will be here all the time."

And that's what they did. They slept in their clothes on the sofa, but didn't eat with us. They took turns going out to eat and sleep. After Mr. Scott spent the night, he left in the morning and returned with fresh clothes. His shirt was neat and his suit, pressed. Mr. Allen, on the other hand, wore the same shirt and suit the whole time he was with us. While one slept, the other stood watch.

And they each had their own way of going about the business of investigating.

"Mrs. Mitsui, I'm sorry, but I have to look through your things," said Mr. Scott as his eyes roamed over the cabinets and shelves that lined the kitchen walls. "I'm afraid I'll have to examine everything. Where would you like me to put things I've examined?"

"The kitchen table, I guess. We can eat in the work area until you finish."

"Okay. You start on the kitchen, Scott," said Mr. Allen. Then he turned to us. "Listen up, everyone. I'm doing the bedrooms. I'm putting everything on the beds after I go through your stuff. So if you have anything on your bed, get it off. Understand?"

I ran into my room and scrambled up the ladder to my bunk to move some books and dolls I had left on it. As I started to back my way down the ladder with my arms full, I realized I couldn't do it without hands, so I dropped my load onto the floor and continued down.

"I hope you don't plan to leave your junk there," Mr. Allen said, looking at the pile at his feet. He doesn't like me, I thought. But that was all right. I didn't like him, either. I picked up my books and dolls, placed them on my dresser, and walked passed him pretending he wasn't there.

During the day, the agents spent most of their time rummaging through our things, and my parents, Brian, and I spent most of our time putting it all back together. They also went through all of our business records and other papers and books. I even saw Mr. Allen looking in the pockets of our customers clothes that hung on the racks.

The "CLOSED" sign remained on the door, but some customers would pound on the door demanding their clothes. On those occasions, Mama would wait on them with either Mr. Scott or Mr. Allen at her side.

Mama couldn't go to the store without one of them accompanying her. She never told me about those trips, but I often wondered what happened. The grocery store wasn't very large and the aisles were narrow. Did the agent wait outside? Or did he follow her around in the store? I imagined that if it were Mr. Scott's turn, he would have carried Mama's basket, and maybe even discussed the quality of the fruits and vegetables and made other idle conversation. On the other hand, I pictured grumpy Mr. Allen following a few paces behind and muttering something like, "Hurry up! We haven't got all day, you know."

I also wondered what the neighbors thought about Mama shopping with a man. Papa had never accompanied her to the grocers. And there she was with a man, and he wasn't even her husband. I would have liked to think that they thought she had a couple of "boyfriends." But it was more reasonable that they thought, "There's Mrs. Mitsui shopping with the FBI agent who has them under house arrest."

In the evening, it was free time for the agents. They were not "searching," but just sitting around reading or talking. Brian had received a bicycle the Christmas before—a gray Schwinn with white-walled balloon tires and chrome fenders. It had a lot of extras like a rear carrier, headlight, taillight, and a horn. He was trying to install the horn.

After watching Brian for a while, Mr. Scott asked, "Want help with this?"

"Sure."

Mr. Scott removed his coat, rolled up his sleeves, and got down on the floor with Brian. "I have a son, Mark, who's eleven just like you. I got him a bike, but it's not this fancy. Where's piece D? You should probably put it with C first."

Mr. Allen sat on the edge of a chair and watched Mr. Scott and Brian. His face was scrunched up in a frown.

"My uncle Ray gave this to me for Christmas. I think I'm his favorite nephew," Brian beamed as he backed away from the pile of parts to give Mr. Scott some room.

"I can see why," said Mr. Scott as he smiled at Brian.

I knelt next to Mr. Scott and peered over his shoulder as he worked. The pomade on his slicked back hair had the sweet scent of roses.

"Is he the uncle that lives in Japanese Town?" he asked. "Do you have a smaller screwdriver?"

"No, that's Uncle Kazuo," Brian answered as he picked the smallest of the screwdrivers from Papa's tool box and handed it to him. "Uncle Ray lives on Monterey Boulevard. He runs a cleaning shop, too. He's my father's younger brother."

"I see," said Mr. Scott. "You mentioned Rev. Nakamura before. How did you know him? Did you go to his church?"

Brian had mentioned Rev. Nakamura having been

arrested by the FBI. Why is he asking about him now? He's questioning us! I thought. Was that our crime? Knowing Rev. Nakamura? Is that why Brian and I were not allowed to leave our home?

"Rev. Nakamura was our Japanese-school teacher. He was a nice man," I said rather loudly, although I was right next to his ear. "We used to go to Japanese school to learn Japanese at the Buddhist Church. My best friend, Jean Ireland, whose father is the captain of inspectors in the San Francisco Police Department, was also a student there. Is there a law against studying Japanese? Is that why you're here? Because we know Rev. Nakamura?"

Papa came running into the room.

"What are you shouting about, Marie. Lower your voice! . . . Oh, Mr. Scott! I didn't know you were here with them. Is she bothering you?"

"Everything's all right, Mr. Mitsui."

I ran into my bedroom and slammed the door. Mr. Scott was just being nice to us to get information, I thought. He's just a sneaky FBI agent. His niceness is only an act! Going to Japanese school is what got us into trouble. We shouldn't have gone to Japanese school! I thought. Then maybe we wouldn't be in this fix.

The following day, I was drawing on a large piece of paper of the kind my parents used to cover clean clothes. I was on the floor of the work area. I suddenly got a whiff of roses. Mr. Scott is nearby, I thought. I put my face closer to my drawing. I didn't feel like talking to sneaky Mr. Scott. Then I felt a tap on my shoulder. I looked to my left and saw that he had folded up his long body so that he was down on his knees on the floor next to me. HIs long narrow face was just inches from mine. His breath smelled like mint.

"I'm sorry if I upset you, Marie. I was just making

conversation. If it were wrong to know Rev. Nakamura, everyone who was in his Japanese school class and congregation would be criminals. Everyone who was a member of his church would be a criminal. That would be silly, don't you think? We would have to pick everyone up! That would be crazy!"

"You haven't 'picked us' up, although you're here. And I guess you're right. I'm sorry I shouted at you," I said. "I made a mistake. I'm glad you weren't 'drilling' us. So why exactly are you picking on us? Does that mean you aren't going to take us away?"

"I don't know. Someone else made the decision. I'm just following orders."

Later that day, a third FBI agent came by. He looked older than Mr. Scott and Mr. Allen. His dark hair was streaked with white and his face had deep lines and sagging cheeks. He had come to speak to Mr. Scott.

"I need to speak with you in private," he said. The older man took Mr. Scott to the front of the store, but we could hear Mr. Scott being scolded.

"Scott, I understand you've been helping the kid with his bike. You're an FBI agent. Your job is not to be a handyman. You need to maintain some distance between members of this family and yourself. Understand?"

Mr. Scott avoided us after that.

After a few days, Brian and I were allowed to return to school. I stood beside Mama as she wrote a note to take back to my teacher. I read her note aloud as I peered over her shoulder, "Please excuse Marie for being absent from school, as she had an upset stomach. . . ."

"Mama, I didn't have an upset stomach!" I said. "Why'd you write that?"

"Shh!" she said in a tone that told me she didn't want to talk about it. It seemed an unnecessary lie. I was sure everyone knew about the FBI. We left school suddenly. Jean and Jimmy brought our homework assignments over and gave them to Mr. Scott. Our cleaning shop was closed and the agents were going in and out all the time. My mother walked up and down Lawton Street running errands with a man that didn't even come close to resembling Papa—-things were not exactly normal at our house. Mama thinks this is something to be ashamed of, I concluded, and doesn't want Miss O'Brien to know! Should I be ashamed, too?

Finally, after a week, Mr. Scott announced that they would be leaving. My guess was that they were satisfied that we were not communicating with the Japanese army, and that we were not dangerous people.

"I'm very sorry we intruded on you like this. I was just following orders," said Mr. Scott. "I hope we meet again under better circumstances." We were all outside, saying our goodbyes to him and Mr. Allen. They were about to leave, when Mr. Allen said he had forgotten something inside.

"Why don't l just go get the car and bring it around," Mr. Scott said and left for the gas station on the corner where the car was parked. Everyone else had gone inside. I stood watching as Mr. Scott walked away for the last time.

Wisps of fog began drifting toward him and reached out like fingers trying to bring him back. I turned and looked up Lawton. The fog doing its usual thing. It was crawling toward us wrapping itself around everything in its path. When I turned back around, I was surprised to find Mr. Allen standing next to me. He leaned over and put his scrunched up pock-covered face next to mine. He could have used a mint. As the mist swirled around him, his green eyes flashed with anger. Just like the Black Tiger in the Shadow movies, I thought. I started to stumble back away from this scary person and was about to run inside. But he grabbed me by the shoulders.

"We're leaving you now," he sneered, "But I hope you suffer even more for what Japan did to us!"

I should have screamed in his face. Or pushed him away. Or run away. Did *some*thing. But I couldn't. For some reason, I couldn't move. I just stood there.

Suddenly, tears began to fill my eyes. They were beyond my control. I could barely see him through the blur. He seemed to stare at me for a moment. Then, without a sound, he let go, turned, and started down the street after Mr. Scott.

I ran inside past Mama, Papa, and Brian into my room, climbed into my bed, and cried until I could cry no more. I could hear Brian saying, "I think Marie liked Mr. Scott."

CHAPTER 6

"Marines' Hymn"
U.S. MARINE CORPS

Patsy McCarthy lived in the neighborhood, but went to St. Anne's, a Catholic school. She was a pretty girl, about my size, with large smiling eyes and long brown pigtails. She also loved to sing. We learned the words to the "Marines' Hymn" we found in a giveaway magazine at the grocery store. Then we locked arms and marched up and down Lawton singing it to demonstrate our patriotism.

"It's good for the war effort!" we told anyone who asked.

Papa and Mama demonstrated their patriotism by buying U.S. savings stamps and distributing them to our customers. They could paste them in a book. When it was filled with $18.75 worth of stamps it could be converted into a bond at a bank. After ten years the bond would be worth $25.00. I could picture most things in my mind, but ten years was beyond my imagination. In any case, these bonds helped pay for the war effort.

One day, not long after our house arrest was over, Mr. Bouchard, the captain of the neighborhood Civilian Defense Committee invited my father to join them. I was so proud. That meant that they trusted him. I imagined that Mr. Scott had arranged it.

First thing, Papa had to learn first aid. He took a class and practiced at home by putting splints on Brian and me. We found out how it felt to have broken legs and arms. Or at least, how awkward it was to be bandaged up. Papa and Uncle Ray had long conversations on the phone about their first aid training. Uncle Ray had been asked to join the Civilian Defense Committee in his neighborhood, too. After Papa completed his training, he was assigned to "blackout" monitoring.

"Everyone has to practice making their homes and shops dark when the siren sounds." Papa explained. "That's so enemy planes can't see us to bomb us. When we hear the air raid siren at night, we have to 'blackout.'

"That means we have to turn out our neon signs," he continued. "Marie, I put you in charge of that and all the lights in the front and work area, because I will be out checking the other stores on this block. When I get back from my rounds, I want to come back to a darkened store." I was so happy that Papa gave me such an important job.

"Brian," he said turning to him, "I want you to be sure the blackout-curtains are drawn in the kitchen. Go outside and see if any light is leaking. If it is, fix it. And be sure the door to the work area is closed."

"Do you and Brian understand your responsibilities? Mama, I want you to see that they do what they're supposed to."

"I'm going to leave my Civilian Defense hat here in the show window, so everyone can see it," he continued. It was a white hard hat with a Civilian Defense sticker affixed to the front. "I don't want you two playing with it. And the Civilian Defense sticker on the window will also let people know they can come to us for first aid."

"I'll absolutely be back before eight," said Papa.

Because Papa and Mama were not citizens, they had to follow rules established for them. They couldn't be outside after eight p.m. The reason they weren't citizens even though they had lived in the U.S. for over twenty years is that the law didn't allow it. But Papa was doing his best to protect us from the enemy anyway. I was very proud of him.

★ ★ ★

One Friday night, after we had all gone to bed. I could hear someone banging on the door out front and people shouting. I hid under the covers.

"Who's out there? What do you want?" Papa shouted. His voice trailed as he ran out front, closing the door behind him. I could then see light trickling in from under the door to the work area. Then I heard the bell. He's going out the door, I thought. There was the rumble of a car driving off and the screeching of tires.

"What happened?" I could hear Brian asking Papa when he returned.

"Nothing. Go to bed."

★ ★ ★

"It was way past your curfew," I could hear Mr. Bouchard telling Papa in a loud whisper. He was on the other side of the wall from where I lay on the upper bunk reading. "It was irresponsible, and I'm afraid that I am going to have to have you resign from the committee." I pressed my ear to the wall.

"Someone was at my door," Papa said. "I thought it was an emergency. So I was just checking. I shouldn't have stepped outside, I know. I wasn't thinking."

"Pete down at the hardware said that you were having a loud party or something. Loud voices and general carrying on."

"That's what I heard, too. It woke me up. But it wasn't me."

"Well, I . . . I'll look into this further. In the meantime, Joe Smith will be taking your turn during blackouts," said Mr. Bouchard.

The following day, Mr. Bouchard was back. "I am very sorry I accused you, Mr. Mitsui," he said. "I asked around. It was Curtis Wright and his friends. They were bragging at the Drop Inn Tavern that they were going to get you. They were drunk. But I have also discussed this with the committee and we all agree that for your safety, I don't think it's a good idea for you to be out after dark. So we're relieving you of your blackout duty. There are too many loonies out there. I'm really sorry."

"I can take care of myself. Why don't you do something about them, instead of punishing me?"

"I'm not punishing you. I'm trying to protect you."

"I don't need that kind of protection!"

"Well, I'm sorry you feel that way, but the decision is final."

The door to the bedroom area opened. Papa came in, slammed the door behind him, and left Mr. Bouchard standing in the work area.

That was the end of Papa's Civilian Defense assignment, but Papa kept his Civilian Defense hat and left it in the window. He never had a chance to actually monitor a blackout. A couple of days later, when I returned home from school, the hat was gone. As well as the sticker.

★ ★ ★

At school, our class was making afghans for children in Europe. For victims of the war. Each of us knit seven-inch squares in different colors, which were patched together to make a beautiful blanket. I chose a beautiful turquoise blue yarn. I went to Mrs. Bagley's to show her what I was going to do. Her variety store wasn't a particularly busy place, and I had often found her knitting to pass the time between customers.

"Do you know how to knit, Marie?"

"No, but I'm sure my mother can teach me."

"I know she's very busy with the cleaners. Let me just help you get started."

"Okay."

She showed me how to cast on, knit, and cast off. She taught me two ways to knit. One way was to loop the yarn around the needle and the other was to hook the yarn. Hooking the yarn was faster. That's what I decided to do.

"You won't have to purl on these squares. Just keep knitting as you did before, when you start on a new row," Mrs. Bagley explained.

With those simple instructions and demonstration, I was off and knitting. Mostly I knitted after I got home from school. Sometimes, I'd go across the street and knit with Mrs. Bagley. We would knit and chat. At other times, I sat in the show-window alcove clicking my knitting needles, creating squares out of lines of yarn. This filled much of my time after school.

"What are you doing, Marie?" customers would ask.

"Knitting an afghan for children who are victims of the war. It's part of the war effort."

"All by yourself? That's a lot of knitting."

"Everyone in the class is knitting squares. It's a team effort."

"I see. Well, keep up the good work."

"I will." I wanted to do the best I could for the war effort. I wanted to prove how much of an American I was. I became a knitting-maniac. At least that's what Brian called me. I was able to knit fifteen and a half squares, which was more than anyone else in the class.

In the middle of February, I overheard Papa and Mama talking about a rule President Roosevelt made about restrictions in terms of where people, "both aliens and non-aliens of Japanese Ancestry," should live. Papa had talked about how he and Mama were "aliens," because they were born in Japan, so I knew what that was. But "non-alien?" I wondered what it meant. The rule didn't mention citizens. How does the rule affect me, I wondered. But I had learned that it was better not to ask my parents questions about anything. If they wanted us to know they would tell us without our asking.

In the days that followed there would be times I would return home and find Papa giving strangers a tour of the cleaners. They would talk in a huddle, so that I wasn't able to listen to their conversations. Papa would be in a nasty mood after those visits by strangers.

Then a few weeks later, Papa was unusually quiet at dinner. He sat crosslegged as usual. He had bathed and was in his yukata. We were having my favorite, rice smothered in tripe cooked in tomato sauce.

Papa cleared his throat, then said very softly and slowly, "We are moving to Stockton to Grandpa and Grandma's. The army says we can't stay here, because we're too close to the ocean. Stockton is okay. It also gives us the chance to be together as a family for whatever happens. Uncle Ray and his family are coming with us." Uncle Ray was Papa's younger brother, who had given Brian the bike. He and his wife were like second parents to Brian and me.

"Why do we have to leave? Can the army tell us what to do? I thought the FBI said we could stay. Isn't the FBI the boss of the army?" The words poured out of Brian's mouth in a torrent.

When Brian stopped to take a breath, I picked up. "We're good Americans. The FBI said so. And we give away savings stamps, you were a Civilian Defense monitor, and I knit afghans. . . . What did we do wrong?"

75

Papa waited patiently until it became quiet. And then he continued. "We just have to follow orders and make the best of it. We have a lot to do as a family, so Friday will be your last day at Lawton."

Oh, no. I have to face my class, I thought. It would be difficult explaining why we were being ordered to leave. We have to move away because we have Japanese ancestors, even if we're Americans? We're dangerous, even if the FBI said we're not?

"Do we have to?" I asked. "How am I going to explain why we're leaving?"

"All you have to do is say you're moving to Stockton to be close to your grandparents." Papa said. "It's been announced in the news that anyone with Japanese ancestry has to leave San Francisco. Your teacher will know. Just tell them we're being good Americans by following the army's orders. You'll feel better if you say goodbye to your friends."

I went to Mrs. Bagley's to tell her that we were leaving.

"That's so unfair," she said, as tears welled up in her eyes. "I'm so sorry you have to go through all this." She put her arms around me and held me for a long time. Then her face suddenly brightened, and she said, "I have a great idea! I'd like to give you and Brian each an autograph book."

"What's an autograph book?"

"It's a book you have your friends write in."

"I don't understand."

"You have your friends write messages to you in it. So you'll have something to remember them by."

"What a great idea!" I said.

She took me over to a shelf that held all sorts of books with blank pages. I selected a maroon one with a spiral wire binding and a larger one for Brian. Mrs. Bagley was the first one to sign mine:

Dearest Marie,

I shall always remember you for your cute smile and wiggly ways. A smart little girl who is most apt to succeed wherever she goes.

Love, Katherine Bagley

★ ★ ★

Brian and I took the books to school as she suggested. On Friday at sharing time I announced that the army had given us orders to leave San Francisco and we would be moving to Stockton to be with my grandparents. This would be my last day at Lawton, I told them. I asked everyone to write me a message in my autograph book.

"We'll be leaving San Francisco next Thursday," I said.

"When are you coming back?" Richard asked through tears. He was the first one to talk to me when I first arrived at Lawton. It was in December and he asked me to help him draw Christmas trees the way I did. I guess you could say he was my first Lawton friend.

"We're actually moving, Richard. We're selling the cleaners and moving." I said. "Stockton will be our new home. The President wants us to leave San Francisco. But we'll be back when the war is over and when we return, we'll visit." I said. I lied. I didn't really think the war would ever be over. I didn't think we'd ever be able to return, either. But it seemed like the right thing to say. I fought hard to keep from crying. I tried to think about something else. Jean had brought a large plate of chocolate chip cookies for my "going away" party. They were sitting on Miss O'Brien's desk and caught my eye.

"When can we have the cookies?" I said turning to Miss O'Brien.

"Would you like to pass them out?"

"May I do it now?"

She nodded with a smile. I placed a cookie on each napkin where a graham cracker would ordinarily go, next to our midmorning milk snack. It would be the last time I had midmorning snack at Lawton.

CHAPTER 7

"Good Night My Love"
SHIRLEY TEMPLE

"Right now, we have to decide what we will be able to take in the car. Remember there are four of us," Papa said. "It'll be whatever is left after Uncle Robert from Stockton picks up all large items such as our beds, bedding, table, and chairs with his pickup." He never mentioned Brian's bike or my Betsy Wetsy.

Brian and I looked at each other and we knew what that meant. Our big stuff had to stay. We would each have to give up our favorite things. For me, it would be my "Betsy Wetsy doll set." Betsy wet when you gave it a bottle. She had eyes that rolled open when she sat up and arms and legs that twisted and turned. Betsy, diapers, bottles, and complete wardrobe all fit in a suitcase and matching buggy. For Brian it would be his bike.

It was not surprising that we would have to give up our favorite toys. Nothing surprised me anymore. Papa always said, "We just have to do the best we can." This was one of those situations.

"Who're you going to give your Betsy Wetsy set to?" Brian asked.

"Jean is my best friend, but she already has more dolls than she can use. And she doesn't play with them. They just sit on a shelf."

"What about Alice? It seems like she's always at the cleaners lately."

"Yeah. She really likes Betsy. Actually I think she likes my doll more than she likes me. I think that's the only reason she comes over," I laughed. Alice was a couple of years younger than me. She was also the youngest of six and didn't have too many things she could call her own. She was cute and wore her hair in one long French braid that began at her freckled forehead and extended down just below her neck. She spoke with a slight Southern accent. That was because her family lived in Oklahoma before moving to San Francisco.

"In that case you know that if you give it to her, she'll take good care of it," Brian said. "I'd give it to Alice."

"Yeah. I guess that's important. She'll take good care of it. What about you, Brian? Who gets your bike?"

"Jimmy." Brian said without hesitation. Blond, handsome Jimmy stood a head taller than Brian and was his best friend ever since we moved here. They met when Jimmy stood up for Brian after he first started at Lawton. Whenever kids tried to pick fights with Brian, Jimmy was there for him. They were in the same sixth-grade class and played baseball and football together. And Brian spent a lot of time at Jimmy's house.

The first time I met him he pointed to his stomach and said, "Marie! Hit me as hard as you can!" So I hit his stomach. It was as hard as a rock. "Come on. You can hit harder than that! Harder! "

"I can't hit you harder than that. I'll hurt my hand."

Jimmy laughed and flexed his muscles. Brian told me he was the strongest boy in their class. Maybe the whole school. I was going to miss Jimmy.

★ ★ ★

"Marie, I want to take you for one last ride on my bike. Get your coat," Brian said. He had me sit "side-saddle" on the crossbar between the seat and the handlebars. I held onto a bar that ran across the handlebars that flared out like wings.

"I'm going to take you to my secret place. I never took you before, because it's on the other side of the hill." Secret place? Brian had a secret and he was trusting me with it. I felt like I was becoming more than just a kid sister, but a true friend.

Brian headed down Lawton and turned right on 25th Avenue. It was flat for about half the block, then suddenly got very steep. He pumped as hard as he could on the flat, then began to tack as the street steepened. He struggled to keep the bike balanced and moving as he pedaled first to the left and then to the right.

"I may not . . . make it . . . to . . . the top," he said breathlessly. "You may . . . have . . . to get off . . . and walk." The bike swayed as he tried to keep it balanced as we slowed down. "Don't . . . hold onto . . . the bar so tight! . . . I can't . . . steer! Just . . . try to balance yourself!"

He kept moving the handlebar back and forth and leaned on me as he pedaled standing up. Suddenly, we were on the flat. "Hooray! We made it!" I screamed.

"What do you mean, 'we made it'? I did all the work!" Brian screamed back.

"Okay. . . . Hooray! You did it! . . . Is that better?"
"Much."

Then he pedaled easily to a shopping center I had never known existed. There were shops for blocks in either direction. It was not one-street shopping like Lawton.

"Okay. Now listen carefully. Stay close to me. I don't want you getting lost. Also, we stay away from the cleaners, the stationery store, and the dress shop. Don't look into those stores even if they shout at us. Okay?"

"This sounds scary. I think I want to go home," I said.

"Nothing to be frightened of. They're harmless, Marie. They shout at me all the time. Mr. Roberts says they're just ignorant cowards." Mr. Roberts was Jimmy's father. Brian stood silently for a moment. "I've got it! I know which stores to go to and totally avoid the bad ones. Okay?"

"Okay."

Our first stop was the soda fountain.

"Hi, Brian. The usual for you? Is this your sister? What'll you have, little sister?" The soda jerk was a friendly man with a bulbous nose and smiling eyes. He was wearing a thin white "overseas" cap and a white jacket, which strained to cover his round belly. The cap could have been larger, too. It was perched precariously on top of his balding head. Each time he leaned over, I was sure it was going to fall into the ice cream. He handed us each our cones and said, "I'm glad Brian finally brought you in, little sister. I hope I see you again soon."

"Thank you, I hope so, too," I turned away quickly so he wouldn't see the tears filling my eyes.

We took our ice cream cones outside and walked around, looking in the windows of some of the shops on the street. We spent most of the time watching the model train in the show window of the toy store. It chugged along a track that coursed through tiny mountain tunnels and towns.

"Wouldn't you just love to go for a train ride someday?" I asked Brian.

"Yeah. I'd like to ride in the caboose," said Brian.

"The caboose? I like the Pullman. It seems like fun sleeping on a train."

Then we went into the drug store to look at comic books.

"Lick your fingers, then wipe them on your dress so they're not sticky." he whispered.

"I am not going to wipe my fingers on my dress!"

"Okay, okay. Then, here, wipe them on my pants." he whispered again. "And turn the pages carefully. You have to be careful how you handle these comics, because kids don't like to buy comics that look used," Brian said, "not to mention how the owner feels about it."

"I know! You don't have to tell me everything!"

"We're each going to buy one. So try to find just one you like."

We sat on the floor checking the ware. Like "Simple Simon." It took a long time to decide on one. There were so many I liked. "Nancy," "Tillie the Toiler," "Mutt and Jeff." And then there was "Green Hornet" and "Flash." I looked up every so often expecting the owner to chase us out, but he never did.

"Okay. I think we'd better get going. Hurry up and choose one. I'm getting the "Dick Tracy.""

I really wanted to buy "Nancy," but I knew Brian wouldn't read it. Then at the last minute, I spotted a "Captain Marvel." I liked the story of Billy Batson and how he became Captain Marvel with all the virtues of Solomon and the Greek gods.

"I want Captain Marvel," I said.

"Good choice! I like Captain Marvel, too."

The trip home was much easier. We were able to coast most of the way.

The next day, Jimmy came over to pick up Brian's bike.

"Here's some polish for the chrome on the fenders and spokes, Jimmy," said Brian. "It can rust if you don't take care of them. And this polish is for the gray painted parts. It'll keep it from chipping. "

"I promise I'll take good care of it. I won't let it rust or get crummy looking. I'll take care of it until you come back."

"It's yours now, Jimmy. Take it and go," Brian said and walked to the back of the cleaners.

When Alice came over to play on Friday, I asked her if she wanted my Betsy Wetsy doll set with the buggy.

"Why would you give it to me? It's your favorite doll."

"I'm moving away and I can't take Betsy with me."

"I have to go ask my mother," she said and ran home.

A few minutes later she was back with her mother, Mrs. Prince, a tall, heavyset woman with gray hair pulled back in a bun. She was dressed in a flowered cotton housedress and navy sweater with stretched sleeves. Mama came out from the back when she heard the bell.

"What's going on? Why're you giving away your Betsy Wetsy doll set, Marie?" Mrs. Prince asked. Then she turned to Mama,

"Did you know she was doing this?"

"We're moving away and we don't have room for big things like Brian's bike and my Betsy Wetsy doll set," I said.

"Well, surely you have enough for your doll. Why don't you take it and leave the rest, if you have to?"

"Brian had to give up his entire bicycle. It wouldn't be fair to Brian. Besides, I'm getting too old for dolls."

"We're only taking what we can fit in the car, and the suitcase and buggy would take up too much space. We plan to do a lot of traveling," Mama said.

"Where're you going that you're doing all this traveling?"

"We're going to Stockton first to join my parents. We may have to leave California."

"Leave California? Why?"

"That's the rumor."

No one said anything. Suddenly, Alice's mother sobbed, "I'm so sorry," and grabbed Mama locking her in an embrace. It was the first time I had ever seen another woman hugging Mama. Her arms stuck straight out. Then she slowly returned the hug. Still sobbing, Mrs. Prince came over to me and buried me in her ample bosom.

When I was able to breathe again, I said, "I'll pack Betsy and all her things in the suitcase for you. Come back later, okay, Alice?"

"Okay. And Marie. I am so happy you chose me. It's the nicest thing anyone has ever given me. I'll treasure Betsy forever."

We had to give the business away, too. That's what Papa said. "One hundred dollars is all we can get for it." And that's what they sold it for. The business, the equipment, most of our furniture, our new refrigerator. . . .

When the World's Fair came to Treasure Island in 1939, Papa bought me a Japanese costume. It was a box filled with a silk undergarment that looked like a kimono and a beautifully patterned lined silk kimono with gold flecks. A collection of brocade, tie-dyed puckered silk, sash, and cord, filled the remainder of the box. It was fifty dollars. Fifty dollars for a Japanese costume, one hundred dollars for a business.

★ ★ ★

It was Thursday, March 26, 1942, a few days before people of Japanese ancestry were no longer permitted to travel. Our moving day. Daylight had just begun to seep through the skylight above my bed.

"Marie! It's time to get up. We have a lot to do."

I pulled my heavy quilt over my head and slid deep under it, like a turtle pulling into its shell. I didn't want to get up. I wanted to stay in bed forever.

"Marie! Get up! You're the last one! Even Brian is up!"

I bolted up and pulled the covers from its moorings and flung them off the bed.

A muffled shout came from below. "What're you doing, Marie? You could have hurt me!"

"Why didn't you get out of the way?"

"This is no time for fighting! Hurry up and get dressed," Mama said. "You need to eat breakfast, so I can clean up the kitchen and get things packed."

I wish she would quit shouting, I thought. It wasn't like her. And it just made things more difficult.

"We don't have time for your tears, Marie. We've got things to do. Uncle Robert is already here with his pickup and the Lees will be here at eight o'clock." The Lees were the new owners of the cleaners.

I pulled on my dress and ran outside. It was a typical San Francisco morning. Thick fog tumbled down Lawton from the ocean moistening everything in its way. Foghorns hummed and groaned in the distance. I stood for a moment to feel the cold, damp mist touch my face and listened to the chorus in the strait. We were moving to hot Stockton. This may be the last time I'll ever see fog, I thought.

"Marie, what are you doing out there like that? You'll catch cold. Come inside and get your things together! Don't make me keep shouting at you!"

Despite my efforts to delay the inevitable, we reached a point where we were packing our car. A huge assortment of things covered with canvas was piled high on the bed of Uncle Robert's pickup as it stood ready to lead us to our new home.

A crowd began to gather in front of the store. Jimmy rode over on the bike Brian gave him. The chrome fenders and spokes glistened in the morning sun whenever it peeked through cracks in the fog. His father and brother arrived on foot a few moments later.

"I see you've been using the chrome polish," Brian said.

Jimmy turned his face away as tears filled his eyes. He grabbed Brian's hand and leaned close. "I'm really going to miss you, buddy. Don't forget to write."

"Me, too." said Brian, wiping his tears.

Jean brought me one of her favorite Nancy Drew books, *The Hidden Staircase,* and insisted I take it.

"I want you to have it and think of me as you read it," said Jean and pulled me into a hug, tears rolling down her face.

"Thanks, Jean. You're my best friend forever," I sobbed.

Soon, the patch of sidewalk in front of the cleaners became totally covered with the Rogers, Irelands, Mrs. Bagley, Mr. Broussard, other shop owners, neighbors, friends, and customers. There were also people I had never seen before. After tears, handshakes, and hugs, Brian and I climbed into the back seat of the car and squeezed in amidst our belongings. Everyone stood at the curb waving as we slowly pulled away. Alice stood in front of everyone with my Betsy Wetsy buggy. I turned away. I felt a terrible sadness having to part with a friend as well as my favorite possession.

"You won't be seeing this neighborhood again," said Brian as we drove away. "Take a good look."

CHAPTER 8

"American Patrol"
GLENN MILLER

It took four hours to get to my grandparents' place in Stockton. We stopped once at the side of the road to eat rice balls and pickled radishes that Mama had prepared. I slept most of the way.

This was a drive we had taken many times before. It was always in anticipation of seeing Grandpa and Grandma and the huge German Shepherds they kept as watchdogs. My grandparents ran a hotel for Japanese farm laborers and visitors from Japan. Grandpa was a farm labor contractor, which meant that farmers would tell him when they needed help, and Grandpa would arrange for workers from among the hotel guests.

I had always looked forward to those visits. But this was different. It wasn't that I didn't want to see Grandpa and Grandma. As much as I liked them, this time we wouldn't be returning home. What was it going to be like, living with them forever?

"Are we going to live in one of the rooms in the hotel?" I asked.

"Grandpa and Grandma own the house next door, and

it's been vacant for a while. They were going to tear it down and build a larger house on the lot before the war started. But they can't do that now," Mama said. "They've fixed it up so we can live there. It has four bedrooms, so it's large enough for both our family and Uncle Ray's."

When we finally reached the outskirts of Stockton, I spotted the huge gas storage tanks to the left of the road that signaled we were close to our new home. The tanks loomed larger and larger. Soon after, I spotted the top of the large three-story red brick building that was the hotel. It towered over the neighboring short, flat houses.

"There it is . . . ," I said softly. "We're almost there."

"You don't have to make an announcement," Brian said. "We're not blind. We can see it, too."

"Well, I saw it first," I said.

We slowed down as we rounded the corner of Center and Lafayette, where the hotel entrance stood. Two cement steps led up to the double doors. It was topped by an enormous transom in which the address "401 S. Center" floated. We passed the entrance to the driveway just beyond the building on Lafayette Street. The gravel on the driveway crunched under our wheels as we entered the parking area. We came to a stop in front of the back door, where two German Shepherds barked and strained at their tethers to announce our arrival. Uncle Ray and his family had arrived just before us and guided us into a parking spot.

The screen door to the kitchen burst open and my grandparents came running out to greet us. Grandpa, tall, husky, totally bald, and neatly dressed in dark pants and white shirt, lumbered toward us. Trailing a few steps behind was Grandma, a round lady with wavy hair pulled into a knot on the back of her head. She wore her usual paisley print smock.

"Welcome. You must be tired from the long trip," Grandma said as she pushed Grandpa aside. "Come in, come in and eat. Food is on the table. You can unload your things later." Grandpa laughed and managed to squeeze in a short "Hope you had a good trip."

Grandma had prepared a Japanese meal of miso soup, broiled mackerel, spinach, pickled vegetables, rice, and tea. She served us in the large dining room where the hotel guests had their meals. There were several long tables in the middle of the room, and a few guests sat deeply engrossed in their meals. Along the left wall was a cash register on a table with a chair next to it. Grandpa usually sat there to collect money from his meal guests. On our frequent visits before the war, Grandpa would be sitting at his post and call to me: "Shizu, come and sing me a song and I'll give you a nickel!" I always managed to go home with a pocketful of nickels Grandpa had taken from the cash register.

No one said anything as we ate. Like the other guests, eyes were fixed on the food, as though it required total undivided attention. Other than the occasional slurping of soup and crunching of pickled daikon, it was absolutely quiet.

"The pickled daikon is unusually crunchy. It makes a nice sound," I said. "You make good pickled daikon, Grandma."

Everyone burst into laughter, although I didn't think what I said was particularly funny.

"I always tell the children that good pickled daikon can be judged by the sound it makes when eaten," said Papa.

Then Grandpa said, "I'm so glad that we're all together. We don't know what's going to happen, but at least we're all together."

"I hope they let us stay here in Stockton," said Papa. "We're pretty far from the ocean now."

"That would be nice. At the moment, all we can do is sit and wait for orders," said Grandpa.

"Does that mean we don't have to go to school?" Brian asked.

"No, I think we should just do what's normal until we get clear orders. Since tomorrow's Friday, you can rest a day and start school on Monday. It's just down the street," said Grandpa.

"You'll be going to the school I went to when I first arrived from Japan," Mama said. "I was twelve then. Just a little older than Brian is now. I had traveled across the ocean all by myself on a ship full of strangers. I didn't know any English when I arrived, but fortunately, they had special classes for children from Japan. It was a good school then. I'm sure it's still a good school." I looked over at Brian and he rolled his eyes as if to say, "Here she goes again, talking about her childhood . . ."

After dinner, we crossed the driveway to the house that was to be our new home. We entered through the back door. To my surprise, it opened to a narrow hallway that was papered with yellowing Japanese newspapers!

"I thought you said that Grandpa fixed this house up for us," I whispered to Mama.

"That's what they said they were going to do," Mama said. "I don't know what happened. At least it's clean." And that was true. It was clean. And if we had been able to read Japanese, we would have been able to catch up on ancient news by reading the walls.

On the bright side, Brian and I would each have our own room. But the house hadn't been lived in for many years, so there was no water or gas. That meant that we could do no cooking in this house. Or anything else. We would also have to use the bathrooms in the hotel.

Mama had four brothers, who were all born here. Three of them lived in the Stockton area. Her oldest brother, William, and his family lived down the road from the hotel, and Uncle Tom farmed in French Camp. Her youngest, Uncle Robert, had recently returned home from San Francisco where he was a student in dental school. Her fourth brother lived in Washington, D.C. Mama's three brothers along with Papa and Uncle Ray would be busy for a while getting the house more livable.

The hotel was at the edge of the shopping district on Center Street, but there were no sidewalks. Once we crossed Lafayette Street, however, there were raised wooden-platform walkways instead of the concrete ones we were accustomed to in San Francisco. Brian was the one who told me about them.

"You've got to see the sidewalks up the street," he said. "They're made of wood and they creak and make hollow thumping sounds when you walk on them. Come on! I'll show you." Brian ran out the kitchen door and driveway and across the street. First, I walked normally so I could hear the creaking. Then, stomped and jumped. It was almost like pounding on drums. The sidewalks also had roofs over them, bouncing the sound back at me. Moviemakers could easily have made a cowboy movie on Center Street, I thought. There was even a rail to tie up horses.

The following week as we walked the two blocks to our new school with Grandpa and Mama, Brian and I walked very deliberately on the creaky wooden boards that led to Franklin. Then we galloped.

"Don't make so much noise when you walk," Grandpa said. "You'll disturb the shopkeepers along the street."

"We stomped all day yesterday and no one seemed to mind," said Brian.

"Yesterday was Sunday. All the shops were closed. If you'll look inside the show windows, you'll see that there are people inside," said Grandpa.

We walked tippy-toe.

"Don't act silly," Grandpa scolded. "Just walk normally. I just want you to be considerate of others. Common sense tells you that noise made directly in front of someone's property is going to be heard inside." Grandpa scolded. Brian and I apologized. I liked it better when he was asking me to sing and dance.

A block later, we found ourselves in front of a large three-story building. It dominated the school yard that surrounded it. Off to one side there was a smaller square building. It had the shape of a building block with windows.

"That's where my classes were held when I first arrived from Japan," Mama said as she pointed to the smaller building. "I don't know what it's used for now. At that time, children like me who didn't speak English were taught here. Grandma had left me in Japan when I was five years old. Grandpa came to America shortly after I was born. . . ." There she goes again. . . .

Brian didn't roll his eyes this time. Instead, he said, "That must have been hard for you to come to a country where you didn't know the language. But you speak pretty good English now!"

"That was twenty-five years ago," Mama said. "When I first arrived Grandpa and Grandma spoke only in Japanese, so I didn't need to know English except at school. And even at school, all my classmates were from Japan. So it wasn't that bad."

As we passed Mama's old school, I could hear the familiar sounds of kids on the school playground. I felt a mixture of excitement and nervousness. Another new school, new kids. We turned the corner and entered the playground. I kept my eyes down.

"Hi, Mr. Nishimura. Are these your grandchildren?"

I looked up and saw a girl about my age standing in front of us. She was "of Japanese Ancestry." She was with two others who were also "of Japanese ancestry." I looked around and almost everyone was "of Japanese Ancestry!" I had never before seen so many kids on a school playground who looked like me in one place before. I soon learned that we were living in the middle of Stockton's Japanese Town!

This is different, I thought. Then, I could feel the knot that was my stomach dissolving. Children began to gather around us, eager to meet the "new kids." Worries about explaining "what" I was and "where I came from" were gone. Worries about explaining why I had moved here were gone. For the first time in months, I could just relax and be myself. Everyone seemed eager to meet us.

Yukiko and Haruko, two sisters who lived down the street from the hotel, became my best friends. Haruko was my age and Yukiko was a year younger. They were both about the same size, but towered over me. Haruko's long forehead was interrupted halfway down to her eyebrows by the straight cut of her bangs, while Yukiko's hair was combed back from her face. They both wore brown boots with tassels. I would have loved to have a pair like that.

Their parents owned a candy store just up the street from the hotel along the wooden walkway. My stomping as I passed the store became a signal for the girls to come running out to join me on our walk to school. On the way home, we stopped by the shop and we each got a piece of candy. I looked forward to that.

My class was a mix of third- and fourth-graders. Of the thirty students in the room, six were not Japanese Americans. Although it was close to the end of the school year, I was able to fit right into the lessons. There wasn't any "catching up" to do. During recess, two teams of kids hit a ball tethered to a pole from both directions in attempts to wind the ball completely around the pole. It was a new experience for me. None of the public playgrounds or schools in San Francisco offered tether ball. We also played a team game called Jintori. The goal was to capture opponents. I had never played that before, either.

When I returned home from school after making my stop at the candy store, I entered the hotel by the kitchen door. Grandma and Mama always had a snack ready for Brian and me. It was usually a rice ball wrapped in seaweed with a pickled plum hidden inside. This would be accompanied by a Nehi orange drink. Delicious.

I wasn't allowed to ever use the hotel's front door.

"Our guests don't want to be bothered by little girls." Grandpa said. "They want to be able to relax in peace."

That seemed a little unreasonable to me. What did he think I was. A tornado? I could enter a room without disturbing its contents. They wouldn't even know I was there. So, one day, I decided to use the front door.

When I opened it, the air, thick with cigarette smoke, made me cough and my eyes water. I just held my breath and squinted. Immediately inside the door was a wooden counter, much like the one at the cleaners except that this one resembled a fancy cabinet with extra pieces of wood along the edges and the middle. The wall behind it was covered with small numbered cubbies. I guessed they were home to the keys to the rooms upstairs. The wall to the right was lined with cloudy windows. These were not "portals to the outside world," I thought, but just providers of light for the tables placed next to them. The tables were for playing games and were littered with money, cards, and overflowing ashtrays. Directly in front of me, a man leaned over and a thin stream of brown liquid shot out of the corner of his mouth into a broad-rim brass bowl on the floor. Had I been a few seconds earlier, I might have ended up with a nasty brown stain on my dress. There were other men in long-sleeved undershirts and overalls, with sun-bronzed heads and faces covered with stubble. Tiny cigarettes were clenched between their teeth, and their eyes squinted against the smoke curling up their faces as they sat hunched over Japanese "hana" playing cards. Hana cards had beautiful simple drawings of flowers and nature scenes in vivid colors on the playing side. The men slapped the hana cards on the table as they played their hands.

As I walked through the room to the entrance of the dining room, one of the men called out to me, "Shizu!" just as my grandfather had always done. It was short for my Japanese name, Shizuye.

"Sing a song for me!"

Just like my grandfather would say! It made me stop. Then he pushed his chair from the table and smiled at me as he pulled a sack labeled "Bull Durham" from his shirt pocket and stretched it open. Then, from a flat package with the words "ZigZag" printed on it in large letters, he slid out a thin piece of paper and held it in his left hand. He poured a line of tobacco down the middle of the paper, put the sack of tobacco to his mouth, and grabbed the short piece of string dangling from the opening with his teeth. By turning his head, and pulling with his hand, he closed the sack. Then he dropped it into his shirt pocket, freeing his right hand. Next, he held the tobacco-lined paper with both hands, rolled it to the outside, licked the edge, and sealed the tobacco in. He twisted one end and stuck it in his mouth. Out came a match from somewhere that he swiped across his pants. The match burst into flame, and he lit the cigarette.

"Shizu!" The sound shattered my concentration. This time it was my grandfather calling me. "Come out of there! This is no place for little girls!"

"Oh, oh . . . ," the card player leaned over and whispered to me. "Looks like you're in trouble."

"You stay out of there," Grandpa said as he came around behind me and guided me out with his hand firmly on my back. "And, you, Nakano," he said over his shoulder, "don't be talking to my granddaughter." We were *both* in trouble.

We stayed with my grandparents for two months until we received notice that we had to move. Again. This time it was to a camp at the San Joaquin County Fairgrounds.

"What's a 'camp'?" I asked.

Nobody knew for sure. All they knew was that we would be able to take only what we could carry. We would no longer have a car.

A couple of days after the order, I was called into Mr. Cecil Owens's office. He was the principal at Franklin. I didn't look forward to seeing him, since principals held bad memories for me.

Mr. Owens was sitting behind a vast book-and-paper-cluttered desk. The light streamed in through the opening in the ceiling like a spotlight on this tall man who had a striking resemblance to Abraham Lincoln. He had dark bushy hair that covered his head, eyebrows, and chin.

"Please sit down, Marie," he said. He looked at me across his desk, hunching his back so our eyes were at the same level. His pale blue eyes twinkled as he spoke.

"Your teacher tells me you're a good student. And I want it to stay that way. I'm concerned there may not be schools where they're sending you." I had only been at Franklin for two months and Mr. Owens was concerned about my welfare. My heart felt full. I thought it would burst.

"I'd like to give you some books," he continued. "I know you like to sing, so I'm including a music book along with others on math, English, and social studies. Then he leaned across the table toward me, so close I caught a whiff of aftershave lotion just like Papa's.

"I want you to promise me that you'll not neglect your studies."

"I'll do my best, Mr. Owens. It's so nice of you to be

concerned about me, when you don't even know me. I'll never forget your kindness."

I wanted to do something, but couldn't think what. Then I blurted, "Do you mind signing the books?"

"Of course," he said. Then in tall, slanted words that filled half the blank page in front of the books, he wrote, "I wish you the best of luck and success in the future, Marie. Sincerely, Cecil Owens May 2, 1942."

★ ★ ★

The local Elks Club served as the headquarters for the registration of Japanese American families in preparation for our entrance into the camp. The government officials assigned numbers to each family. We received labels with that number which we would dangle from buttonholes on what we wore. It was also painted on every loose item we had. Suitcases, folding chairs, boxes were all identified with numbers. Instead of Marie Mitsui, as far as the government was concerned, I was now a number.

Our luggage was limited to what we each could carry. The government also issued a list of items we were required to take. My father made a box out of wood that he said he would use to make furniture at the camp. He and Mama would carry that, and Brian and I would each carry a suitcase. The list also included pots, pans, and dishes, so everyone in our extended family brought mess kits. They were oblong, shallow metal containers that had a collapsible handle which secured the lid. The lid became a plate. Within were various utensils and smaller plates. We also purchased metal cups and canteens. All of this took up precious space and weight. We had already pared our belongings down when we left San Francisco. Now we had to throw away even more to make room for compact kitchenware.

"I'm taking my princess coat, no matter what! I don't care if I have to leave everything else!" I told Brian. It was bulky and really left little room for anything else in the suitcase I was to carry. If I packed my coat, I would have to pare down to one dress. Other dresses, sweaters, my bed linen, towels would not be able to make the journey with me.

"You can't remove those things from your suitcase," Mama said.

"Don't worry about it, Marie. You can always wear it," suggested Brian.

"It's 90 degrees!"

"Well, do you want your coat or not?"

"Whatever you don't take, we can put in the basement of the house," Grandpa assured us. "We'll board it up, so it will be safe until we return." Was he kidding? I was taking my coat with me. Otherwise I'd never see it again. What made Grandpa think we'd ever come back? We didn't even know anything about where we would be tomorrow, much less "when we came back." Talking about "coming back" was just crazy talk. I was only nine, but even I knew that.

We took four folding chairs. Between the chairs and the mess kits, pillows, blankets, and sheets, we barely had space for a few items of clothing.

CHAPTER 9

"Don't Fence Me In"
BING CROSBY

On May 5, everyone from our neighborhood, including my uncle and family from down the street, and my uncle from French Camp, assembled in front of my grandparents' hotel, because of its central location and large parking area. We all waited for the bus that would take us to our new home. The large stiff pieces of paper identifying us by number were attached to our clothing like price tags we had forgotten to remove. Our suitcases, boxes, packages, and trunks had matching tags or were boldly emblazoned with family numbers.

Finally, the wait was over. The bus arrived. But immediately behind it was a group of soldiers with knife-tipped rifles. The tall men with black bands on their arms with the letters "MP" imprinted in white approached us. Everyone stood frozen. No one said a word.

Then one of the soldiers spoke.

"We're here to see that you get on the bus. I have a list of your numbers, so when I read yours, come forward with your baggage." It was a slow process as people checked their labels when a number was called.

Brian leaned over to me and whispered,

"I prefer the FBI. They don't come at you with bayoneted rifles!"

"I'm scared," I said. "Do they intend to spear us or shoot us, if we get out of line?"

"Just don't get out of line, unless you want to find out!" Brian said.

We all boarded the bus, and it took us the short distance from the hotel to the San Joaquin Fairgrounds. We came to a halt in front of a huge structure, which was the entrance to the camp. There were armed MPs as we boarded the bus, as we got off the bus, and as we entered the camp. There were MPs everywhere. The army must have thought we were very dangerous people to guard us with so many soldiers.

We soon discovered that the entrance to the camp was also the exit to life as we had known it: roller skates, car rides, stores, telephones, trips to the beach . . .

In the administration building there were stations set up to check our baggage for "forbidden objects" (guns, knives, etc.). They also gave us our room assignments and other instructions. It also served as a "shooting gallery" where we received our vaccinations and typhoid shots.

"You'll have to take off your coat for your shot, little girl," said a nurse. "Actually, why in the world are you wearing a coat in this heat?"

"It's my favorite coat, and there wasn't room in the luggage."

"Of course."

Many became ill after receiving their shots. Mama was one of them. She ran a fever and became bedridden. It was hot, we hadn't unpacked, and Mama was sick.

Fortunately, Grandma was assigned the room next to ours, so she was able to help us get settled and nurse Mama.

A chemical was also put in the water that made many others ill. This resulted in long lines at the bathrooms. Some people figured out that if they let the water stand in a pot for a while before drinking it, the chemical in the water disappeared. That's what we did.

We were assigned to one room in a six-room gable-roofed barrack. Block 6 Barrack 108 Apartment D. My new address was 6-108-D, Stockton Assembly Center, War Relocation Authority, Stockton, California. But it really wasn't an apartment like ones in San Francisco. Those had bathrooms and kitchens. A camp "apartment" was just one room. Furthermore, I don't think the builders finished their work. The walls that separated the apartments ran only part way up, stopping at the point where the roof began to slope. Basically all of us in the barrack were in one large room separated only by partitions, pretending they were walls.

The doors were level with the ground outside and opened out, so the dirt in front of the door had to be cleared constantly. The floors were made of material used to pave roads. When we walked on the grit that slipped easily into our apartments from the dusty outdoors, our footsteps were accompanied by a sound resembling the rasp of sandpaper on a woodworking project. I could hear a constant din of shoe scraping against floor as others shuffled around in their rooms. A thin coat of dust settled on everything, including the inside of my mouth. I could feel the grinding of fine bits of sand when I brought my teeth together.

It was summer in hot, humid Stockton, so the room was always like a stuffy oven.

"Lights out" was at nine p.m. I would lie in bed and watch the shadows disappear from the ceiling, one by one, as the lights went out in the rest of the barrack the closer we got to zero hour. Everyone whispered, but private conversations were impossible. The tunnel formed by the open space above our rooms permitted sounds to travel freely into the rooms below.

The woman in the next room woke us each morning as she retched into a pail, and the sound and smell of her discomfort wafted over the wall.

"Mrs. Sato has 'morning sickness,'" Mama said.

"'Morning sickness'? Mornings make her sick?" I asked.

"She's pregnant. She's going to have a baby. Some women get sick when they're pregnant," she said.

Mrs. Sato sounded miserable. I don't think I would ever want to be pregnant, I thought.

Grandpa, Grandma, and Uncle Robert lived in a room of similar size to ours on the other side. It was built for four people, so they had to share it with a bachelor. It was very crowded in there. My other uncles and their families were assigned housing remote from us. It was a challenge locating them. But thanks to Uncle Robert, we found them.

Uncle Robert was almost a dentist. He had been a student at the College of Physicians and Surgeons in San Francisco when the war began. Although it was the next to last year for him, he wasn't allowed to finish. He had to leave like everyone else. Here he drove a watering truck around the camp to help settle the ever-present dust. Everyone looked forward to his drive down the space between the barracks. The truck had an enormous tank with a hole-riddled rod from which he released a long, cooling fountain of water. The spray pulled the dust out of the air and removed the heat from the ground. His visit was the highlight of the day.

The toilets and showers were in a building located in the middle of our block, which was a cluster of barracks. Several toilets lined a wall in the washroom. There were no doors. A long metal tub with six faucets draining into it was our wash basin, and they lined the other wall. The showers were in a separate area. There were several of those and they, too, were unpartitioned.

I felt uncomfortable seeing others shower—all ages,

sizes, and shapes. So I often bathed in the middle of the afternoon when no one else was around. If I heard anyone else in the shower when I entered, I left. Between trying to make time in the afternoon and finding others in the showers when I did, I didn't shower as often as I should have.

★ ★ ★

We didn't need to pack pots and pans or mess kits. All our food was prepared for us in mess halls. These were large buildings in the middle of each block and with enough space to feed just one-third of the block at one time. There were three calls for meals, announced by the striking of metal rods, triangles, or gongs. For about two hours the metallic sound of varying pitches reverberated throughout the camp. We learned to identify our particular sound. The third "bell" was ours. We stood in line in the hot summer sun and slowly inched our way into the hall. Although we had to wait until others finished their meals to make room for us, we didn't feel as rushed, since we were last.

"I'm glad we have last bell," said Brian. "We can have seconds."

We picked up plates at the end of a counter. As we pushed them along, servers plopped dollops of stewed meat of some sort, along with creamed corn and rice. Breakfast was fried potatoes and runny oatmeal, at first. Then little boxes of individually wrapped cereal appeared. Kellogg's Shredded Wheat was my favorite. I would carefully peel back the cardboard and waxed paper and pour milk directly into the box.

We sat at tables with attached benches. At first, my mother tried to find places at the ends of the benches, because sitting between people was a challenge. The challenge was to climb into the space between the bench and table without kicking neighbors in an attempt to not reveal her underwear.

Finding a place to sit became less complicated when she figured out a "lady-like" way to sit. She placed her right knee on the bench as a turning point, pushing it toward her other leg as much as possible. Then she pivoted her right calf to the inside of the bench and lowered her foot onto the floor. Next, she would face the table and lean on it. Finally, she would rest her left knee on the bench, then rotate that calf under her other leg. With both feet where she wanted, she would smooth her skirt and sit down. That was too much trouble for me. I would climb up on the bench and slide down. Until I caught a sliver.

We rarely ate as a family. Mama and I ate together. But I don't know when Papa ate, because he was always off somewhere working on community activity projects. Since Papa had experience with theater and had organized shows and such before the war, he was recruited to help out. People tapped into his background to help them set up programs to entertain everyone in camp. Brian ate with us at first, but soon ate with his friends, and we rarely saw him.

★ ★ ★

Brian and I spent the first couple of days exploring the camp. The top of the grandstand provided us with a bird's eye view of our new surroundings. It was an enormous place built around a race track. Some barracks were confined within its circle. Others spilled outside its perimeter. But most of the camp was cloaked under cover of trees, so we couldn't really tell what was out there. We decided to find out.

We discovered that our boundary was set by a continuous cyclone fence topped with barbed wire. It was a barrier that separated us from the rest of America as well as the rest of Stockton. Every few yards, there was a guard tower with soldiers, their bayonets glistening in the sun. We walked under the canopy of trees up to the fence to look out. Beyond it was a busy street. Life seemed unchanged for those on the other side. It seemed they drove down the road going to wherever they were going and doing normal things, like we had been doing days earlier. There was a war being fought somewhere, but it was impossible to know that by looking out. It felt like those of us who were on this side of the fence were the only ones whose lives were affected by it.

"Do you think those people out there notice us? I wonder what they think we're doing in here?" I said.

Before Brian could say anything, a deep voice bellowed from somewhere above us,

"Hey! What're you kids doing down there? Get away from that fence!"

Brian and I craned our necks to see where the voice was coming from. We discovered we were standing a few yards away from a guard tower! Every few yards, it turns out, there was a guard tower with soldiers, their bayonets glistening in the sun.

"Didn't you hear me? Get away from that fence! You kids shouldn't be out here!"

Brian grabbed my hand and pulled me along as he ran.

"Come on, Marie. Let's get out of here!" I stumbled trying to keep up with him. He reached down and pulled me up. Soon we were out of sight of the guard.

"I don't know what others think about us," Brian said as he tried to catch his breath. "But one thing I know for sure. We may not be wearing clothes with black and white stripes, but we're in prison!"

CHAPTER 10

"Sleepy Lagoon"
HARRY JAMES AND HIS ORCHESTRA

Most evenings, after dinner, folks gathered outside their apartments. People brought their chairs outside to escape the heat trapped in their rooms. Some sat on benches crudely hammered together, while others stretched out on lawn chairs they had managed to squeeze into their luggage. The sun dropped behind the barracks and the ground, dampened moments earlier by Uncle Robert's watering truck, smelled fresh and cool. Strains from the song "Sleepy Lagoon" rippled in the air from 6-108-F, a couple of doors down. The clear, sweet voice of Harry James's trumpet surrounded us.

The soft blare started with the bubbly sound of a gentle brook, and gradually erupted into a dazzling fountain of notes. Marsha, the teenager in 6-108-F, had packed her record player and one record. She may have had other records, but "Sleepy Lagoon" was all we ever heard. Mama said Marsha was "lovesick," whatever that meant. Grandma and Grandpa, pregnant Mrs. Sato, Marsha and her parents, Papa, Mama, and Brian all sat outside fanning themselves and chatted. But Mrs. Uyeda and her sister, Mrs. Uyeda, sisters who were married to brothers, dominated the scene. They charmed everyone with their soft laughter and colorful Japanese dialect. I understood little of what they said, but the lilt and rhythm of their words were pleasant and soothing. They made everyone feel comfortable and at ease. Evenings in front of our apartment made me feel transported to another place—cool, beautiful, and dreamlike. It was my favorite time of day.

★ ★ ★

My cousin, Jean, lived in the next block. She was fifteen and knew a lot of important things that no one else would tell me. I could ask her anything and she would patiently explain. She was the one who told me what our mailing address was at Stockton Assembly Center, and what she thought was going to happen next.

"The government is preparing camps for us in other states," she said, "We don't know exactly where as yet, nor when we're expected to move. One thing is for certain. We're not going to be here very long."

"When you find out where we're going, will you let me know?" I asked.

"You'll be the first," she said.

On my way to her apartment one day, I heard a familiar voice calling me.

"Shizu! Shizu! Sing me a song!" I looked among the people clustered in the shade of a huge umbrella of a tree outside the apartments. There were unshaven men in their undershirts clustered around makeshift tables made of random pieces of wood with uneven legs to accommodate the roots of the tree. Wisps of smoke from each man joined a bluish cloud trapped in the space between the tree branches and their heads.

"Shizu! Over here!" the voice repeated.

And there he was, sitting by himself, just beyond the others. It was the card-playing Bull-Durham-smoking man from Grandpa's hotel that had called to me before! It was Mr. Nakano! He was sitting next to a bowl filled with small twisted, squashed tubes placed on an orange crate. On it was also a board smeared with an amazing mix of colors, and he was dabbing at it with a brush. He managed a broad smile with a cigarette clenched between his brown teeth. His bare, bronze head, sprinkled with bits of black and white snips of hair like salt and pepper, glistened with sweat. The stubble continued down his face, increasing as it continued to his chin. His overalls and sleeveless undershirt were streaked with colors in a random pattern. As he watched me walk toward him, he set his board down, picked up a round wooden fan, and poked at it with his brush. As I got closer, I noticed a strong, sweet, oily, strangely familiar smell in the air. I sniffed deeply to fill my head so I could examine it. Then I remembered! It reminded me of Joey lying in his bed with a box on his ankle.

"Do you have a broken ankle?" I asked.

"What?"

"I smell a broken ankle. My friend had a broken ankle once and this is the smell."

"What you smell is the paint. They're oil paints!" Mr. Nakano said as he laughed. "Smell of a broken ankle . . . that's a good one!"

He carefully placed the fan in a can, then found an empty spot on a paint-stained rag and wiped his brush. He rested his hands on his knees and looked up at me with full attention.

"How are you, Shizu? Are you going to sing a song for me, today?"

I was beginning to tire of that. He doesn't really want me to sing. I guess that's all he can think of to say to me. But I mustn't be rude.

"If you want to hear me sing, you'll have to go to the 'singspiration' they have at the grandstand."

"Then that's what I'll have to do," he said with a laugh. "I'd like to go listen. Let me know when you're singing."

"Actually, you can join us at the 'singspiration.' You can sing, too. We do that every Friday evening at the grandstand. Just follow your ears! But that's enough about singing. I want to know what *you're* doing!" I said, pointing to the fan he had just placed in the can. He picked it up and held it up for me to see.

"Oji-san!" I said (Oji-san was the equivalent of "mister" in English), "that is really beautiful!" It looked complete, but he said that he was in the process of putting the finishing touches on the flaming red poppies in a field at the base of a mountain.

"Where'd you learn to do that?" I asked.

"I was a painter in Japan," he said as he took a tube of reddish paint and squeezed a tiny blob on his paint-smeared board. A smaller amount of yellow was added to that. He picked up a tool that looked like a knife with dull edges and pressed the colors together until it resembled one of Brian's red marbles with yellow streaks. Then he took one of the many brushes he had sitting in a can and wiped it with a rag. This brush was small and had bristles that came to a point. He poked his brush into the pigment, then dabbed at the center of each flower.

"You painted pictures in Japan? So, why did you leave?" I asked.

"I couldn't sell enough paintings to support my family. I have a wife and a little girl who was about your age when I left. I came here to get rich and then return to my family and my painting . . . but I just can't seem to save enough."

"Oh," I wasn't sure what to say to that. So I continued to ask about his family in Japan. "So they must all be in Japan.

110

I'm really sorry that you aren't all together. Who's taking care of them, if you aren't there?"

"I left Japan twenty years ago," he said. Then he stood up suddenly and said, "Would you like a fan? I've made lots of them. You could choose one you like." He motioned for me to follow as he walked across the way to his apartment. "Come on and I'll show you what I have." He led me into the room he shared with three other men. Dense burlap covered the windows, so little light penetrated the room. I stood for a moment looking at them.

"They keep the room cool," he said.

"It doesn't feel very cool to me," I said. "Wouldn't it be cooler if you just opened the windows?"

"We open all the windows at night. In the morning, we close up the room and cover the windows. It would be a lot hotter if we opened the windows and let the hot air in during the middle of the day."

Beds were lined up against the walls with boxes and suitcases between. The beds were covered with army blankets without bedspreads or blanket covers. One man was sitting on his in the semi-darkness, writing something, using his lap as a table. The other beds were empty. Oji-san's bed was in the far corner and next to it was a box filled with decorated fans, like a vase filled with flowers. He lifted a corner of the burlap curtain so that a hot stream of light shone on them. Oji-san laid the fans out on his bed. They were all about the same size, made entirely of wood, including the handles. But each was painted with a different picture. There were blooms of flowers, majestic mountains, portraits . . . everything you could imagine.

"This is incredible! Is there nothing you don't paint?" I asked.

Oji-san smiled and said, "Take any one you like."

"Are you sure? Don't you want to sell them?"

"I want you to have one. Choose whatever you like."

I examined each one carefully. It was a difficult choice. So many and so beautiful. Finally, I picked one with cherry blossoms. I turned it over to discover red peonies and two small yellow butterflies on the other side! The colors were vivid and the subjects very clearly drawn, stunning in their simplicity. They were exact copies of pictures found on hana cards.

"I like this one!" I said.

"Ah. You like the hana-card picture," he said as he laughed. "Take it. It's yours."

"Are you sure? It's so beautiful. Maybe you'd like to paint the entire deck. You might want this, if you do."

"It's yours, Shizu. Take it," he said. He looked pleased that I had found one I liked. Then he stood silent for a moment and just looked at me.

"Shizu, if you're interested, I could teach you how to paint with oil. Is that something you'd want to do?"

"That would be so great! I'd love it! I'd have to ask my parents first, of course. But I'm sure they won't mind. Thank you so much!"

I ran home to tell Mama.

"Look what the man from the hotel gave me!"

"What man from the hotel? Where've you been?" When I told her what had happened, she became very upset.

"You shouldn't be taking gifts from strangers, and you certainly shouldn't be going into a man's room!" She snatched the fan from me.

"Where's he live? This fan has to be returned!"

"He lives just beyond the mess hall on the way to Uncle William's to visit Cousin Jean. He sits outside his apartment painting. But I don't understand! He's not a stranger. It's Mr. Nakano. He used to live at Grandpa's hotel. What did I do wrong?"

"You are never to go into a man's room again! Do you understand? He could have hurt you!"

He didn't hurt me. He was a very generous man. He offered to teach me to paint. But Mama just didn't understand. She wouldn't listen to me. And I didn't dare disobey Mama. Particularly since she was so upset about it. I would have to find another route to my cousin's. I hoped I would never see him again. I was so embarrassed. Thankfully, I never did. But Mr. Nakano did go on to teach other children to draw without hurting them.

★ ★ ★

Since it was summer, there was no formal school, but there were some organized activities for children, aside from Mr. Nakano's art class. About a week after we arrived we reported to the stables, which were nestled under the trees. We were divided by grade level and sang or played games. These sessions were held in the morning in the stables or in the grandstand. They were over by noon, because the afternoons were so hot. So we were on our own during the heat of the day.

One hot afternoon, I bumped into Haruko, who had been in my class at Franklin School. She was a very pretty girl with long, thick lashes that shaded her round eyes like the black bill on my brother Brian's baseball cap. The sausage curls, tied in bunches on either side of her head with bows, cascaded down past her shoulders and bounced when she walked. The bows always matched her pinafores. The freshly starched ruffles arched over her shoulders like the wings on a delicate butterfly. Her mother must have spent hours on her pretty daughter, I thought. I guessed that if I were as pretty as she was, Mama might have spent as much time on me.

We spent many afternoons on the race track jumping partitions. They were used to separate horses at the starting gate when our camp was a fairground. The partitions were high so we had to pull ourselves up. They were wide enough to stand on and far enough apart from each other that it was a challenge to leap from one to the other.

The goal was to develop a rhythm, so we could leap them one after another without stopping. I would place my hands on a partition, jump up so I could straighten my arms and support myself, then kick my legs up. Then I would help Haruko. It was more difficult for her because of her dress. It would get caught under her legs as she tried to hike up. All we could do is jump one partition at a time. After a day of play at the starting gate, Haruko's pinafore would wilt like an abused flower. But she was always back the following day, freshly starched and vibrant.

One day one of the more agile kids who had been leaping partitions somehow fell backward and injured her back. We stayed with her until an olive green ambulance with a large red cross on it arrived to take her to the hospital.

"I don't think we should play here anymore," I told Haruko. "It's too dangerous. We've got to find somewhere else to play."

"I know another great place," said Haruko. "It's cool and grassy. It's very close to the fence and almost looks like it's 'outside.'"

I wasn't sure I wanted to be anywhere near the fence since my experience with Brian, but decided to go along with Haruko anyway.

"Why haven't you said anything about it before?"

"Well, that's because it's so different from anything else in the camp. Not many people go there. I want to keep it that way. I don't want too many people to know about it," she said, "It's my secret place, so you have to promise not to tell."

"I won't tell anyone else about it, if you don't want me to. But what about my brother? Is it all right to tell him?"

"Especially your brother! We don't want a lot of boys invading the area. Boys will be wanting to play baseball and wrestle and be rowdy. We want to be able to play croquet there in peace. It'll make my mother happy, too. She's been after me for messing up my dresses."

"Okay. I get it."

"It's so much safer than jumping partitions," Haruko said.

"Anything is safer than jumping partitions. Why don't we go to this place now?"

We left the race track and headed toward a wooded area near the edge of the camp. Her secret spot was different, just as she had said. It had towering trees and green grass with a large white house set back against the fence. It was a two-story building with green trim around the shuttered windows. Stock and pansies blanketed the roots of enormous drooping willow trees. It looked like someone's home. But there wasn't anything that said it was off-limits to us. No signs, no fences. As we drew near, coolness and dampness radiated like an ocean breeze. It was surely the most comfortable spot in the camp. On the wide expansive lawn, a croquet course was set up with wickets, balls, and mallets placed at one end. There was no one else around. We would have the whole area to ourselves.

"Are you sure it's all right for us to be here?" I asked Haruko.

Just then a loud voice bellowed, "Hey!"

The last time that happened, it was an armed guard.

"Let's get out of here, Haruko." I grabbed Haruko's hand and pulled her along. "We shouldn't be here."

"Hey. Wait! Don't go! Look up here. In the guard tower!"

"Come on, Haruko. Let's go!" Haruko tried to remove my hand from her arm.

"Come ON! Haruko! We're not supposed to be here. He'll probably shoot us!" I shouted at her.

"I'm not going to shoot you," said the voice from the tower. "It's all right."

"He says it's all right," said Haruko. "Just calm down."

I was frightened, but curious. The last time I had encountered a guard in a tower was still very fresh in my mind. I thought then that I was going to die. But this guard did seem a little different.

"What's your name?" he shouted from above.

"Haruko."

"Marie."

"My name's Arky."

"Archie?" I asked.

"No, Arky. A-r-k-y. I'm from Arkansas, so all my friends call me Arky . . . short for Arkansas."

"Where's Arkansas?" asked Haruko.

"It's a long way from here. In the middle of the United States."

"Oh. Well, I think we'd better get going," Haruko said. And started to walk away. I followed.

"Come back again, girls."

We walked out of sight of the tower and sat on the grass for a while before we headed back to the barracks.

"That was strange," I said. "talking to someone who's supposed to be guarding us. The last time Brian and I met one of those people, I thought he was going to shoot us!"

"I think he's just lonely," said Haruko. "There isn't anyone around to talk to."

"Do you think we should come back tomorrow?"

"Sure. Why not. It's cool here and we could always play croquet, if we want."

"Oh, yeah. Croquet."

Haruko was waiting for me outside my mess hall after lunch the following day. We walked the hot stretch across the race track into the cool green area.

"I've been thinking about an idea I have," said Haruko. "What? What's your idea?"

"Let's try to get the guard to come down out of his tower!"

"What? That's crazy. Why would we want to do that? . . . Besides, he would never come down."

"It could be a kind of game."

"What do you mean, a 'game'?"

"A game. You know. It'll be a game to see if we can get him to come down."

"So you mean, if he comes down, we win, if he doesn't, he wins? I don't know, Haruko."

"Actually, I want to see what a guard looks like up close. Wouldn't you like to see what he looks like up close?"

"I've seen a lot of guards up close, and frankly, I don't like what I see. They're mean and scary."

"But this one's friendly. Don't you want to see what a friendly guard looks like up close? Come on, Marie, it'll be fun."

"I don't know . . ."

"Let's just try!"

" . . . Okay." What's the harm, I thought. Anyway, he's not going to come down.

The following day we went directly to the guard tower. Arky was looking our way as we approached.

"Hi, girls," he shouted. "Good to see you." When we were close enough so he didn't have to shout so much, he told us about his family and why he was in the army.

"Arky, I'd like to talk to you some more," said Haruko after a short while, "but you're so far away. Why don't you come down here and talk to us?"

"I can't do that. My job is to stay up here. In case some-one tries to escape."

"No one's going to try to escape. And besides, how

many people have you seen around the fence besides us?" I asked. "Anyway, we have to go now. Goodbye." I turned and grabbed Haruko's hand. "We have to go now," I said as I led Haruko away.

"I don't think he's coming down. He isn't stupid. He could get into trouble," I said as we walked away. "Let's play croquet."

"Oh, he won't get into trouble. You worry too much," she said. "Let's come back tomorrow."

We returned the following day and the day after that, each time trying a different way to get him to come down. We complained that our necks hurt, that it was hard to hear what he was saying, and that we had never talked to a friendly soldier before. All the others we've seen have been mean and unfriendly, we told him. But he never came down.

On the fifth day, Haruko said,

"I would really like to see what you look like up close, Arky. You're a special soldier and I want to be able to remember your face and shake your hand. . . ."

Then, to my surprise and horror, he moved from his spot in the tower next to the window and headed toward the door! I could see him slipping his arm through the strap on his rifle and across his chest, so it hung down his back. Then he started to back down the tower ladder. The bayonet caught the sun on its slick surface and bounced it in my eyes. It seemed to take forever for him to reach the ground.

As I stood there watching his slow descent, I began to feel an indescribable uneasiness. Much like when I took the "long cut" through Mrs. Jensen's apartment in San Francisco. We had been trying to get him down from the tower for days. And now that we had succeeded, it didn't feel very good. What had been just a game for us was losing its appeal. Since I didn't really believe he would do it, I hadn't thought through what it would be like to actually have the soldier down on the ground with us. I stood frozen, filled with a mixture of fear and overwhelming stupidity.

"What have we done!" I whispered to Haruko. "What are we going to do now?"

"Don't worry," said Haruko. "It'll be all right."

I thought about what Mama had said about Mr. Nakano. If gentle Mr. Nakano could hurt me with paint brushes and a few tubes of paint, imagine what a soldier with a rifle could do!

When he finally reached the ground, he turned and stopped for a moment and just looked at us. Then he stepped slowly toward us placing each foot deliberately on the ground as if testing its firmness. He wobbled slightly as he walked. My fear melted. He's more terrified of us, than we of him! I thought. As he drew closer, I was surprised at how old he looked. He must be Papa's age, I thought, but not as outgoing and confident. He had a gentle face, round and covered with little holes. Scars left by pimples, just like Uncle Robert, I thought. Mama had explained that to me. It was the result of popping pimples as a teenager. The soldier removed his army cap, revealing a forehead that extended to the top of his freckled head. What little hair he had was reddish brown.

His pale face turned beet red as he extended his hand to Haruko. "How do you do, Miss. My name is Arky." Then he turned to shake hands with me.

"We're so happy to be able to shake your hand!" Haruko said, bobbing up and down and making her curls bounce.

That made him smile and seemed to settle him down.

"It's a real pleasure meeting you both," he said. "I truly enjoy these visits with you. But I am sorry that I am meeting you under these conditions. These are difficult times, but I hope that you get through them all right. I'll say a prayer for you." He seemed very relaxed about being on the ground as he spoke. But it made me nervous. What if he got caught out of his tower? My original fear *of* him was transformed into fear *for* him.

"I think you'd better get back up in your tower," I said. "I wouldn't want you to get into trouble."

"You're right. I'd better go before someone sees me," he said. "But I'm glad I had this opportunity to shake your hand. Being in the guard tower is a boring job. You two have made it all worthwhile. I hope you continue to come by."

We watched him climb up to his perch. Then we left.

We didn't return to see Arky the following day, because Haruko was absent from the activities class. And I wasn't going to go see Arky alone. The singing group was preparing for a recital and my afternoons were filled with rehearsals after that.

A few days later, my cousin Jean came over with the latest news. "Have you heard?" she said. "We're all going to be shipped to Arkansas!"

"Arkansas? Arkansas! That's where Arky's from!"

"Who's Arky?" asked Jean.

"Oh, no one. Just someone Haruko and I met. I've got to go, Jean. I'll talk to you later," I said and left her standing in front of our apartment. I ran to Haruko's.

CHAPTER 11

"Once in a While"
FRANK SINATRA

"Hey, Haruko. Where've you been? I've missed you."

"I was sick," she said.

"Are you okay now?"

"Yeah."

"Well, have you heard? We're going to Arkansas. Let's go tell Arky."

"Wait. You're going to Arkansas? We're going to Arizona!" Haruko said. "I can't stand it! We won't be in the same camp!" She began to cry. I tried to comfort her.

"You'll meet a bunch of new people. You probably won't even remember me after a while. . . ." Haruko was new to this. It was clear she had never moved before.

"I won't forget you, Marie! Never in a million years!"

"Let's go see Arky, anyway!" I said. "C'mon. He'll probably be glad to see us."

As we crossed the cool green lawn and approached the tower, we could see that the guard in it was taller. Arky was no longer there.

"Stand back! You girls shouldn't be here!" shouted the guard.

"Where's Arky?" I asked.

"Didn't you hear me? Get away from here!" he shouted. "Go play somewhere else! This is a restricted area!"

"Arky must have gotten into trouble for talking to us," I said. "We were responsible. We shouldn't have talked him into coming down to talk to us," I said as we walked away.

"Yeah. Someone must have seen him come down. I hope he's all right," she said. "Or maybe he's just been assigned to another guard tower. We could go look for him," she added with a smile and a bounce. "Let's do that!"

"That sounds like a great idea," I said. "Let's go!"

We walked along the perimeter of the camp, but never found him.

★ ★ ★

I awoke the following morning, but didn't have the energy to pull myself out of bed. It was as though the strength in my muscles had been drained out of me during the night. It was an effort to even talk. It had also turned cold and the sheets felt like ice. "Mama, can you get me another blanket," I said.

"Another blanket?" Mama said in disbelief. "It must be 100 degrees in here!"

"Mama, I'm cold. I need another blanket," I said.

She put her hand to my forehead. "You're burning up!" She covered me, stuck a thermometer in my mouth and put a wet towel on my forehead.

After Mama took my temperature, I fell asleep. When I awoke, two strangers were peering down at me. One was a very pretty lady who wore a white coat over her dress. The other lady seemed timid and hung back. She wore a white uniform and cap. A nurse, I thought. The woman in the white coat smiled as she introduced herself. "My name is

Dr. Suzuki, and this is Nurse Komura." Then she turned to Mama, "What's her temperature?'

"105. And she has the chills," Mama said. Dr. Sato then unfastened my nightgown and looked at my chest.

"See how the rash covers her trunk?" she said to Nurse Komura. I strained to see what they were looking at. My chest was uneven and red like the back of a cooked Dungeness crab. Ugh.

"This is a classic case of German measles," Dr. Suzuki announced with a smile, "Textbook . . ." She was clearly pleased. I wondered why she was so happy that I had German measles and what that had to do with books. But it was too much of an effort to ask. Then she turned to my parents.

"I'm afraid she'll have to be quarantined. I want to make sure German measles doesn't spread throughout the barrack. I'm particularly concerned about Mrs. Sato next door because she's pregnant. We'll have to put your daughter in the hospital."

I drifted into sleep again after the two left and was awakened by two men lifting me onto a cot with wheels. Then I was placed in the olive green ambulance with a huge red cross painted in a white circle. It took me to the camp hospital.

I was placed in the isolation ward, which was an enormous room with empty cots and one other patient. Only people with the German measles were placed there. The emptiness of the ward indicated that quarantine was working, the nurse said. The other patient was a boy I had never seen before. I was puzzled. It seemed logical that my roommate would be someone I knew. But the nurse told me that the incubation period was longer than the stay in the hospital, so the person from whom I caught it would have already gone home.

It was the only time I had ever spent even one night away from my family. I couldn't remember ever feeling so alone.

Added to the loneliness, I felt like I was sinking into a huge space and there was nothing to hang onto. My dreams were invaded by enormous white, towering blobs that leered down at me. I tried to escape from them, but there was no place to go. When I awoke my eyes burned, so I had to keep them closed. Then I'd fall asleep and the monsters would return.

My parents came to see me every day. That's all they were able to do. See me, that is. They had to peer at me through a small diamond-shaped window cut in the door close to my bed. I never saw Brian, because children were not permitted to visit.

A couple of days into quarantine, the nurse brought me two cars my father had carved out of wood. They smelled strongly of fresh paint. One was black and the other red. Each was about a foot long, flat, sleek, and round. They were plain without movable parts, but Papa must have spent hours carving, sanding, and painting them. Beautiful. But . . . cars? I think he had me confused with his other child. What was I supposed to do with cars? I didn't want to hurt Papa's feelings, so I cradled the hard, smelly objects like they were dolls, whenever the nurse warned me that Papa and Mama were coming to see me. The rest of the time I left them on the table between my roommate and me. They became a conversation piece for my otherwise non-talkative companion. He tried to guess what model and year they were.

"I think they're cars of the future," he concluded. "They're more modern than anything I've ever seen. Anyway, that was really nice of your father to go through all that trouble to make them for you. Can I hold them?"

"Sure," I said.

The day before my release the nurse took them away.

"They're covered with your German measles germs, so we have to sterilize them," she said.

When she returned them to me, they were warped,

crinkly, and sticky. Papa came to pick me up. He took one disgusted look at them and said they were ruined and threw them away in a trash can on our way out of the hospital. I shouldn't have cradled them, I thought. Then they wouldn't have needed sterilization. I felt badly.

Papa looked at me and said, "Don't feel sad, Marie. I can make you new ones when we get to Arkansas." Then he squatted in front of me and told me to climb on his back.

"I can walk," I said.

"No, you can't. It's a long way and you're still weak," he said sternly. He became my ambulance home.

"We're leaving for Arkansas this afternoon after lunch," he told me in gasps, as we cut across the race track toward our barrack. I wasn't very big, but neither was he. It was clear it wasn't easy for him to carry on a conversation and carry me. "You don't have to talk, Papa," I said.

"We've all been packing and cleaning up, so you just need to take it easy until we leave," he continued as though he hadn't heard me.

Finally, we reached our barrack. We spotted Mama cradling a bundle of catalogs, boxes, and other odds and ends, on her way to the trash bin.

"Oh, there you are. That was a long way from the hospital. You both must be tired," she said. "You should go lie down. I'll join you quickly. This is the last of the trash. . . ."

Papa gave me a final boost and headed toward the apartment. Suddenly I remembered. Oh, No! My coat!

"Papa, where's my coat?" I straightened my legs to release my grip around his waist and scrambled down. Papa almost fell as a result of my sudden dismounting.

"What?"

"My coat! Where's my coat!" Without waiting for his answer, I dashed to our apartment.

It was not at all as I had left it to go to the hospital.

The windows were bare and the cots stripped of linen and blankets. The beds had been transformed into a pile about as high as the benches in the mess hall. They were stacked, thin, legless frames layered with the thin mattresses and topped by Brian, lying spreadeagle like a squashed spider. The table and chairs were gone. In their place was the wooden container that had held most of our belongings when we arrived. Suitcases stood on either side like sentries. The room looked much as it did when we first got here.

"What happened to it?" I shouted. "Did it get thrown out?"

"You talking about your coat?"

"What else would I be talking about!"

"It's right there where I put it," said Brian as he got up and walked toward the hook on the wall just inside the door. I turned, and there it was. I pulled it down and clutched it to my chest.

"Thank you, Thank you, Brian. You're such a great brother!" As I started to move toward him, one arm cradling my coat, the other outstretched, he staggered backward, wheeled around, and bolted out the door.

"Where's Brian going in such a hurry?" asked Mama who was just outside the door with Papa.

"I think he thought I'd hug him," I replied.

"What? Oh, I see you found your coat. Brian made sure it didn't get left behind. Don't forget to thank him."

"I'll give him a big hug!"

"When Brian gets back, have him bring the brown suitcase outside." said Papa as he lifted one end of the wooden box filled with our belongings. He motioned to Mama to pick up the other end and they trudged out the door.

I slipped my coat on as I slowly took one last look around at what had become home for the past five months. Amazing what one can get used to. What next? I wondered.

CHAPTER 12

"Chattanooga Choo Choo"
GLENN MILLER AND HIS ORCHESTRA

For my first train trip, I had always imagined that I would enter a magnificent train station. Beautifully dressed people would be rushing across gleaming marble floors, their sounds bouncing against walls that soared to unreachable ceilings. Like I'd seen in the movies. In the distance, trains would be signaling their arrival with wailing whistles, followed by the gentle ringing of their engine bells as they glided into the station. Departing trains would rumble and grumble as their engines labored to move stubborn cars seemingly stuck to the tracks. Stationary trains would have sleek, streamlined cars flanked by courteous, uniformed porters, who would smile and extend a hand to help me board.

But today, there were no marble walls or floors. No trains coming and going. No courteous porters. This one-track train station was without floors, ceiling, or walls. We stood outside in the hot mid-day sun in a treeless, open field. There, among a chaotic jumble of people, suitcases, bundles, boxes, and armed soldiers, we waited to be transported to some unknown place deep inside of our own country. We would board an old, paint-faded wooden thing of a train car that looked like it had been dragged out of a junkyard. I felt embarrassed even to get onto it and hoped that no one would see me riding in it.

Instead of porters helping us, soldiers stood guard at the train steps, with blank expressions and rifles with pointed bayonets at their sides. Another soldier, armed with a clipboard, called out family names.

I wore my favorite "princess" coat. The beige, double-breasted, hooded wool coat trimmed with dark brown velvet that my parents had bought for me two days before Japan attacked Pearl Harbor. It was the coat I wore into Stockton Assembly Center, and now I was wearing it to Arkansas. It was a little cooler now, but this was a particularly hot Indian summer day. I pulled the hood over my head to protect it from the sun directly above. The beads of perspiration that kept forming on my nose ran together and trickled into my mouth. I kept pulling my hood away from my head so that my dampening hair wouldn't cling to the velvet lining. But I didn't care as long as I was able to keep my coat.

Brian was carrying his trademark tennis ball in his right front pants pocket. That's why the lines in his heavy corduroys bulged out.

"I need it to play catch when I run into friends," he'd say if anyone asked. He also wore his gray wool zippered jacket with the square pattern of thin blue lines. The jacket barely covered his belt and its sleeves were a couple inches above his wrist, but it was the one he always wore.

Papa, in his three-piece suit, tie, and matching hat, stood out alongside other men who were in shirtsleeves or windbreakers. That was the only kind of clothing Papa owned. We were people from cold San Francisco traveling with people from the hot rural towns outside Stockton. My mother wore her brown wool coat and brown hat with the curly duck feather.

Finally, it was our turn to board. I had to pull myself up onto the stool placed below the lower step of the train. From there I was able to grab the train's handrail and climb up the steps onto the entry platform. After I turned and entered the car I was surprised to see what looked like maroon velvet upholstery peeking out from between the people moving up the narrow aisle and into their seats on either side. Maroon velvet? That was just like the soft comfortable seats in the Alhambra Theater in San Francisco! Grade A and grade B double-feature movies, Looney Tunes cartoons, cliffhanger serials, and Movietone news with pictures of the war in Europe and refugees boarding trains all appeared in my mind's eye. . . .

"Marie!"

That was Mama's voice. I turned and looked up to see where it was coming from. She was right behind me. "Pay attention!" she said as she nudged me down the narrow aisle with the suitcase she was carrying. As we moved, she brought her face close to my ear and explained that the soldier in charge said that every fourth seat had to remain empty for baggage.

Half of the seats had been pulled forward, like on streetcars, so that two seats faced each other forming a unit. For our family of four that meant one of us would have to sit with strangers. There was a young couple with no children in the unit in front of what was to be ours. My parents had decided that I should be the one to sit with them.

"I hope you don't mind having Marie ride with you," Mama said to the couple. Turning to me, she said, "Marie, this is Mr. and Mrs. Okamura."

"Glad to meet you, Marie," said Mrs. Okamura from her seat next to the window. "But don't call me Mrs. Okamura. That makes me feel old. Please call me May. And call my husband Tom."

"Okay."

"Why don't you sit next to the window so you'll be across from me," May said with a laugh and turned to Tom. "Move our suitcases, Honey."

He leaned over and pulled them onto the aisle seat over a small mound that was all the padding left on the seat after years and years of pounding by many, many behinds. Not at all like the soft, beautiful Alhambra seats. The seating on the train had lost most of its color to the sun, most of its velvet hair to people brushing against it, and all of its softness to people sitting on it. That's what May told me later.

"You're blocking the aisle!" a loud voice boomed from behind us.

The soldier was glaring at our family and motioning wildly with his rifle to clear the aisle.

"You'd better sit down, Marie," Mama said. "Be a good girl, now. Don't give them any trouble." Then she turned to May and Tom and bowed. "Thank you very much for letting her sit with you."

Papa removed his hat and bowed.

"Thank you," he said before he, my mother, and my brother moved on to their seats.

I quickly climbed over the Okamura's bags and removed my coat. It felt good to take it off. There was a shallow shelf and a hook over the window for hats and coats, but I couldn't reach them. Anyway, I wanted to keep my coat close to me. I folded it inside out so it wouldn't get soiled and placed it carefully on their bags and sat down. I pulled my coat toward my face and rested my cheek against the smooth and silky, but slightly damp, lining and closed my eyes for a moment. It felt good. It also felt cool in the train after standing in the sun so long. But that wore off, and I began to notice that the air in the car smelled like damp, salty dust. We could use a little fresh air in here, I thought. I stood up and examined the window to see if I could figure out how to open it. I removed my shoes and started to climb up on the seat to see if there was a latch on the upper edge of the sash.

"You can open it now, but once we start moving, you'll have to close it and draw the shades," May said with a laugh.

"What?"

"They don't want us to be seen by people outside the train, I guess," May said. Again, with a laugh, "Or maybe, they don't want us to look out, because they suspect we're spies!"

"I don't think they suspect us of being spies," I said. "The FBI put us 'under house arrest' back in January. That's what everyone called it. They moved in with us for a week. Brian and I weren't allowed to go to school and my mother had to shop with an FBI agent. After one week they decided we were not spies or anything like that. So I don't think they suspect us of being spies. They already took care of that. But it's okay that we pull the shades. I'd rather not be seen riding this train anyway."

"Oh," said May and smiled.

I thought about it for a while. Then I began to wonder: would the shades be drawn as we passed through Los Angeles? My best friend in San Francisco, Beverly Jensen, had visited Los Angeles once and she said that the sidewalk curbs were very high and jumping off them on skates was difficult. Will I be able to see that for myself?

I asked May.

"Earlier," May replied, "a soldier told us that we would have to pull down the shades when passing through towns, cities, train stations, roads paralleling the tracks—anywhere there was the possibility that people would be around. So that would include Los Angeles and probably most of California, I would guess. But there are large stretches of desert in Arizona, New Mexico, and Texas we should be able to see.

And open our windows and enjoy the desert air. It won't be so bad. We can still have a good time," she said with a laugh.

I soon discovered that May loved to talk. So time passed quickly, despite not being able to look out. May was a pretty lady, with large, laughing eyes and pencil-drawn eyebrows. Her mouth was held in a perpetual smile. And when she spoke, a hearty laugh punctuated her sentences, even though what she said was not always funny.

Although Tom wore glasses, he was as handsome as May was pretty. He had eyes that angled out slightly, giving him a gentle, kind look. Deep dimples formed in both cheeks whenever he smiled or stretched his lips a certain way.

May and Tom had not been married very long. May was born on a farm near Lodi, a town outside Stockton, and Tom had grown up in Japan, so their childhoods were very different. Tom had been sent to Japan when he was six years old to be raised by his grandparents. He returned to the United States just before Pearl Harbor. He spoke in Japanese, mostly. May, on the other hand, had never been to Japan. Her Japanese was at the same level as Tom's English. Tom would speak to May in Japanese and she would answer in English. It seemed to work. But he was very quiet and didn't have much to say. He and May rarely spoke to each other at all, but that may have been because I was there.

May also shared what seemed every detail of her childhood with me. She had grown up on her family farm with two brothers and four sisters. They were assigned chores and were responsible for the care and feeding of their chickens and cows, as well as helping with the grape harvest. She described the steps involved in her tasks, so that I felt if I ever lived on a farm, I would know exactly what to do. May also told me about how she and her siblings got into a fair amount of trouble. She and her brothers and sisters were always hungry, she said. Once they cooked some sweet potatoes on a fire in the barn on the hay-strewn floor. Their carelessness resulted in a fire that almost destroyed their barn. She showed me a scar on her leg.

"This is a permanent reminder of my misbehavior," she said.

In exchange for having May tell me her life story, she wanted to hear mine. It wasn't as interesting as hers. Since I grew up in the city I didn't tend animals or do anything interesting like that. I didn't do any chores to speak of, so I was of absolutely no use to my parents or my family. I just played.

"How lucky you were that you didn't have to do chores!" May said

At that moment, Brian appeared in the aisle.

"What's going on?"

"Nothing." I said. "What do you want?"

"Actually, I want my ball. It's under your seat."

The seats rested on metal legs that were nailed to the flat wooden floor. Brian and his friends were playing catch in the aisle. Whenever Brian or his friends lost control of his ball, it rolled freely like the steel ball in a pinball machine, down the aisle and in the open spaces between packages and boxes placed under the seats.

"Get it quick, Marie, before it rolls away!" Brian shouted.

I slipped down onto the floor and scooped it up. As I reached over to give it to him, he asked, "You want to play?"

"No."

"You're missing a lot of fun. . . ."

"I don't think so."

He had found boys to play catch with him, so he didn't really need me to play with him, anyway. Sometimes, some of the seated adult passengers also joined in and caused a commotion. They would play "keep away" by throwing the ball to each other instead of returning it to the boys.

The aisle had become a playground. For Brian, it had

become his home away from home. He played catch in it, ran through it, and sat in it. He even stretched out and slept in it. It seemed the only time he was in his seat was when a soldier appeared.

Brian would scramble over our luggage into his seat the moment a soldier stepped through the door.

"Stay out of the aisle!" the soldier would shout if he saw the kids were not in their seats. But it didn't take long for them to figure out when the soldier was coming. He had a schedule. He appeared once every hour and whenever the train began to slow down. Occasionally, though, the soldier would surprise us. I never knew when he would appear and shout at Brian. It was like watching the scary Abbott and Costello movie *Hold That Ghost* where dead bodies unexpectedly fell out of closets. After that, I covered my eyes whenever someone was about to open a door in a movie. Neither doors opening in movies nor the sudden appearance of soldiers seemed to bother Brian.

★ ★ ★

After sunset, a soldier lit the hurricane lamps at each end of the coach and ordered us to lower the shade. Whatever light left outside trickled in through the narrow windows along the bottom of a flat dome built on the roof of the car. When that light faded, it was time to go to sleep, because it was too dark to do anything else. I used my coat as a pillow. I would put it against the window or against May and Tom's bags, but I really couldn't lie down. I also slept in my clothes, so technically I hadn't gone to bed. Therefore, the following morning, I saw no need to wash up or even brush my teeth. And I didn't.

On the other hand, May would be the first one out of her seat as soon as the darkness was broken by the growing light of dawn. With disheveled hair, smeared eyebrows, and rumpled clothes, she would remove a few things from her suitcase and put them in a bag. Then she would disappear into the telephone-booth–sized lavatory that was stuck in the corner of the car. A long line of passengers would begin to fill the aisle. Finally, she would emerge fresh and beautiful. Like a butterfly out of a cocoon. Or Superman out of a phone booth. But May never made a comment about my poor hygiene. Nor did anyone else.

It was May's idea to teach me to play rummy. It happened when we were stalled in a train station. An armed soldier entered our car and stood guard at the door. That happened whenever the train slowed down or stopped. Tom, who dozed or read through most of the trip, didn't doze or read when soldiers were in the car. His eyes grew large. Better to see the soldier and follow his every move, I thought. A spot on his jaw below his ear would begin to bulge in and out as though there was some creature trapped inside trying to pound its way out. As Tom watched the soldier, I watched Tom.

"Honey, let's play cards!" May said with a laugh.

"What?"

"We can play rummy."

Then she turned to me. "Do you know how to play rummy, Marie?"

"I know how to play fish. . . ."

"Rummy is a lot more fun. Come on. We can teach you. Can't we, Tom."

"Yeah. Sure."

She stood up and rummaged through her purse that was hanging on the hook above the window and pulled out a deck of cards. Then she reached over and grabbed several large *Saturday Evening Post*s from the pile of reading material stacked on top of their baggage. She set them on our laps to use as individual tables. She dealt the cards and explained how the game was played. Although rummy was a little harder, May was right. It was a lot more fun than fish. . . .

But the hardest part of the game was keeping the cards from sliding off the slick cover of the magazines. I had to concentrate on keeping my knees together so my "table" wouldn't collapse. But I wasn't the only one. Tom's table would collapse, too. And May would collapse with laughter when that happened.

"This takes concentration, Tom," she said. "Focus on the game. You can do it!" She laughed again.

He turned to her and sighed.

"Let's just play."

Just when I was close to "going out," our stationary train felt like it was struck by another train. Tom and May were almost pushed out of their seats by the jolt, and our cards became a scrambled mess.

"I guess we've finally hooked up with an engine," May said as she gathered the cards together.

We never spent a day or night without crashes, jerks, and rapid chugs of locomotives trying to grip the tracks with their spinning wheels. That was the feel and sound of one train detaching us and another attaching. And that was how May explained it. Our train would stop, then back up onto a spur line. The main train would unhook us and leave. What seemed like hours later, another train would back into us with a crash to ensure proper coupling, then move forward with a jerk to test the union. Then we slowly chugged off toward Arkansas.

The train eventually worked through the slips and stumbles and found an even rhythm. The wheels began to click a steady beat. Eventually, a soldier came through the car announcing that the blinds could be raised. May reached over and pulled on the shade and then released it. It snapped up to the top of the window revealing what resembled a beach without the ocean. Sand dotted with short, stubby plants.

"This will probably be all we'll see for a while." said May. "I think we're in some kind of desert."

"I guess that means we won't be stopping for a while," she continued. "Let's see if we can finish a game this time."

Our cars, filled with people rejected by our country, were rejected by one train after another as we slowly made our way halfway across the continent. I told May ours was a "train of rejection."

"I wouldn't go so far as to say we were a 'rejection train,'" said May. "I would rather call it a 'buttermilk train.'"

"A what?"

"Let me explain. Milk trains stop at every station to pick up milk at towns along its route. I know that from experience," she added.

"This one stops at all the stations, but with all the jerking, bumping, and shaking going on, the cream in the milk would surely be butter by now. Butter and milk. Buttermilk. Get it?" She threw her head back and laughed at her own joke.

Then she went on to explain how she would skim the cream off milk back on the farm, and shake it in a jar until it turned to butter.

"Try that the next time you get milk from the store," she said. "Just pour the cream off the top . . ." She stopped in mid-sentence.

Would I ever be able to go to a store again, I wondered. Would I ever be able to skate on sidewalks again? Would I ever be able to do anything normal again?

It was as if she had been listening to my thoughts. She leaned forward to pull me close for a hug, just as the train came to a grinding halt without warning. I tumbled forward onto her, and we found ourselves nose to nose. We just looked at each other for a moment. Then she began to laugh, and her whole body began to shake in rhythm with her laughter. The feeling of her laughter made me laugh. Together we laughed until our blended tears rolled down our cheeks.

Suddenly, I was struck by the silence. Something was not right. There was not the usual bump, jerk, and chug that followed our stops. We had not been notified of the stop, nor told to lower the shades. Had we had reached our destination? Were we in Arkansas? I looked out the window. We were still in the desert. No houses. Nothing. Are they going to let us off here in the middle of nowhere?

"May, is this it? Is this our new camp?" I shouted.

At that moment, a soldier entered our car. "We're stopping here to stretch our legs."

I sat back and felt my whole body relax and melt into the seat.

"What a relief!" I said. Getting off the train sounded good. It was three days into our journey, and I had not walked on anything but the pitching, rolling train floor. This is great! I thought.

As we lined up to leave, I waited until my parents and Brian were right behind me, so we could all get off the train together. Brian and I might be able to play tag or something, I thought. But as I started to step out the door, out of the corner of my eye, I saw something flash. I turned to see a blade catching the sun just inches from my face. It was attached to the rifle of a soldier standing on the ground below. Obviously, this was not the first armed soldier I'd ever seen, but this was the closest I'd been to his weapon. Then I saw other flashes in the distance, out in the desert. Several other soldiers, bayonets gleaming in the sun, stood like posts of an invisible fence.

"Don't stop there! Keep moving!" the soldier shouted as he motioned with his rifle. As he swung his rifle I kept an eye on his bayonet so I wouldn't get hurt. Then I moved away quickly, but not too quickly. Away from this soldier. Down the steps. Onto the stepstool and down to the ground. He would just as soon poke me with his bayonet as look at me, I thought. Playing tag with Brian would not be a good idea, either, I decided.

I stepped away from the train and waited for Mama. It didn't feel good standing outside the train surrounded by armed soldiers. We're like corralled animals, I thought. I could feel my stomach churning with a mixture of fear and anger. As soon as Mama got to the ground I ran to her and threw my arms around her waist.

"Why are they doing this to us, Mama? Why!" I shouted at her between sobs.

Mama just held me close and stroked my head until I calmed down.

"I just want to return to the train," I said. "I don't want to roam in their corral."

We were the first ones back on the train with the others right behind. Even Brian returned to the train without exploring the edges of our outdoor desert prison. I sat at the window and watched the people in lines waiting to board the train with the armed soldiers slowly moving in behind them.

CHAPTER 13

"Be Careful, It's My Heart"
FRANK SINATRA

Two days later we finally arrived at the Rohwer Relocation Center. It was October 6, 1942. My tenth birthday. Rohwer was located in the southeast corner of Arkansas, in the middle of the Mississippi River bottomlands, in the middle of a forest, in the midst of barbed wire fence and guard towers.

Our train stopped at the edge of a clearing. From the top of the steps, I could see black tar-paper houses much like the ones in Stockton Assembly Center. After days of bright desert, the black buildings set against the background of dense trees seemed dark and gloomy. It heightened my fear and indescribable loneliness. I looked around for Mama.

"Marie!" Brian snapped. "Over here! Don't just stand there. Come on! We need to stay together." I said a quick "good bye" to May and Tom and ran to be with my family.

There was a long line to board the trucks to take us to the administration building. Here we would be "processed" again. They would check our luggage and give us our apartment assignments. In order to get to our new homes before dark, we couldn't dawdle. This was no time for daydreaming.

We finally boarded an army truck that resembled a

covered wagon. From an old wooden train onto a covered wagon to our home in the forest. Just like the movies about the olden days, I thought. We climbed aboard and sat on the wooden benches in the rear of a covered truck filled to capacity with people who had not bathed or changed their clothes in four days. The air was stifling. Mercifully, a few moments later, we were getting off at the administration building. We emerged only to line up again to enter the building.

Once inside, we were directed to a table where Papa and Mama were required to sign a bunch of papers. Brian and I looked over Papa's shoulder and helped him when a section seemed unclear.

A questionnaire asked what kind of work experience people had, so they could be put to work in areas they were familiar with. We also got our housing assignment.

After processing, we stood in another line to be driven to our new home. We were the last to board another truckload of unwashed people. Being the last ones on had its advantages.

We traveled a road between clusters of buildings, each surrounded by a moat. Like a castle would have. Except there was no water in the moats. Why would we need empty moats, I wondered.

Our first stop was at a block in a clearing that had almost no trees. I followed Mama and Papa as they climbed down. This isn't bad, I thought. It seemed cheery with the sun shining freely and abundantly. Then I learned it wasn't our block. We were just making way for those in the back of the truck. After driving up and down roads through shaded blocks and sunny blocks, we were finally dropped off in the most densely forested part of the camp.

Our new home was in Block 8 in the farthest corner of the camp at the edge of the wilderness.

The trees were so dense, the sky was barely visible. Leaves

on the branches fanned out trying their best to block out the sun. The gloom I felt when we arrived, returned. This was to be our permanent home. "For the duration," Mama said.

"What does that mean?" I asked.

"That means 'until they decide to let us out.'"

"You mean until the war ends?"

"Yes. I think so. That's how others think of the 'duration.'"

"Oh. I see," I said. But I didn't really see. I didn't understand. I realized there was a war going on in Europe and the Pacific, where there was shooting and bombing and people getting killed. But there was also an invisible war going on in the United States that I didn't understand. It was unseen and mysterious, because there were no battles. It was this invisible war that made us prisoners and caused things to happen to me and my family. The army of my country decided we were the enemy, although we never attacked them or did any harm to anybody. The FBI even proved that we were not enemies. But that didn't matter. That invisible force was strong. It was an enormous thing like the white blob that invaded my dreams when I was sick. It invaded my mind then seeped down into my stomach and sucked it empty, leaving me alone and afraid. It was like a fog that covered us completely and controlled us. I couldn't imagine that we would ever be released. How does one get rid of something one can't see? We were going to be here forever. The blob would be with me forever.

★ ★ ★

We were dropped off at the back entrance of the mess hall next to a pile of coal. The barracks, six on each side of the mess hall, were placed perpendicular to it, and a laundry building that also housed the men's and women's bathrooms was behind it. Each pair of barracks faced each other. And each barrack had six apartments with a pair of apartments sharing a porch. The tiniest apartment for two or three persons and the largest, built for families of five, were paired and located at the ends of the barrack. The middle pair were twins, so to speak, built for families of four. Mounds of dirt formed paths that ran the length the barracks. Papa led the way to our apartment checking the paper with our address on it against the markings on the barrack. We walked on the raised path that branched off the main one to a porch in the middle of the barrack.

"8-2-C. Block 8, Barrack 2, Apartment C," said Papa. "That's it. Our new home." The main path from our barrack led directly to the mess hall exit. The entrance was on the other side. The bathrooms were kitty-corner in the farthest part of the block relative to our "apartment."

Just like the assembly center in Stockton, an apartment here was just a room. In the corner of our apartment were four collapsed cots, mattresses, a pile of army blankets, and a stack of huge white boards. Next to the inside wall stood a round black-metal wood-burning stove, which came up to my shoulder. It was tall and trim. It didn't have a "pot," so it couldn't be called a pot belly stove. There was an opening at the top for depositing coal, wood, or trash and one at the bottom for removing the ashes.

The outside walls had exposed studs that formed the skeleton of the building. Two-by-fours ran up and down and diagonally, naked and uncovered. Thankfully, the walls separating the rooms extended to the ceiling. Our conversations would not be permitted to travel the attic tunnel to the rest of the barrack as they had in the assembly center.

★ ★ ★

Uncle Ray arrived to greet us. He and his family had preceded us by several days. Back in the assembly center they had been living close to the hospital, because my cousin was only six months old at the time. The section close to the hospital housed people from the farming areas surrounding Lodi, near Stockton. Since the schedule assignments to depart the assembly center had been based on location, they had arrived in Rohwer ahead of us and were housed together with their communities. Uncle Ray and his family were assigned to this same block and had arranged to have us live close by.

So now we were going to live among people from the farming area surrounding Lodi. My grandparents and Uncle Robert lived in the area where Stockton people were assigned, Block 33. Block 8 was another new community for our family. I would have to make a whole new set of friends.

★ ★ ★

"Before you bring your baggage in the room, we have to cover your walls with the plaster boards," Uncle Ray said pointing to the stack. A couple of other men appeared from nowhere to help. "It'll help to insulate the room from the heat as well as the cold."

Soon the walls were transformed into a series of white panels. The skeleton got its skin. When they were done, we were left with the task of cleaning up chunks of plaster and paper that were trimmed from the boards. We had no cleaning tools, so Mama, Brian, and I painstakingly picked up as much as we could by hand. Mama used her handkerchief to clean up the fine chalky powder. We then unfolded the cots and set them up in pairs, so they were perpendicular to the outside walls. The beds were unmade, but Brian and I had the same idea. We each leaped onto a cot and stretched out. It felt good to be able to actually lie down after four nights of sleeping upright.

"Mama, I have to use the bathroom," I said as I sat up suddenly.

"Why don't you and I go look for it," Mama said As we headed toward the mess hall, we met a woman who lived in the end apartment of our barrack. A cotton kerchief covered her head and pulled her hair away from her dark wrinkled face. She wore a flowered apron that covered most of her upper body. Her dark pants were tucked into black rubber boots that rose halfway up her calf.

"Excuse me," Mama said. "We just moved in. My name is Mitsui and this is my daughter, Marie."

"Welcome to Block 8. My name is Oyama. I have a daughter about your age," she said as she put her hand on my head. "I don't know where she is now, but come by later so you can meet her."

Terrific! I thought. I'll have a friend that lives in the same barrack!

"We're just learning our way around." Mama said. "Can you tell us where the bathroom is?"

"Of course. Go down past the mess hall and you'll see another building. It's U-shaped. Enter and turn right and there'll be another door. That leads to the toilets and showers. The toilets are to the left. You want to go past the first two rows to the ones that face the wall, unless you like to look at someone else facing you as you're sitting. There aren't any doors on the stalls. A bunch of us were talking about making curtains or something. I think Mrs. Nakamura has already ordered some fabric from Sears Roebuck. Again, welcome. And let me know if there's anything else I can do to help you," she said.

Then, as we began to head toward the bathroom, she added, "Most people have ordered chamber pots from Sears Roebuck, if you don't already have one. Otherwise it's a long way to go in the middle of the night."

It was a long way to the bathroom. Farther than at the assembly center. When we arrived, there was no one else using the toilets, so Mama and I were able to get the last ones in the row that faced the wall. No one would be walking past us, either. The wash area was equipped with real sinks and mirrors. There were two rows of them. About fourteen in all.

We also decided to check out the bathing area. There were four tubs and eight showers. Just as some of the toilets faced each other, the shower stalls faced each other as well. I wondered if curtains were going to be made for those, too.

As we left the bathroom, we saw that at the end of the corridor formed by the base of the "U" there was a door to the laundry room.

"Let's go take a look," I said to Mama as I dragged her by the hand and leaned forward using all my weight to pull her toward the laundry.

"I really think we should get back to our room."

"There's nothing to do right now. Our luggage isn't here, yet. Come on, Mama."

"Okay. We'll just take a peek. And then we have to get back to the room."

I was surprised by the size of the laundry room. It was an enormous area with eight pairs of double-sink washtubs occupying only half of it. There were only two women scrubbing clothes, totally absorbed in their work. One woman was busy near the entrance and the other at the far end. They didn't seem to be aware of each other.

"Hi," I said to the woman closest to the door. She was bent over her washboard in sudsy water. She was scrubbing a sheet, which she twisted tightly before snaking it gradually from the suds into the clear water in the next tub. Although she had her hair wrapped in a navy blue bandana, a few wisps hung in her face. As she straightened up she tried to move the hair out of her eyes by sticking her lower lip out and blowing.

The mischievous strands fanned out for a moment, then fell back into place to further annoy her. She then brought her sudsy hand out of the water and used her dry forearm to push the hair out of her eyes.

"Hi," she said with a smile. She exhaled forcefully causing her shoulders to drop. She seemed happy to have a break.

"You must be the new folks. The Mitsuis? The Ray Mitsuis are my next door neighbor! Isn't that a coincidence?" she said with a polite laugh. "My name is Yamamoto. Welcome to Block 8." She bowed to Mama.

"My name is Mitsui," Mama said as she returned her bow. "How do you do?"

"And who is this?" Mrs. Yamamoto said, turning to me.

"My name is Marie. How do you do, Mrs. Yamamoto. Do you have any daughters my age?"

"No," she laughed. She wiped her hands on her apron and started to redo her bandana. "I have a daughter, but she's in high school."

"This is a very large laundry room." Mama said. "All these washtubs . . . I've counted sixteen. Is it always this empty?"

"Heavens, no." She said. "Sometimes every single wash stand is in use, and at other times, it's like this. I haven't figured out a pattern yet."

"Oh. Then it's just the luck of the draw as to whether you have to wait for a sink? And what is all that empty space back there?" Mama asked as she pointed to the expanse beyond the tubs.

"That's supposed to be for ironing. But there aren't any ironing boards. I hope they weren't expecting us to provide our own. I certainly didn't pack one. Did you?" Then she released a deep, hearty laugh that rolled through the empty laundry room like thunder. The woman at the other end looked up, shook her head, and returned to her wash.

Ironing boards never arrived. The empty space was eventually filled with ping pong tables that some of the men fashioned out of boards and saw horses. Mama did her ironing using her very firm bed as a board. I guess others did the same.

"You said you were neighbors of my in-laws. Can you tell me which is their apartment?" Mama asked.

"We're right next door. We share a porch. We're in 8-3-F, so they must be in "E," she said. "They're a great couple. And the baby is so cute. He never cries."

★ ★ ★

Auntie Asayo screamed with delight when we arrived at her apartment. She was a very pretty lady with laughing eyes and a tiny pointed nose that tipped up. There were little toys peeking out of the pocket of the blue smock she wore over a flowered dress. My cousin, Ray, Jr., crawled on the floor behind her. When he caught up to her, he pulled himself hand over fist up his mother's dress until he was standing. He wobbled like a drunkard as he turned and reached into his mother's pocket. Out came a small car. He squealed with delight, sat down with a thud, and began chewing on his newly discovered toy.

"It's so good to see you, both!" she said, as tears streamed down her face. "Come in, come in," She pushed the screen door open. Then she suddenly held her hand out to stop us. "Do you mind taking off your shoes? Little Ray still crawls on the floor. He's such a slow child. He's almost a year old and he still isn't walking." She always talked like that. It was clear she was bursting with pride about little Ray, but she never bragged about him.

"What do you mean?" I said. "Look at him. He's standing! Mama says Brian didn't start walking until he was eighteen months. And look at the floor!" I said as I stared at it in disbelief. It gleamed like a polished table top. "How did you get it to look like that?" I asked.

"I use floor wax. And I wash it down every morning." she said as she waved us into the room and gestured us to sit on her bed. "Ray sanded it down first so the baby wouldn't get slivers. Then I waxed it. But never mind the floor. When did you get here?"

We told her how we had already seen Uncle Ray and how he was helping us get settled. Then we talked about our train trip from Stockton.

"While you went south, we took the northern route," Aunt Asayo said. "We were able to see the Great Salt Lake and Colorado. The scenery was beautiful. And we were here in three days."

"All we ever saw was desert and it took us four," I said.

"I think the train went faster because there were babies and sick people on our train," Aunt Asayo said. "Because we had little Ray, they gave me and the baby a Pullman berth, so we could lie down. But Big Ray had to sit throughout the trip like everyone else. I feel guilty that we were given special treatment, and that your trip was so long and uncomfortable."

"It must have been uncomfortable for you, too, having to care for little Ray in cramped quarters," Mama said. "But we're here now, alive and well. I guess that's all that's really important." Then Mama stood up suddenly as she looked at her watch. "Look at the time! We'd better get back!" We both hurried out the door.

We returned to our apartment to see that our luggage had arrived. Papa was disassembling the crate that held most of our belongings. There was a mountain of clothes, bedding, and other odds and ends piled high on the beds.

"I'll build a table with wood from this box like I did before. Ray and Brian have gone to scavenge some wood scraps to make shelves," Papa said, as he tugged at a stubborn nail. He braced his foot against the box and gave it a healthy yank. Out it came as the nail released its grip suddenly, sending Papa backward, so that he almost fell. He regained his balance, then turned to look at Mama. "It certainly took you a long time to go to the bathroom. Did you get lost?"

"No. I'm sorry we were gone so long. We bumped into a lot of people. We even stopped by to talk to Asayo," Mama said.

"Are they all right? How's little Ray doing?"

"They both seem to be settled in nicely. The baby seems on the verge of walking. He's pulling himself up."

"I'll have to go over there and pay my respects, too. I'll do that later."

Mama and I finished setting up our apartment, as Papa continued with the box. She found some clothesline amidst our stuff and we pulled a section of it across the room so we could hang a blanket to create separate spaces for sleeping and waking activities. Mama also tacked pillow cases over the windows.

"It's a good thing we brought all these sheets and pillow cases from the hotel," she said. "I'm sure we'll find other uses for them, too. But I might order fabric from Sears Roebuck later and make some decent curtains. For the time being, though, this will give us some privacy." Mama said.

"And don't forget to order a new chamber pot," I said.

When Papa and Ray finished our projects, they left to begin working with the other men of the block doing community carpentry. They cut boards into three-foot slats and nailed them to logs stripped of their branches to place on the paths that connected the apartments to the common buildings. Then they became lumberjacks and were off into the woods to collect logs for firewood. These would be cut into uniform pieces, then split with an ax. The firewood would be laid in a cross-hatch pattern until a huge pile stood like a stack of Lincoln Logs at the far end of the laundry/bathroom building. This wood would be used to fuel the boilers in the bath and laundry rooms.

Every so often a lumberjack would get lost in the dense woods. It was a treacherous combination of marsh and forest with bogs and snakes. If it was after nightfall, curfew would be suspended and everyone was permitted to leave their lights on. Since our block was the closest to the forest, we were constantly involved. People would wave their flashlights and call into the darkness. Thankfully, no one ever got permanently lost.

We ate our meals in two shifts. The mess halls were not large enough to handle our entire block at one sitting. Ours was the second bell, and Mama, Brian, and I ate together. Papa was hired as a cook, so he ate with the kitchen crew. He had worked in a restaurant in his youth and entered that on his questionnaire, even if his experience was only as a busboy.

We could always count on creamed corn for dinner. It was the stable staple in our diet. I imagined that the cooks mined a bottomless pit of the stuff somewhere deep in the woods. Mercifully, when the crops grown by some of the internees reached harvest, our meals became more varied.

There was always a surplus of bread. Every day platefuls placed on each table were left uneaten and piles of bagged loaves were left by the exit from the mess hall for people to take back to their rooms. Bread pudding was a regular, as was stuffing, toast, and anything else the cooks could make with leftover bread. It didn't take a genius to figure out we didn't eat much bread, because we were rice eaters. The only time we ever ate bread back in San Francisco was when Mama made a sandwich. I'm sure that was true for everyone else. The rumor was that someone in the administration was related to the owner of a bread factory. Eventually, rice made its way to our tables, but that didn't replace the bread. A plate of bread continued to appear at every meal.

Papa came home one evening and announced that we were going to have turkey for our first Thanksgiving dinner in camp. That was exciting news. We had always had turkey back home in San Francisco, so it would be like a little piece of home in Arkansas.

"I'm so glad I'm working in the kitchen. My experience at Pig 'N Whistle Restaurant will come in handy with the turkeys," he said. "All this reminds me of the days when I first arrived in San Francisco."

"I thought you were a busboy at Pig 'N Whistle. Did you also cook?" I asked.

"I spent a lot of time in the kitchen, so I watched what the cook did. I learned a lot from just watching. And sometimes I helped cook," he said.

We learned from Papa that there was more than the usual amount of preparation involved for the big Thanksgiving dinner. So Papa was at the kitchen most of the day. At one point he came home very upset.

"Those idiots," he said. "They're going to ruin the turkeys. They want to overcook them. They probably never prepared turkeys before. But I know that the worst thing you can do is overcook them. The meat gets dry and tasteless. I can't convince them to cut down the cooking time." He paced a bit, then returned to the kitchen.

Ultimately, he was able to get his way. They turned out to be "the most delicious succulent turkey anyone had ever eaten." Everyone raved about it. It had red juice coursing through some of it, but no one minded. In the words of one person, "It was like a medium rare steak." Papa was not bashful about taking the credit and sharing how he persuaded the chief cook to shorten the roasting time.

Two hours later, Papa's hero status came to an end.

Dozens of people got sick from having eaten the undercooked meat. There was a lot of heaving going on. Everywhere.

The following day, Mr. Ota, the chief cook, came to our apartment.

"Mr. Mitsui," he said, "We are all simple country folk here in Block 8, and you are from the city. I think you should get a job in an office or something and leave the cooking to us simple country folk." With those words, Papa was fired.

After that Papa refused to set foot in the mess hall.

That meant that Mama had to bring his meals home. My uncle had always brought their meals to his home to eat because of little Ray. And people who were sick had their meals in their apartments. Papa was neither a baby, nor sick, but no one complained about this special treatment.

Another effect of Papa and Mama not working was that our family no longer had any income whatsoever. Brian and I were entitled to a clothing allowance of $3 a month each, if at least one member of a family worked. No one worked, therefore, no clothing allowance, either.

One evening about a month later, Mama came running into our apartment after going to the bathroom.

"The kitchen is on fire!" she said. "I could see flames in the kitchen area!"

"Have you told Mr. Ota?" Papa asked.

"No, I thought you should do it . . . ," Mama said.

Papa bolted out the door yelling, "Fire! Fire!" as he ran to Mr. Ota's apartment a few yards from the kitchen. I ran outside and watched people pour out of the other apartments surrounding us.

"Where? Where's the fire?" they shouted.

"The kitchen!" Someone yelled out of the darkness.

Mama ran after me and led me back into the apartment. "Stay inside. You'll get in the way!"

The fire was caught in time and there was very little

damage. Papa was a hero. Particularly since the memory of the mess hall in Block 6 that had recently been destroyed by fire was fresh in everyone's mind. The residents of that block were scattered to surrounding mess halls for their meals. Everyone in our block was happy to have been spared that inconvenience.

The following day, Mr. Ota, the chief cook, came to our apartment to personally thank Papa and asked if he would return to the kitchen. There was an opening for a pot washer.

"Actually, it was my wife that discovered the fire. You should offer the job to her," he said. Mama took the job.

★ ★ ★

But as one problem was resolved another developed.

We shared our porch with a young couple, Ken and Masako Nakamura, and their two preschool children, Taro and Sumi. They were a Japanese-speaking family. Ken was a quiet man who always dressed in neatly ironed shirts and pants and polished shoes. He smiled a lot, but rarely said anything. He reminded me of Tom, my train mate. Ken's wife, Masako, was six months pregnant, but was always in motion. If she wasn't sweeping the porch and steps, she was scurrying around in their apartment with muffled footsteps.

"Since the children play on the floor, we always take our shoes off before entering," Masako said. "So please remove your shoes, Marie." It was a routine that everyone had to follow when visiting the Nakamuras, just as it was at my Uncle Ray's. She was very meticulous and all that shoe polishing and ironing filled the spaces between child-rearing chores. Taro and Sumi were amazingly quiet, like their parents. Or maybe I never heard them over our own din. Brian and I spoke in shouts, when we were close enough to whisper. Papa and Mama seemed to argue more than ever. Brian and

I had developed a strategy to bury Papa and Mama's fighting and divert attention to ourselves. This we did automatically. It wasn't anything we had planned. Papa and Mama would suddenly discover that they couldn't hear themselves argue because of us. They would turn to us and Papa would say something like, "Keep your voices down! You're disturbing the neighbors. I don't know what's happening to you kids. This camp life is ruining you."

When we were back home in San Francisco, I hated when they argued, but I hated it here even more. Family arguments were no longer contained within the family. It was as though everyone had their ears to our walls. Lately, their fights were about what Papa was doing while Mama was working. He checked with administration each day about a job in Community Activities, but they were still organizing and not ready to hire him.

Papa spent most of his spare time visiting with Masako. Whenever she padded across the floor of her apartment and opened the screen door with a squeak, Papa would peek to see if she was carrying something. If she was, and she was, most of the time, he would be hot on her heels. Most of the time, she was on her way to the laundry room. He would offer to carry her load. And after she was done, he would, of course, carry her load back. He probably even did her wash, though I never checked. Sometimes I saw them just sitting and chatting.

Naturally, Papa and Masako's friendship did not go unnoticed by others in the block. It seemed people had nothing better to do than gossip. The idle talk crept into Mama's ears and set off an explosion.

"You're the talk of the camp!"

"She's pregnant. Since I'm not doing anything, helping her is the right thing to do."

"Well, you wouldn't be doing 'nothing,' if you got a job."

"I'm waiting for the Community Activities job. You know that. It takes time for the administration to get it organized."

"You should have taken this job as pot washer when the Block Manager came around. Yeah. You should be washing pots instead of me, instead of following that woman around like a lost puppy."

"I'm just showing compassion! You should have some compassion for Masako, too."

"I don't recall your showing *me* much compassion when I was pregnant. I worked every day in the cleaners, and cooked and cleaned. I don't remember much help with any of that. You weren't even around when Brian was born. You were gallivanting with your actor brother from Japan on that tour. . . ."

Papa seemed not to hear what Mama was saying.

"You should be showing Masako some compassion, too. The least you could do is keep our half of the porch swept."

"That woman is complaining about my not sweeping the porch? If the porch needs sweeping, *you* should sweep it!"

One day, when I returned home from school, I noticed a stack of empty boxes on the Nakamura's side of our porch. I could make a neat playhouse out of them, I thought. Maybe the Nakamuras have the same idea. Or maybe . . . they're moving! I knocked on their door. Ken answered.

"Hi, Marie. What can I do for you?"

"What're you going to do with all those boxes?" I asked. Ken smiled. "We're moving."

"Moving? No. Are you really? Are you leaving camp?"

"We're just moving to Block 39, which is close to the hospital. An apartment opened up there. With the baby coming and all, we thought it would be convenient."

"Wow! That's really great!" I said. Then I realized that didn't sound quite right. "I mean that's great that you're going to be so close to the hospital. Of course, I'm sorry to hear you're moving. I'll miss you all."

What I wanted to say was, "That's the greatest news I've heard in a long time! With your wife gone, we can have some peace and quiet around here!" I'm sure the Nakamuras were glad to be rid of us as well. Everyone could breathe a great sigh of relief. Except Papa. He was very sad.

"She reminded me of Mama when she was young," he confided to me one day. If that was meant to make me feel better, it didn't.

CHAPTER 14

"Over the Rainbow"
JUDY GARLAND

The Sakais moved into 8-2-D soon after. They were an older couple along with their married daughter and grandson. Their daughter's husband was in the army, fighting in France. Our barrack got considerably quieter.

And Papa finally got the job he was waiting for. He was hired as director of Community Activities. Mama also moved out of the kitchen as pot washer and into the administration building as a clerk typist. She had been to business college before she was married. Mama's salary was increased to $16 a month from $12. Papa also made $16 a month. Only professional people like doctors made the top salary of $19 a month.

Mama greeted the news of being hired in the office with mixed feelings. She was pleased that she would be out of the kitchen, but worried about her wardrobe.

"I didn't bring much in the way of 'presentable' clothes." She held up the two dresses she brought. One was a sleeveless black thing gathered at the shoulders, and the other, a brown dress with large brass ornaments on the right shoulder and waist, "I may have to order some dresses from Sears Roebuck . . ."

"Buy new clothes? That makes no sense! You might as well stay home! Or maybe you can get your old job back!"

"You spent all that money on your clothes when we had the cleaners and I never said anything! I should be able to buy new clothes now, if I want!" They were at it again . . . would they ever stop fighting? It made my stomach turn. No doubt it would be the grist for the gossip mill tomorrow.

Mama decided on the brown dress to wear to work the first day. It looked like a party dress to me. Both her dresses did. But she had little choice. The second day, she wore her usual skirt and blouse.

"Most of the people in the office are young, single women. I'm the oldest clerk typist there. Everyone dresses casually," she said. She didn't have to buy new clothes. All that arguing for nothing.

★ ★ ★

Shortly after our arrival at Rohwer, I met a girl who lived in the apartment next to the entrance to the mess hall. She was my height, but chubbier. She had eyebrows that met in the middle and a nose that exposed its nostrils to the fullest. She would swipe at her nose with the back of her hand, pushing it farther up her face. Her hair was bobbed in a dutch boy cut. I assumed she was my age, because of her size, but something was not quite right about how she talked. Then I discovered that she was only six to my ten! Even among Japanese Americans, I was a shrimp. Much to my further disappointment, I soon learned that there were no girls my age in the block. There were several girls who were a year older or a year younger and they were classmates at school. I, on the other hand, had no one like that. So, I had a life in school and another in our block.

Outside of school, I spent a good deal of time visiting

with older people. Ruby Matsumoto was in high school. She was a cheerful teenager who always had a song on her lips. She would either be belting one out or singing just under her breath. She walked with a bounce that set her loose pageboy in motion. Her wavy bangs barely touched her eyebrows that sat high above her slender eyes, set in a permanent smile. She was one of the most cheerful people I had ever met.

Ruby made her own pleated skirts, with applied silk-screened patterns of her own design.

Although Ruby was a very popular girl with many friends, she always had time for me. She often invited me to her apartment so I could watch her work. She sketched and carved a pattern, then glued it to a silkscreen. Then she would place fabric under the screen, put a line of paint on it, and pull it across the cloth with a squeegee. She used a squeegee just like the one Papa used when washing the show window back home at the cleaners. Lifting the screen left the design on the fabric. She also did stenciling that was not as elaborate but also involved cutting a design out of stiff paper and applying paint to the cut-out area.

I told her about the man in the assembly center who painted fans.

"I'm really sorry you weren't able to keep that fan. It sounds very beautiful."

"Do you ever oil paint?" I asked Ruby.

"Actually, if I were to paint a picture, I would use my silk screen or do block printing. Whenever I make any kind of print, I never know exactly how it'll look until I complete it. I find that exciting." Her dream was to someday design clothes to sell to people.

I also visited with Terry, a young mother with a five-month-old daughter. Terry was a pretty, rather dark-com-plected lady with thin sparkling eyes framed by heavy arching eyebrows. She wore her hair in an upsweep pulled forward into two enormous pompadours. Her baby daughter, June, had very round, closely spaced eyes and was not as pretty a baby as I would have thought Terry's would be. Terry's sole occupation was to take care of June, so I often found her at home. I would visit my aunt and cousin, then share what I had learned with Terry. For example, I told her about the little folded origami objects my aunt made from old newspaper that she had colored with crayons. These were hung by thread and tied to branches close to the doorway, so they would twist and turn with the breeze. It would keep little Ray occupied for hours. It worked with June as well.

★ ★ ★

Although we had frequent rain showers, in late November, the rains arrived in earnest.

"In order for it to be green and lush, there needs to be a lot of moisture," Papa said. The once empty moats brimmed with water and the bridges across them became barely passable. I wasn't allowed to walk on them during heavy rains.

"You're so little, if you slipped off, you would drown," warned Mama. That was enough to keep me away from them. The driveway behind the kitchen was the only way out of our block for me. The ground also became a soggy mess. Water moccasin snakes lurked in the moats and in the puddles that developed under our barracks. Wood piles shrank as the temperatures dropped, and the smell of burning wood filled the air. Lightning crashed through the trees and occasionally hit its mark. A tall majestic tree behind our barrack was struck with such force, the trunk split into two pieces. The weaker half separated cleanly from the rooted portion. Fortunately, it came to rest parallel to the barracks. We were spared.

"Lush growth and tall trees are a curse," I told Papa. "They bring torrents of water, lightning, bogs, and snakes. There isn't one thing good about it!" I longed for the clean lines of concrete sidewalks, the apartment buildings, and the stucco homes of San Francisco. I missed Jean, Maxine, Alice, and all the other kids at Lawton. I missed being able to go to the store and to visit my friends. I missed the sand and the beach. . . .

One morning, I was awakened by Brian who was shouting in my ear.

"Marie! Wake up! It's snowing outside! Hurry up and get dressed!" I sat up in my bed and looked out the window. From there I could see the roof of the barrack across the way. It had been transformed from a dull gray to a glistening white. I slid up out of my tightly tucked blanket cocoon and ran barefoot across the icy floor to peer out the window. Small white particles were floating down from the sky and landing on the whiteness that already covered the trees and everything on the ground. I had never seen snow before. It was magnificent. I poured a little hot water out of the kettle on the hot plate into my wash basin and dipped my toothbrush in it. I ran my brush quickly around my teeth and splashed a little water on my face. Then I pulled off my nightgown, slipped into my warm long-sleeve sweater, knee socks and skirt, boots, and my princess coat.

"I don't think you should wear that coat out there," Mama said. "Wear your rain cape." She was referring to my long blue waterproof cape with attached hood.

"It's snowing, Mama. Not raining," I said. "I'm not going to get wet." Then I bolted out the door. Brian was already outside. When I stepped onto the porch, the bits of ice that landed on my coat looked like tiny pieces of rice. As if to read my mind, Brian said, "It's sleet. It isn't snow. Snow comes down as flat flakes."

"Oh," I said. "Are you sure?"

"Yeah," he said. He sounded disappointed.

"Well, whatever it is, it's beautiful," I said and pulled my hood up over my head.

"Let's go over to the rec hall area," Brian said.

There was a large clearing there, behind the laundry room. It was a gathering spot for kids. When we arrived it seemed as though every school age kid in our block was there. And more. Snowballs were flying from the vicinity of the wood pile to the rec hall. I was immediately drawn into a war. My high-school-age friend, Ruby, her brother, Brian's best friend, Frank, and some boys from another block were there.

"Marie! Come help us. Be on our team!" Ruby said from behind a pile of logs. "Help us make some ammunition!" By that she meant snowballs.

"Wow, you look really pretty in that coat, Marie," Joey said. He was Ruby's friend from school. "You're as beautiful as Ruby!" I was so glad I wore it.

There were also logs to be moved to enlarge the fort to accommodate newcomers. I pitched right in. It was great fun, but getting hit by snowballs and moving dirty logs was a wet and messy business.

When I returned home Mama had a look of disbelief as her wide eyes scanned my coat.

"Look at it! It's ruined! I'm not going to be able to clean it, you know. We aren't in the cleaning business anymore!" I took it off and examined it. And Mama was right, it looked terrible. There were dark brown stains on the pale beige sleeves and front from carrying the logs. I should have listened to Mama when we were at Sears, I thought. I should have picked a darker coat, then the stains would not be so prominent.

Because it was wool, after the coat dried, it was misshapen. It was clear where the snowballs and sleet had soaked it. The shoulders and upper back were puckered and the sleeves had shrunk so much the lining was showing. It was grotesque. My princess coat was now truly fit for a clown.

CHAPTER 15

"Stars and Stripes Forever"
JOHN PHILIP SOUSA

School started very soon after we arrived at Rohwer. Two of the blocks had been adapted for use as schools. The elementary school for our side of the camp was in Block 35. Half was for the high school and half for grades K–6.

The classroom walls were bare except for the flag. The only furniture in the classrooms was benches without tables. But there weren't any books, either, so it didn't matter that much at the time. The rainy season had begun in earnest and running around outside was not an option, so our teacher had us march to "Stars and Stripes Forever." It was a great way to keep thirty restless children under control. She taught us marching terms like "Atten . . . hut!" "Mark time, harch!" and "To the left, harch!" When books and other supplies finally arrived, we didn't march as much. By then we had tables to match the benches, and our marching space was gone.

A group of girls at school who had been taking baton lessons before the war organized a baton-twirling class after school. I had enjoyed marching, so I joined the group. Papa carved a baton for me out of wood with a knife from the kitchen and sandpaper he had brought along. The wooden baton was twenty-six inches long including the oblong ball at one end. It worked reasonably well except that the inside of my elbow was in constant pain from being battered by the wooden ball as it passed under my arm. I longed to have a baton like my fellow twirlers. Theirs were not only made of metal mottled to reflect and scatter light like crystal, but were topped with a soft rubber ball. The Sears Roebuck catalog listed them for $3.50, but Mama thought that an extravagance.

"We need to be saving our money for a time if we are ever released from camp," she said.

But she was soft-hearted. Yet not so soft-hearted that she bought the one I wanted. There was a less expensive one in the catalog and she ordered it. It was $1.95, 32 inches long with a huge metal sphere at the business end. It was her surprise gift to me. Unfortunately, it was totally unusable. It was a drum major's baton . . . too long to twirl under my arm and the metal ball on the end was a menace. Not only to me, but anyone who happened to be in range when the poorly balanced rod was thrown in the air. Intentionally, or unintentionally. But I pretended to use it. I would take it to baton practice and simply watch the others. I eventually stopped going. Besides, I also needed white majorette boots, which my parents would never have bought me. In any case, that was the end of my baton-twirling career.

Sears Roebuck, Montgomery Ward, and Spiegel catalogs provided me with a window into a fantasy world. When I was feeling sad, I could get lost in their pages of furniture, stoves, and dishes. I pretended I lived in a house like Jean Ireland's and "ordered" things for it from the catalog.

★ ★ ★

While thumbing through *Mechanic's Illustrated*, my father came across an article about getting rich selling salve. That was a medicinal jelly that came in a tin. It was great for cuts, insect bites, burns, and any other minor wound.

"Marie," he said. "Take a look at this. If you want to make some money, sell some salve. Then, if you need a baton or anything else, you can use your own money."

"That sounds like a great idea, Papa," I said. It cost five dollars for ten tins or fifty cents each. I was supposed to sell them for a dollar a piece. When those were sold, I could order more.

"Where am I going to get five dollars?" I asked.

"I'll give it to you. It's an investment, so it's worth spending. I'm sure you'll have no trouble selling it."

I could buy the baton I wanted and have money left over! After the first ten were sold, I could order more and even buy some boots! I could hardly wait for my tins of salve to arrive.

When finally they did, I took them to all my adult friends. I told them what a great product it was and said all the things the company told me to say. No sale. I reduced the price, but even when I offered it for fifty cents, no one was interested. Actually, I couldn't even give it away. I sold only one tin and that was to my aunt.

What a waste of money! With the five dollars spent on the salve, I could have gotten the baton I wanted and maybe the boots, too, if I counted the money for the baton Mama bought me. Instead, all I had was nine cans of salve and a useless baton. What were my parents thinking?

★ ★ ★

The warmth of spring warned us of the hot days ahead. It became warmer and more humid with each passing day. Sudden showers sent everyone scurrying. It soon became a common practice to cut three-foot-by-three-foot openings in the walls of our homes at the level of the floor for better circulation. Openings were also cut in the walls of our classrooms.

I learned very quickly that I had to choose between sweltering in the middle of the room or getting a bug up my dress by catching a breeze sitting next to an opening. There were no screens, and insects flew or crawled inside and willingly shared any kind of space. I chose to swelter. At night we slept under mosquito nets that protected us against the cool night air as well as mosquitoes. More sweltering. Chiggers were another menace. I never quite figured out how they managed to slip into my pores to suck my blood. The barely visible tiny red blood-sucking insects caused intense itching and were next to impossible to extract. I wasn't sure which was worse, Rohwer's summers or winters. Spring and fall were nice, though.

★ ★ ★

My grandparents lived in Block 33. That's where Stockton people lived. May and Tom, my train friends, were in Block 33, too. Actually, they, from Lodi, should have been in Block 8, and we, from Stockton, in Block 33. That must have been the trade that was made in order to accommodate Papa's and Uncle's Ray's request. It didn't matter, though, because few of my Stockton friends came to Rohwer. Most were sent to Arizona.

Grandma said that I needed to be a good homemaker. She felt that camp life deprived me of the necessary experiences, so she had me visit her whenever possible to "train" me. She taught me things like putting chopsticks in a chopstick holder with the points down, so people wouldn't touch the working end of it when they removed a pair. She also taught me how to wash rice so the grains didn't get broken. Her table was covered with a flower-print oilcloth. I learned to clean the part that hung loose down the sides as well as the top. Grandpa always grinned and snickered as Grandma instructed me. He thought Grandma took things too seriously. He seemed much more relaxed since the days at the hotel before we left Stockton. On the other hand, he looked older. His back was rounder and he could no longer walk without a cane. And even with his cane, his walking was labored.

One day, I arrived at their apartment to find Grandpa in bed.

"Are you sick?" I asked.

"Not really. Grandma thinks I should stay in bed, though. Just because my toe is sore. My feet get cold, so I was using a hot water bottle. The cloth wrapped around it came off and my toe got burned," Grandpa said.

"I had a sore toe once," I said. "But it went away. It hurt a lot at the time, but it mended."

"That's what I keep telling Grandma. But she is so serious about every little thing." Then he threw back the covers. "You want to see my toe?" I walked over to the foot of the bed and peered at his foot.

"It's all bandaged."

"Oh, yes. So it is. Let me take the bandage off."

"No, Grandpa, that's all right."

Thankfully, just then, Grandma walked in. She was accompanied by a man in a white coat. I knew immediately who he was. A doctor. They're probably going to take him away to the hospital, I thought.

"Marie," Grandma said. "You'd better get along home. And tell your mother to come over as soon as she can."

"Shizu, don't listen to her. There's nothing wrong with me, except that I have a sore toe," Grandpa shouted to me as I went out the door.

They took him to the hospital, like I thought they would

and didn't allow children to visit. Grandpa died after a while. He had gangrene. I missed him terribly. He was always so cheerful. Now there was no one to call me "Shizu."

A funeral was held at the Buddhist Church that was set up in one of the recreation halls. Mama had to wear a black dress and a black hat with a veil. She didn't have a veil, so she took a piece of black lining material and pinned it to her hat. The "veil" totally covered her face so that no one could see it. She couldn't see anyone else's face either, unless she lifted the opaque material. I asked Mama what the funeral was going to be like.

"Grandpa will be lying in a large wooden box," she said.

"How do we know Grandpa is in it?" I asked.

"The lid will be open," said Mama.

"You mean, I have to look at dead Grandpa?" I asked. The only dead people I had ever seen were in the movies. *Hold That Ghost* with Abbott and Costello was one of the last movies I had seen before the war. People were murdered and hidden in closets or in secret panels. Every now and then, a dead body would suddenly appear and I would scream. For most of the movie I covered my eyes when someone approached a door, because I feared that a dead body might suddenly fall out. Their unnaturally white faces with startled looks and gaping mouths, along with their sudden appearance, frightened me. As much as I loved Grandpa, I didn't want to look at his dead face. I didn't want my last memory of him to be a ghastly one. The last time I saw him, he was laughing. I didn't want anything to replace that.

At the funeral we lined up to view his body. My legs felt weak and wobbly as I waited my turn. Then I had a brainstorm. I decided that I would close my eyes and not look at him when the time came. I stood behind Mama. She moved up, and I closed my eyes. I heard the rustle of Mama's dress as she walked away. Brian was behind me.

"What are you doing?" he whispered. "People are waiting." He gave me a little shove. This made me stumble. My arms extended to break my fall caused my hands to land on Grandpa's casket! My fingers gripped its open edge. I could feel soft, slippery fabric. I opened my eyes to see what it was. It was the casket's beautiful white satin lining. Just inches away was the dead body. To my surprise, it wasn't a "dead body." It was Grandpa, who looked like he was sleeping! He looked so peaceful. I expected him to open his eyes and say, "Shizu, sing me a song." The next thing I knew, Brian was taking me by the hand and leading me to my seat.

★ ★ ★

There were two Caucasian girls who passed through our camp. They both happened to be in my class. Not at the same time. They were children of people who had been recruited to work at Rohwer from outside the camp. Both became very good friends of mine.

My friendships with them did not go unnoticed.

"Why do you make friends with them?" a classmate asked.

"Why shouldn't I?" I told them. I remembered how difficult it was to be different from everyone else.

Anette was a tall, slender girl with a Texas drawl. Blonde and bright. Her height and "Caucasianness" reminded me of Jean, whom I missed very much. But she had a manner that didn't endear her to the others. She would say things like, "Don't you know it isn't polite to eavesdrop?" and "I beg your pardon?" where others in the same situation might say, "I wasn't talking to you," and "What'd you say?" They thought she was putting on airs. She wasn't. That was just the way she talked. I visited her often at her "quarters."

Her home was white clapboard, not black tar paper like

ours. It was a true apartment with a kitchen, bathroom, living room, dining room, and separate bedrooms. It was on the opposite corner of the camp, beyond the administration building. Whenever I visited, her mother was napping, although it was the middle of the day. Anette said that her mother didn't like Rohwer. One day, Anette was gone.

Frances arrived later and was shorter than Anette and wore her dark hair in French braids. She taught me to braid mine in the same way. Her hazel eyes were like an eagle's. They fixed on something or someone, then quickly darted to something else. They continuously scanned the classroom or wherever we were, collecting observations. She would ask me about them later.

"Why do so many girls wear the same dark blue dotted swiss dress? What does it mean? Do they belong to a club or something?"

"The blue dotted swiss dresses are 'government issue.'"

"'Government issue,'" Frances repeated. "That's 'G.I.,' isn't it? 'G.I.' means soldiers, doesn't it? That's confusing."

"That's true, but it's also anything the government gives us. We're allowed about $3 a month for a clothing allowance. Some families take it in the form of clothing and others take the money, like we do. My mother works as a secretary for the administration and makes $16 a month. My father arranges community activities and also makes $16 a month. They're trying to save money in case we ever get out of here. We've had to buy boots and rain gear and warm clothes and mosquito nets and stuff like that. Fortunately, my mother can sew. She orders fabrics from Sears and then stitches them by hand, because we don't have a sewing machine."

"We have a sewing machine," said Frances, "maybe she can use ours."

"Thanks, Frances," I said. "That's really nice of you to offer."

"I noticed you don't have a bathroom in your apartment. What do you do, if you have to 'go' in the middle of the night?"

"One of the first things we ever bought from the Sears Roebuck catalog was a chamber pot. It's a small bucket with a rounded edge and lid. That's what we use at night. Sometimes it's used during the day, too, when it's especially miserable outside. Then there's the devil to pay, because somebody has to empty it. The bucket gets heavy and . . . You really don't want to hear the rest."

"Eyew . . . That sounds disgusting, Marie. I'm glad we have a bathroom. I wish I could share ours with you."

Frances was not long at Rohwer, either. One day, she, too, was gone without a word.

★ ★ ★

The only other non-Japanese visitor we had was Miss Finch, my teacher. She dropped by one evening.

"I make a point of visiting the families of all my students," she said. "I was once a part of the Christian Mission in China and Japan." It was the first time in my life that a teacher had ever visited our home.

Miss Finch was about the same age as Mama and had a round, rather flat face with eyes that peered. That is, her gaze seemed to be fixed so that the upper part of her iris never showed. She accomplished this by pulling her chin in at all times. She had a rather large mouth, which she kept in motion most of the time. This gave others little chance to talk. She also spoke with my parents in the same manner she spoke to students in her classroom. During the course of the evening Papa told her that his first job in San Francisco was at a restaurant on Kearny Street. It seemed she didn't hear much of what Papa had said except that he mispronounced "Kearny

Street." Miss Finch went into a long explanation about the early history of San Francisco and how "Kearny" is an Irish name and is pronounced "Carney" rather than "Kerny." Papa and Mama didn't say anything as she rattled on and on. Suddenly, Papa stood up and said, "Look at the time. I have an assignment tomorrow that starts at seven a.m.!" Miss Finch looked surprised. Then she stood up and said, "Oh. I'm terribly sorry. I didn't realize how late it was. I really enjoyed meeting you all." Then she quickly left.

As soon as she stepped out the door, Papa exploded. "Who does she think she is? How dare she correct my pronounciation. Nobody in San Francisco says 'Carney.' And even if they did, she should have kept that to herself. I'm not a child. She thinks she can insult me just because I'm Japanese and a prisoner here!" It was not clear what Miss Finch's purpose was in visiting us. But I'm sure it was not to upset my father.

My uncle Robert, the former dental student, volunteered for the army as soon as the government permitted it. At the beginning of the war, all Japanese American soldiers were discharged from the U.S. Army. Then the government changed its mind. About a year after they put us in camp, they distributed a questionnaire for everyone to fill out to determine the loyalty of potential recruits. My uncle must have filled it out correctly, because he was accepted into the army. My mother's other brothers, Uncle Tom and Uncle Keith, also volunteered.

Uncle Keith lived in Washington, D.C., with his family and was working for the Bureau of Indian Affairs when the war started. Although he was almost thirty years old, married, with a daughter and two sons, he left them to volunteer for the army.

A square fabric banner bearing three blue stars hung in my grandmother's window. That meant she had three sons fighting in the war. A neighbor had a banner with a gold star. The blue star turned to gold when her son was killed in action. I hoped that my grandmother's stars never changed color.

My uncles trained at Camp Shelby, a special camp across the river in Mississippi set aside for Japanese American soldiers. Even as soldiers, they were separated from other Americans. Their unit was called the 442nd Regimental Combat Team and they fought in Europe. Uncle Robert and Uncle Keith were both wounded in action and awarded Bronze Stars in addition to Purple Hearts.

Everyone in camp was required to fill out the questionnaire intended to determine who might be suitable candidates for the service, regardless of their advanced age or sex. Even my grandmother. Mary Komura was a friend of the family. She lived in our block and worked for the administration. She was also responsible for finding the office job for my mother.

"You must not answer the questions about loyalty in a negative way, unless you want the government to send you back to Japan," Mary explained to Papa and Mama. "Some people are angry with the U.S. for putting us in camps and then asking that they sign a loyalty oath. But you must put your anger aside and think of the consequences." And Mary was right. People who answered the questionnaire in such a way that meant they wouldn't fight for the United States were all sent to one camp called Tule Lake in California. From there, many were to be sent to Japan.

Papa and Uncle Ray had many conversations about pledging their loyalty to the United States. Renouncing their Japanese citizenship would leave them without citizenship in any country, since they had been denied citizenship in the U.S. even after living here over twenty-five years.

"And if Japan wins this war, we're in big trouble," Papa

said. "We will be considered traitors, since we're citizens of Japan. But since we made America our home and decided years ago that we wouldn't be returning to Japan, it won't matter. Just hope the U.S. wins. . . ." With that, they pledged their loyalty to the United States.

Mary was a very good friend. She and I visited each other's apartments often. Mary was about thirty years old, but not yet married. She was tall and slender, with a long face and nose. She was always cheerful and had a certain rhythm about the way she walked and talked.

She had a collection of jewelry that she kept carefully arranged in a wooden box. Whenever I visited her in her apartment, she explained the different ways stones were cut and mounted. My favorite was the ruby ring that she wore most often. Each time I saw her with it I said something about it. One day, to my surprise, she removed it from her finger and gave it to me!

"You like it more than I do, Marie. It's yours. I want you to have it as a reminder of our friendship. If I ever get married and have a daughter, I would want her to be just like you!"

"That's the nicest thing anyone has ever said to me! That means more to me than the ring! But I'll take good care of it and it'll always remind me of you." It was a heavily faceted oval stone in a bezel setting. That means it was cut at angles in many places so that it reflected light from all directions and was held in place by a continuous piece of gold, rather than just prongs. The inside of the ring was faceted just like the exposed surface. It wasn't a cabochon, which is a stone sliced in half. I wound tape around the inside of the ring so it wouldn't slip off my finger. But it was on and off my finger constantly so I could admire and more fully appreciate the wonderful gift and what it represented. I would hold it up to the light and peer through it. One day, I set it down instead of replacing it on my finger. I never saw the ring again. I was so ashamed. I never told Mary what I had done. Instead I told her that Mama had it for safekeeping.

Among those who answered the questionnaire in such a way that they were transferred to Tule Lake was Jim, a friend of Brian's friend Dave. Jim wrote that he was enraged that his father had wanted to return to Japan. Jim decided that he would run away, although he was only thirteen at the time. He and a couple of friends planned to "hop a freight train" to Oregon. It might have worked, had not other kids learned of it and tried to join them. Three would-be escapees grew to a crowd of twelve. They all appeared at the appointed time without warning. Rather than abort the plan, Jim and his friends decided to go through with it. They managed to squeeze under the barbed wire, and down the road toward the tracks. But word of their planned escape had spread to adults, who alerted the sentries.

"We could have made it if it weren't for those other kids tagging along. They slowed us down. But I'll tell you, I was never so scared in my life as when all those soldiers in tanks bore down on us with their guns and lights. They yelled at us, 'Halt! Or we'll shoot!' Man, I didn't have to think twice. I stopped so suddenly, I fell down," Jim wrote in his letter to Dave. Poor Jimmy. I hope he doesn't get shipped to Japan, I thought.

As a result of the questionnaire there was a lot of shuffling of families from one camp to another. Some of the people who lived in Tule Lake and didn't want to go to Japan were moved to other camps to make room for the new inmates. Our block received two such families.

One of them, the Sanos, was a family of three. They had a daughter, Ann, who was nine, a year younger than I. She was very pretty, although some said that she and I resembled each other. Poor Ann.

We never became friends. Perhaps because she hated

it when folks made comments regarding our resemblance. There was no doubt in my mind that it was an insult to her. We were also in different grades.

Another latecomer to our block was a large family from Hawaii. They arrived one rainy day, dressed in Hawaiian clothes. Short-sleeved shirts, shorts, cotton dresses, and split toe sandals. The rest of us were bundled in coats and boots. One of the children was a girl about my age. She had long, dark brown hair that flowed in soft waves past her shoulders. She had eyes that never stopped smiling. It didn't matter if she was laughing or frowning. I kept my fingers crossed that she was also a fifth-grader. She wasn't. She was in fourth grade. There were now four girls in fourth grade in our block. I was the only one in my block in the fifth.

The other two girls in the fourth grade were Martha and Teruko. They both lived on the other side of the block and were from large families. Yoshiye was the oldest of six and moved and talked like a boy. She wore dresses that hung amazingly loose on her body. From her broad shoulders, they would drape straight down as though there was nothing to break their fall.

Martha had dark eyebrows that arched over large deeply set eyes framed in thick dark lashes. She was beautiful.

I usually bathed late in the evening when there were few people in the bathroom. One evening I decided to go right after dinner around six. As I entered the shower room, I could hear shouting and laughter. Martha was standing naked at the entrance to the showers, beaming. Donna and a couple of other high-school-aged girls were pointing at the swelling around her nipples, celebrating the fact that her breasts were developing.

"What about you, Marie? Let's have a look!"

I turned around and left. They called after me calling me a poor sport. I decided I hated showers. And I hated those girls. That was the last time I entered when they were around.

Not long after that incident, I was going to the bathroom after there had been a heavy rain. I could hear men's voices coming from the women's lavatory.

"What's going on?" I shouted. "What are you men doing in there? It's a girl's lavatory you're in, you know. I have to go. . . ."

"There's a snake loose in here. You girls need to keep the outside door closed! Especially during a storm!"

Between leering teenagers and snakes, the bathroom was not a pleasant place.

★ ★ ★

In the fall of 1943 our family received an enormous package from San Francisco. Jean Ireland's parents had arranged to have our large Gilfillan radio shipped to us. It was the talk of the block. No one ever before had received anything like it. Wrapped separately were some loose-knit sleeveless sweaters and wool plaid skirts for me. Just what Jean would wear, I thought. Jean had also included letters from some of my Lawton classmates. I felt like I was back at Lawton when I read them. For them it seemed nothing had changed. The kids were just as they were when we left, except we weren't there anymore. The letters made me cry. I never wrote back, because I felt embarrassed to tell them what it was like here.

The radio was my link to the "outside." I kept up with the latest songs by listening to the "Hit Parade" and pressed my ear to the radio in an attempt to learn lyrics. Fred Allen and Jack Benny were also my favorites, and I was able to get a glimpse of what those on the outside were experiencing through their comic routines. However, as much as I enjoyed listening to them, I was always left with the feeling that I was the "outsider," an eavesdropper. The programs touched on common experiences Americans shared that didn't include people like me. Programs ended with patriotic messages like "Buy War Bonds" or "Save your grease to make ammunition." It reminded me of that brief period after the war started when we were living in San Francisco. A time when I felt like I was doing my part in the war effort. That seemed so long ago.

★ ★ ★

Papa had a job with the Community Activities department because of his acting background. CA was responsible for providing entertainment to the internees. One could say we experienced the evolution of the movies in camp. Early in our stay, we didn't have "talkies" (movies with sound). He and his committee did things like provide sound for silent movies. It started with crashing waves. Papa and his coworkers simulated the sound of the ocean with rocks rolling around in a washtub. He also did voice-overs. He added dialogue to a full-length Japanese silent film, *47 Ronin* ("47 Samurai"), which someone had brought into camp. All the characters, including women and children, were done by men. Rehearsals often took place in our apartment. It was pretty silly. My father's voice did not sound anything like a woman's, no matter how squeaky high he raised it. But they seemed to enjoy themselves, and I guess others enjoyed their work, too, regardless. They played to packed houses.

After a couple of years, CA was able to rent movies. Papa would bring catalogs home from movie companies such as United Artists and Columbia that released their films in 16mm format. I would pore through the books and tell him which movies I wanted to see. I spent a great deal of time reading the short descriptions and determining who the starring actors were. Many of the movies I selected were actually screened. Henry Fonda, Walter Pidgeon, Maureen O'Hara, and James Stewart were among my favorite actors, so my choices of *Grapes of Wrath, How Green Was My Valley,* and *Mr. Smith Goes to Washington* were very logical picks. I also chose Abbott and Costello's *Hold That Ghost* and *Flying High,* which I had remembered seeing just before the war. The early movies were limited to those available in 16mm because of the small size of our "theaters." They were converted recreation halls. Each block had a recreation hall, but a few blocks had to sacrifice theirs for the common good to be used as churches, canteens (mini-stores), and movie theaters.

The movie theater in our area was in Block 10. We were fortunate because the people in that block built rows of seats on gradually elevated risers to imitate theater seating. There were no bad seats in that house. Later, with the construction of a large auditorium in the center of the camp, more recent 35mm movie releases became available to us. The first to be shown was *Lost Weekend,* starring Ray Milland. I didn't see it, since it was all about a man who has a problem because of his love of alcohol.

CHAPTER 16

"Dream"
PIED PIPERS

Alcohol was no stranger to our household. Many of the arguments between my parents were about Papa's drinking. When we lived in San Francisco, Papa really enjoyed his beer and Japanese sake. He settled down every evening comfortable in his yukata, sitting cross-legged in his chair, savoring his drink.

But it only became a problem when he was drinking away from home. A particularly frightening episode occurred in San Francisco on our way home from a visit with Uncle Ray. He lived on Monterey Boulevard. Our home was in the Sunset. Somehow we found ourselves at the entrance to the Twin Peaks tunnel at West Portal Avenue. It was designed for streetcars, only. The tracks sat above ground in the tunnel and blended into the pavement that rose to meet their level as they exited the tunnel.

As we drove home after Papa's drinking all evening, Papa attempted to enter the tunnel and drove off the pavement into the track area. We were all in the car and I recall thinking we would be crushed by a streetcar charging out of the tunnel before Papa could free the car from the tracks. By some miracle, he was able to get back on the pavement and back out of the tunnel. Things like that didn't happen often, but it was frightening when they did.

In camp there was no beer or sake. There wasn't any kind of alcohol. And, of course, there were no cars, so concerns about Papa drinking and driving were not issues. But one day Papa made a surprising announcement. "I'm going to make my own sake!"

The word "sake" isn't just for "rice wine" but can be used for any kind of liquor. Holy moley, I thought. Papa wants to make "moonshine!" Just like Lonesome Polecat and Hairless Joe! They were characters in the Li'l Abner comic strips. They were bootleggers and made "kickapoo joy juice," which was whiskey. It was made in the light of the moon. That's why it was called "moonshine." They had to make it at night to avoid being caught. The bootleggers were on constant guard against "Revenoo'ers," special police who were on the prowl for "moonshiners."

"Isn't it against the law to do this?" I asked. "Won't 'revenoo'ers' be looking for you?"

"Revenoo'ers?"

"In L'il Abner, revenoo'ers are always looking for bootleggers," I said.

"What are they going to do?" asked Papa. "Put me in jail?" Then he laughed.

"Hey! Isn't Dogpatch supposed to be in Arkansas?" said Brian. "Only, they're in the Ozarks. But Ozarks, bottomlands, what's the difference. Arkansas is Arkansas! It's the perfect state to have a still!" Then he laughed. "Maybe someone will create a cartoon about Papa and his version of 'kickapoo joy juice'!"

"It's not funny, Brian! It's against the law! Suppose he gets caught! They might send us to Japan!"

"You're right, Marie, this could be serious." Brian said.

"Hey, Pop, remember when you used to talk about Mr. Shimizu and how he got blind from drinking poorly made whiskey during prohibition? You're no expert in whiskey-making. Suppose something goes wrong?"

Then, suddenly, Papa said, "A chamber pot! I'll make it in a chamber pot! It would be perfect! It's just the right size and I can keep it under the cot. No one would know I was brewing."

"I'm confused, Papa. How can you get a whiskey-making contraption under a cot?" asked Brian

"I'm not going to make whiskey. That's distilled liquor. For that, you need fancy equipment and there's boiling and catching the liquid from tubes. And temperature is critical. With Japanese sake you just let rice rot," Papa said.

He had been talking to Mr. Kobayashi on the other side of our camp. Not only had he made sake before, but he also had a key ingredient he was willing to share with Papa. Sake is fermented rice, I learned. Together with what he received from Mr. Kobayashi and some rice from the kitchen, he was ready to start his own brew.

"How will you keep the buckets separate? They both stink. You might accidentally use the wrong one!" his friends teased when Papa told them his plan. "You won't find me drinking from your chamber pot!"

"They don't have to drink it. I'll just enjoy it by myself," he said after they left. "It'll be their loss. That much more for me."

It still didn't seem right. But at least I wouldn't have to worry about him driving drunk. From the Sears Roebuck catalog, he selected a gray-and-white-mottled pot, distinct from the other navy-blue-and-white one. He had Mama get some rice from the mess hall. He placed the rice in the pot with water and the ingredients he received from Mr. Kobayashi. Each morning he carefully washed his hands before he removed the lid to stir the mash. On the third day, the faint stench of sake escaped when he opened the pail.

One evening after two weeks had passed, he announced, "I think it's ready." He carefully pressed a piece of cloth down onto the surface of the liquid, which filtered through to the top. He scooped some of the clear liquid with a cup and handed it to Mama.

"Here. Heat this," he ordered. The pot of water she had placed on the hotplate was boiling. She removed the pot from the heat and placed the cup in the hot water without scalding her fingers. She had done this many times before in San Francisco and was an expert.

"How is it?" Mama asked.

"Hmm. I can't really tell," said Papa. "Heat some more." This continued for a few glasses.

"This is really strong stuff!" Papa said a short while later. "It's gone to my head. I've got to lie down." Mama had to help him to bed.

The following morning he complained he didn't feel well. Of course, he's not feeling well, I thought. He's "hung over." I continued my usual morning routine to get ready for school. After getting dressed I squeezed some toothpaste on my toothbrush, grabbed my soap case, and draped my towel around my neck. I was about to go out the door. Mama and Brian had already left for the bathroom. Papa was looking at himself in the small mirror hanging on the wall.

"I can't seem to close my right eye," he said. I could see part of his reflection. There was a definite droopy look to his right eye.

"Let me take a look," I said. He turned and when I saw his face, I felt like I was watching a scene from "Dr. Jekyll and Mr. Hyde." In it, Dr. Jekyll watches his face transform into the grotesque Mr. Hyde character. I had to step back. Half of Papa's face looked as though something was pulling it down, while the other half was normal. As he tried to speak, saliva spilled from his drooping lips.

"Something's wrong with my face!" he said. Just then Mama walked in the door. I could see the horror in her eyes when she looked at him. "Oh, my goodness! We have to get you to the doctor!" she said.

"I'm not leaving the house looking like this," Papa said.

"Don't be difficult. You have to see the doctor."

"Have the doctor come here!" Papa said. "Tell him I'm too sick to go to the hospital."

"Okay, okay . . ." Mama said reluctantly. "I'll go get him. In the meantime, go back to bed," she said. "And, Marie, you go wash up and get ready for school. There's no need for you to be here. You'll just be in the way."

"But, is Papa going to be all right?" I whispered.

"I don't know. But there's nothing you can do, so go on to school."

"Maybe I should stay with Papa while you get the doctor."

"I don't need anyone to stay with me!" Papa shouted. "Just do what Mama says!"

When I returned home that day, I learned that it wasn't serious. That is to say, he wasn't going to die. He had just lost control of all the muscles on that side of his face. The doctor diagnosed it as Bell's Palsy. Since Papa didn't tell him about his "moonshine," we never learned whether or not there was a connection. But no one else hesitated to make it.

"I'm glad you tested it first," said Uncle Ray, when he came by to see him. "Something must have gone wrong with the brew."

"Nothing was wrong with the sake!" Papa insisted.

"Are you sure you didn't use the wrong pot?" Uncle Ray continued and laughed. I guess he thought he could tease Papa about it because his illness wasn't serious. To him. But to Papa, it was dead serious. He became the laughing stock of the block. Papa had gotten sick drinking his questionable brew, everyone said. He had gotten the pots mixed up, they added, thinking that was funny. That's the story that made the rounds.

Papa was a sensitive man and was totally humiliated. He refused to leave the house. He gradually regained partial use of his facial muscles and was able to control his drooling, but he remained a recluse.

Papa had always been fastidious about his appearance. He always kept his mustache well trimmed, and his face smooth. But now he stopped shaving, and his face went gradually from stubby to bristly and then to a flowing beard and long whiskers. He languished all day in his yukata, never getting dressed. When he gave up his yukata so Mama could wash it, he sat around in his one-piece sleeveless underwear with trapdoor. He didn't even leave the apartment to go to the toilet. He had thrown out the sake, so we had two chamber pots to empty. Occasionally he slipped out of the apartment in the dead of night to shower. His crankiness made our apartment an unpleasant place to be. We never had visitors anymore, and I spent as little time as possible at home. I went to Tomoko's as often as I could.

Tomoko lived in Block 1 and had joined our class in sixth grade. She had enormous eyes that bulged slightly and a face that sloped inward toward her chin. With her thick French braids hanging down her back, she always looked like she was leaning forward. She was a towering giant of a girl who clearly outweighed everyone in the class, including the boys. Everyone was intimidated, and she took best advantage of it. She bossed us around mercilessly. Especially, me. Perhaps because I was the smallest in the class, she chose me to be her special servant. I sharpened pencils for her and gave up prized possessions when I was stupid enough to bring them to school. She would elbow me every now and then to let me know that she could really hurt me if she wanted.

She told everyone that I was her best friend. I always thought of her as my best friend, too, because she was my only friend. Others avoided me because of my connection to her.

Her mother had been a Girl Scout leader before camp and wanted to organize a troop. We turned out to be the only two-member troop in the camp. But Mrs. Otani, Tomoko's mother, turned out to be one of the kindest, most gentle persons I had ever met. She looked older than my mother, with her gray hair and thin face streaked with deep lines, and she spoke English without an accent. She just generally seemed more in tune with everything than my parents. She reminded me a lot of the adults I knew in San Francisco. Because of her, I was able to tolerate Tomoko. I was able to talk to Mrs. Otani about anything and everything. I felt safe with her, because I knew that whatever I told her would go no further, since she lived seven block communities away. She was wise and sympathetic to all the little things that troubled me. Tomoko had the ideal mother. I couldn't figure out why Tomoko was the way she was.

I often talked to Mrs. Otani about my father.

"I hate going home. He's always so cranky. We have to walk around on tip toes, and I can't say anything without his going into a rage."

"It's a terrible thing when your face gets distorted," Mrs. Otani said. "That happened to my sister. She was so embarrassed about it, she wouldn't leave home for months. In your father's case, no one seems to have any sympathy because of his 'home brew.' Everyone seems to think he brought it on himself. He's going through a very difficult time, Marie. You just have to be patient. He'll recover soon."

"I hope so."

One day, when I returned home from school, I found the floor covered with newspaper. Papa had begun practicing his Japanese calligraphy.

"When I was a child in Japan, my father always praised me for my fine calligraphy," Papa said. "He was the principal of our school and very strict. He rarely complimented me or any of my seven brothers and sisters. So I must have been very good to have impressed him enough to praise me."

He would make his own ink. He did this by pouring water into a specially made stone that had a well gouged out at one end. Then he took a charcoal stick, dipped it into the water, and rubbed it on the stone. Gradually, the water became inky black. He took his fat brush with flared gray bristles and placed it in his mouth. It emerged moist and pointed. This he dipped into the reservoir of black ink in the stone and alternately dipped, raised, and rotated the brush until it was completely black.

He had always written large signs for the Japanese plays and movies he was in charge of. For that he would use a broom and poster paint. But now he wrote from images in his head, seemingly without purpose. He knelt before the paper first and just stared at it for a while. Then he leaned forward and began his strokes with his brush held straight up from the paper and pressed, pulled, and lifted in very studied, graceful movements. Once he started a piece he did not stop until he was finished. It was one continuous flow of writing. If it pleased him, he tacked it on the wall. If it didn't, he folded it up neatly and placed it in the corner with others he planned to dispose of later. There were as many in that stack as were posted.

There was beauty in the way he applied the ink to the paper and beauty in the product. I have no idea what he wrote, because I couldn't read Japanese. It didn't seem to matter. This continued for a while.

When I told Mrs. Otani what my father was doing, she asked if I was interested in calligraphy.

"Well, yes, but I don't know how to read or write Japanese."

"How about English calligraphy?"

"What do you mean?"

Mrs. Otani rummaged in some boxes in her closet and returned with a pen, black ink, and a sheet of paper. The nib was flat and cut at an angle instead of being a rounded point. She dipped the tip of the pen in the ink and began writing my name in fancy letters.

"That's beautiful, Mrs. Otani. Is that English calligraphy?"

"You could call it that," she said as she reached for a small booklet from her bookshelf. "It's called Old English Lettering."

"How would you like to do some lettering for a Brownie patch?"

"Could I? That would be terrific! Thank you, Mrs. Otani!"

"Take this book and study the strokes. You'll find arrows around the letters to show you what direction the strokes should go."

"I'm so excited! Thank you so much!" I said and threw my arms around her neck.

"Just take good care of the book," she said as she unraveled my arms. "It's the only one I have. I've had it most of my life."

I took her book home and copied the shapes and forms of all the letters, as best I could, before returning it to her. And I went to her house whenever I had time and practiced lettering in "Old English." I never owned a pen of my own, so I found that tracing the outline of the letters and cutting them out with one of Papa's razor blades was almost as satisfying as actually writing them. I worked with black construction paper and a tin-foil background using gum and cigarette wrappers scavenged from friends.

★ ★ ★

In the meantime, Papa discovered that the Gilfillan radio shortwave band to Japan worked, although we were almost half a world away. The early morning news broadcast from Japan could be heard late in the afternoon in Arkansas. When I returned home from school, all his writing material had been put away. Instead, I found Papa sitting with his ear pressed to the speaker, slowly turning the dial like a safe-cracker listening to tumblers. With patience, the crackling buzz would dissolve into a rising and falling voice of a man who sounded like he was under water. A slight slip of his hand, and the static would return.

Listening to the Japanese newscasts became a daily routine. Word spread quickly that we were getting broadcasts from Japan. The apartment began to fill with a different set of people. They were men who were not working. Either elderly or lazy, I thought. They listened to reports of battles in Luzon and Mindanao in the Philippines, from which Papa drew elaborate maps and followed the course of the war. These replaced his calligraphy on the wall. I was uncomfortable and confused. America treated us like we weren't really Americans, but Papa had pledged loyalty to the United States when he signed the questionnaire. He said he would fight for the United States, like Uncle Robert and Uncle Keith, if the government asked.

"What are you doing, Papa! I thought you were rooting for America," I blurted. "If you keep this up and you get caught, we could all be shipped to Japan!" I expected to be scolded for my rude outburst, but instead, he answered, almost in a whisper, "It's been confusing for me, too. I've been thinking a lot about Grandfather and Grandmother in Japan, lately. I worry about what will become of them."

★ ★ ★

I remember it was a Tuesday. I returned home from school to find the apartment empty. The maps and charts had been stripped from the wall and Papa was gone! They've taken him away! I thought. The authorities found out about his listening to Japanese broadcasts and have taken him away! I ran next door.

"Papa's gone!" I said. "Do you know anything about it? Did they take him away?"

"Take him away? No, no, of course not. He returned to work," Mrs. Sakai said. "Aren't you glad?" She held me as I sobbed.

CHAPTER 17

"You're a Grand Old Flag"
GEORGE M. COHAN

In the fall of 1944, I started junior high. That meant I had to travel to the farthest corner of camp for school. Occasionally I was able to hitch a ride on a transport truck that took office workers like Mama to the administration building located diagonally across camp. It was just beyond Block 31, where the junior high was located.

There were no girls my age or even a year older than me from our block. The only other girl who was a junior high student was a ninth-grader. That was Bertha. Occasionally, she invited me to walk to school with her and her friends. I wasn't really included in their social life and they often whispered to each other. But it gave me great comfort to be with them. They called me "Little Mitsui." You might say that I was their mascot.

Junior high presented a new set of problems. There were two blocks set aside for schools. Half of Block 35 was an elementary school and the other half, the camp high school. Half of Block 31 was elementary and the other half, the junior high school. All the children from Stockton Assembly Center went to the Block 35 elementary and most from Los Angeles to Block 31.

Since there was only one junior high, suddenly we were all thrown together. The kids from Los Angeles seemed more mature and assertive. The boys, particularly, were constantly wrestling with each other or pushing each other around. And they were not timid about challenging the teachers. The girls seemed older and smarter. None of my friends from elementary school were in any of my classes, except for one. Tomoko.

A very large boy, who was to be in most of my classes, immediately identified himself as the supreme bully of seventh grade. He intimidated everyone.

On the first day of school, I was walking down the aisle between the chairs with my eyes fixed on an empty seat in the back of the room. Suddenly, I felt myself being catapulted through the air and my books flew down the aisle in front of me.

"Why don't you watch where you're going, stupid! Couldn't you see my leg in the aisle?" said a voice behind me.

As I scrambled to pick up my things, a girl sitting close to where I had fallen whispered, "Don't pay any attention to him. That's Ken. He's a bully. Just act like nothing happened."

I followed her advice, collected myself and quietly sat down. No sooner had I settled in than Tomoko entered the room. I almost didn't recognize her. Her long, thick French braid had been replaced by sausage curls that cascaded part way down her face and back. She looked like a poor imitation of an overgrown black-haired Shirley Temple.

"Marie!" she shouted as she started down the aisle. Just as she was about to pass Ken, the bully's desk, his foot darted out like the tongue of a frog catching a fly. Tomoko went down with a crash.

"Ken! You did that on purpose!" she screamed.

"We meet again!" Ken chuckled. "Where've you been this past year? Almost didn't recognize you with your new hairdo."

"You're as mean as ever!" Tomoko shouted.

"You want to make something of it?" he shouted back. Tomoko burst into tears. Then he rose out of his chair. He was enormous. He looked like Paul Bunyan. Only the ax and Babe, the blue ox, were missing. He was tall and round. But unlike the gentle lumberjack hero, Ken was brutish. He started to lean over Tomoko. I thought he was going to hit her. Fortunately, the teacher walked in.

"I want everyone to take their seats," she announced. Saved by the teacher. Whew. She saw Tomoko picking up her things and sniffling. Mrs. Wolf walked toward her and offered her hand to help her up.

"Are you all right?" She asked.

"He tripped me!" She screamed, pointing at Ken, the Bully.

"Is that right?" Mrs. Wolf asked as she turned to Ken.

"My foot was in the aisle. I guess she just didn't see it," he said softly.

Then he gestured in Tomoko's direction.

"I was about to help her up when you came in."

"I'm terribly sorry you didn't see my foot," he said turning to Tomoko. "I hope you're all right." Not only was Big Bully Ken nasty, he was also quick and conniving. Scary combination.

When we were dismissed, I ran to catch up with the girl who cautioned me about Ken. Tomoko stayed behind to talk to Mrs. Wolf.

"Hi. Thanks for your great advice," I said. "I think you saved my life. My name's Marie. What's yours?"

"Rhonda." She replied. She was about my size and wore bangs and hair that hung straight to her shoulders. There was a flatness to her face, but she was cute.

"I've been in classes with Ken before, and you can't challenge him," said Rhonda. Once you get on his bad side . . . watch out! Everyone's afraid of him, so they avoid him. Tomoko used to be in our class, but she transferred to the Block 35 elementary, because Ken was giving her such a bad time. I don't know what she'll do now."

The next day, Tomoko was gone. She had been transferred to another group of seventh-graders. I didn't see much of her after that.

I decided I would be nice to Ken, in hopes he wouldn't make me his next target. The next time I saw him, I smiled and said, "hi." It was as though no one had ever done that before.

"Well, 'hi' yourself!" he said raising and lowering his voice as though he were singing. I thought I would be sick. For better or for worse, I had definitely put myself on his good side. He thought I liked him. I guess that was better than being beaten up. Since he was in all of my classes, I couldn't avoid him.

Mrs. Wolf had us begin the day with the Pledge to the flag. She also had us learn a song. We learned at least one song in each grade we passed through. In fifth grade, it was "Stars and Stripes Forever"; in sixth, it was "Monkeys in the Zoo"; and now, in seventh grade, she was going to teach us "You're a Grand Old Flag." I guessed she felt we needed to be reminded that we were Americans and needed to express our patriotism with the Pledge and the song.

Mrs. Wolf was also our social studies teacher. As part of one of her lessons she asked, "If you could travel to another country, which country would it be?"

"England," I said, although I had no particular desire to go there.

"Very good, Marie. That's where I'd like to go, too," she said.

I wondered what she would have said if I had answered, "Japan." No one else did, so I could only guess.

It was a stupid question, though. Here we were in prison, not knowing what our future held. We couldn't travel outside

Arkansas, much less to foreign countries. Was this her way of testing our loyalty, I wondered.

★ ★ ★

Whenever Ken was around me, his anger and need to bully others seemed to subside. At least that's what others said. That silly look replaced his frown. And he seemed to be everywhere I went. I decided to try out for a part in a play. And there he was. He tried out, too and we both got parts. I think he would have followed me home for lunch, too, if he didn't live on the other side of the camp.

Then one day, Brian came home and said, "There you are, Marie. There's a big oaf of a guy outside looking for you. I think it's that Ken guy you've been talking about. Do you want to see him?"

"Are you kidding? You didn't tell where we lived, did you?"

"Well, I thought I'd better check with you first."

"You're such a great brother, Brian. Thank you, thank you, thank you!"

"What do you want to do? I think he's going to find out where you live, sooner or later."

"Next time you see him, tell him I go to Grandma's everyday after school."

"Okay. That might work."

That visit from Ken kept me cooped up in the apartment for days. I dared not go outside, lest he not believe the Grandma story. Fortunately, he stopped coming.

★ ★ ★

By the end of 1944 many people in our block were finding work outside the camp and leaving, even though the war raged on. California would not let us return, but most of the other states were accepting Japanese Americans. Most of the folks who left were young, single people. One young woman who had moved to Michigan had been attacked and murdered. That slowed down the exodus from our block for a while.

"It's not safe out there," Mr. Ashikaga said. "If the government can't assure our safety, we're not leaving."

Many others felt that way, too.

★ ★ ★

On May 2, 1945 the war in Italy ended. It was reported to have been the longest and most bitter of all the European campaigns. My two uncles were among those wounded in battle. VE Day, Victory in Europe, followed six days later on May 8, 1945. Victory in Asia could not be far behind. The exodus from camp began in earnest. Brian was fourteen and I was twelve.

"Why are we staying here, while others move out?" Brian asked Papa. "Let's get out of here, too."

When the Sakais, our next door neighbors, left, Brian and I became more vocal about it. Papa then cut a doorway between our room and the vacant one next door and gave the newly acquired space to Brian and me. He must have thought that would somehow placate us.

"It's nice to have more space, but it's not a substitute for leaving this place," Brian said. "I don't want us to be the last ones out of here." It was getting to be a contest, the last one out of camp being the loser. Brian and I agreed that we would try to push harder for Papa to get a job. So each day we would ask, "When are we leaving?"

In response each day, Papa would come home with some crazy idea for a job outside.

One involved harvesting cypress-mushrooms in the area surrounding the camp. It would mean that we would move out of camp only to settle in rural Arkansas.

"We could live in the town of Rohwer down the road, and I could go into the forest and pick mushrooms."

Earlier, camp authorities had given us a leave to visit the outside. "Outside" meant the town of Rohwer. When it was our turn, we rode a covered truck along with several others into the tiny town. There was a "five-and-dime" store and not much else. We spent our entire hour there. The owner was a very friendly woman who reminded me of Mrs. Bagley in San Francisco. We bought some bobby pins and barrettes from her and sat down to a strawberry ice cream soda. It wasn't made with strawberry syrup or strawberries and vanilla ice cream. It was strawberry ice cream and soda, but it was a treat, nonetheless. However, the town of Rohwer was definitely not a place I wanted to ever call home.

"No, Papa," Brian and I both said. "We don't want to live in Arkansas. That would be like moving just halfway out of camp."

Papa turned down the mushroom-job offer.

Then he came home with the idea of working on a farm in New Jersey. It was called Seabrook, and many from camp had settled there.

"You don't know anything about farming, Papa," Brian said. "Besides, I don't want to live on a farm."

"Neither do I," I said. Mama wasn't crazy about the idea, either.

"Chick-sexing" in Alabama was next. That was a job that involved examining newly hatched chicks and sorting them according to sex. It was said to be very hard work, but very lucrative.

"It pays real well," Papa said. But we made it clear we didn't want to live in Alabama.

Finally, Mama came home from work one day, excited with what she had learned at the office.

"Someone told me that there is a request for a presser and silk finisher in Denver, Colorado!"

"Perfect!" Brian and I said in unison. "Papa, you have to apply!"

The administration arranged for interested people to interview for jobs "outside." Actually, that was supposed to be their mission: to "Relocate" us. That's why we were in "War Relocation Camps." Papa was permitted to travel to Denver for the interview and was hired along with Mama. With the assistance of the admininstration, he also found an apartment for $12 per month. He was gone for a week making the arrangements.

We were permitted to leave as soon as there were enough people headed west to fill a railroad car. Five days after his return from Denver, our family gathered in the area behind the kitchen, next to the coal pile. The same spot we arrived two years and nine months earlier. A cluster of people assembled to see us off as we boarded the covered truck. Giving folks leaving camp a "send off" had become a ritual. Lately, I had been a member of several of these send-off groups. At last, we were the ones being sent off. It felt good.

The truck carried us to the railroad tracks on the other side of camp, retracing the path we took when we arrived. But the view had changed. What had been barren barracks when we arrived had been transformed into homes surrounded by vegetable gardens and flowers, alive and vibrant. I felt a tinge of sadness as I watched it all recede into the background. Soon we were at the tracks on the other side of the administration building, where we joined a group of others waiting to board the train. A soldier helped me up the steps. That was my last encounter with the MPs.

CHAPTER 18

"Ac-Cent-Tchu-Ate the Positive"
JOHNNY MERCER

Once again, we stood at an outdoor train station next to the railroad track that ran just outside the camp. From the top of the steps, I turned to look back. It didn't look or feel as I had remembered. The climb up the steps was easier. They had lost their steepness. And I was filled with excitement. We were headed for Denver to a normal life. It was not a journey to nowhere.

We were a mix of people headed west. We, to Denver, and others, to St. Louis. We arrived first at St. Louis and had a short layover. We were allowed to alight.

We were actually in a real train station. It had a roof that soared to the sky. It was also the first time in three years we were without an armed escort. I looked around thinking they were lurking about somewhere and would suddenly appear. As I scanned the crowd milling about the station, I felt that this must be what it is like to be in a foreign country. Then I spotted a group of people with Japanese faces.

"Hi . . . My name is Amy. Welcome to St. Louis!" said a cheerful lady breathlessly as she raced toward us ahead of the others.

"We're also from Rohwer and thought you might like a snack during your layover." She found us seats among people waiting to board their trains and presented us each with a little brown paper bag stuffed with sandwiches and fruit. Seeing her and the others gave me a feeling of being wrapped securely in their protective warmth. Being "outside" felt like suddenly being thrust in the ocean after being in a swimming pool. No sides to swim to. Although we were meeting for the first time, she and the others felt like family. They gave us a tour around the station and chatted until it was time to leave. Our next stop was Denver.

There, we were greeted by a couple of kind, generous men, also former internees. They had come in their trucks to drive us and our belongings to our new home. It felt strange to be in a car. It was close and stifling. And there were so many other cars surrounding us. So close to ours. It was a miracle that they didn't crash into us or each other, I thought. We finally came to rest on a busy street in front of two stores that flanked a skinny door like two thick slices of bread and a sliver of filling. Upon the grimy glass transom was written "1920" in digits large enough to be seen a mile away, if buildings were transparent. We were on Lawrence Street. 1920 Lawrence Street, Denver, Colorado. Our new address.

The entrance to the building was at street level next to a tofu factory. Once inside, stairs led up to our apartment on the second floor. I trudged up the steep staircase and waited at the top for Papa to lead the way. He walked down the dimly lit hall to a padlocked door. He fiddled with it and the tumbler dropped out. Without the tumbler, he was able to unlatch the door. He picked up the pieces and put it back together.

"Actually, we don't need a key for this lock. Just jam something into the hole and pull the tumbler out," said Papa. Although I was anxious to see our new home, I waited, along with Brian and Mama, for Papa to pick up the pieces of the lock before we tried to enter.

It was an old room with faded wallpaper and a tall, narrow window on the far wall to the left. Upon the clean oriental carpet, whose intricate pattern was interrupted by threadbare areas, was placed a double bed, a well-used bureau, a small table, and four chairs. Directly opposite the door was a sink, next to a small cabinet topped by a double gas burner. Just inside the room was a doorway to the right that led to another room just large enough for a double bed and bureau. It was decided that Mama and I would share the bed in the front room and Papa and Brian, the other.

"Where's the refrigerator?" I asked Papa.

"There isn't one. We just can't buy any more than we can eat at one time. And there can't be any leftovers. We will just have to shop carefully."

He walked over to the window, pulled the lacy curtain back and pointed to a store across the street.

"That's the fish market," he said. "The grocery store is just a block away, so it won't be that bad."

"That means we'll have to shop everyday," said Mama. "How am I going to do that when I will be at work? I may not get home before the store closes."

"Marie can do the shopping," said Papa, without skipping a beat. It was as though he had considered this before he rented this place.

"She's big enough now. You just make a list for her and she should be able to take care of it."

We were just released from camp. I hadn't had any chores to do and suddenly, I'm responsible for buying groceries.

"I guess that will work," Mama said. "It will have to work. Marie, we're all counting on you. Actually, it all seems so strange. Having to go buy groceries and having to cook after all this time having it done for us."

"What's really strange is asking me to do it! I don't know anything about shopping, I wouldn't know where to look for things," I said. "Why can't Brian do it? He's older."

"Because he's a boy," Papa said.

"What does that have to do with anything?" I said. "I can find things in a store more easily because I'm a girl? That doesn't make any sense."

"You can ask the store clerk for help. Don't worry. It's not that difficult," said Mama. "I'm really sorry to have to ask you to do this."

"I'm not stupid, I guess. I guess I can manage. I'll just have to remember to get correct change," I said. "But I still think Brian should be the one to do it. . . ."

★ ★ ★

It was frightening to me, and I was nervous about it. At the same time it felt good to think that everyone thought I could manage it. It also felt good to be useful.

Eventually, I was allowed to plan the menu as well. I bought a lot of fish at the Granada Fish Market that was directly across the street. I fried river smelt, which was ten cents a pound. Squid was also very cheap. We had a lot of squid sashimi. Fish could also be bought without ration points, unlike meat. But every now and then I bought hamburger at the grocery store on Larimer Street. That was also where I bought Chef Boyardee spaghetti. It was a kit with spaghetti, sauce, and grated cheese. We ate a lot of that, because it was simple to make.

There was a single faucet over the only sink in our apartment, and it was not connected to a drain. A five-gallon bucket caught the used water. It had to be emptied into a toilet that was located about fifty feet from our apartment. Fantastic! A five-gallon bucket, I thought. Not a dinky little chamber pot. We wouldn't have to empty this as often. We once allowed the bucket to fill up. It was then we learned that it was nearly impossible for any of us to carry a bucket that size, much less empty it without creating a huge, sloppy mess. Papa and Mama slid a broomstick through the handle of the bucket to share the load, and left a soggy trail on the old patterned carpet that ran the halls to the toilet as they fought in vain to keep the waste water from sloshing as they walked. They then managed to flood the floor around the toilet as the water poured out uncontrollably when they tipped the bucket to empty it. There were twelve other apartments on our floor and we shared that one toilet. A line had begun to form as the other tenants waited for us to mop up the mess.

"That was so inconsiderate of us," Mama said. "That must never happen again! It was a terrible inconvenience for everyone."

We also shared a "bathtub," an old, darkened, slimy barrel that had been sliced in half and set in a makeshift closet whose walls were lined with large metal signs scavenged from who-knows-where. The words "7 Up" on one of the signs peered through a large ventilation hole cut high up in the door.

Most of the tenants on our floor were single women, with the exception of one woman, Bernice, and her six-month-old baby. They lived down the hall and around on the other end of the floor. Our hall ran into an enclosed porch, which extended about twenty feet to the left to the room with the "bathtub." To the right, was the toilet. Outside the toilet was the common sink. Another hall extended from there, parallel to our hall.

Bernice's apartment also looked out onto the street. She had just come outside from the Amache Relocation Center in Granada, Colorado. Her husband was serving in

Europe with the 442nd, and she was awaiting his return. Her pencil-thin eyebrows arched high over her almond-shaped eyes, and she wore her lipstick outside her natural lipline. Her hair was rolled in pompadours in the front and fell in a pageboy in the back. She spoke with a rasp as though she had a permanent cold. When she laughed, she sounded like the actress Betty Hutton.

"As soon as Jim comes home, he'll take us out of this dump," she said. She walked over to the large calendar with the words "GRANADA FISH MARKET' emblazoned across the top.

"Take a look at this. See this day with the red circle around it? August 31? That's when he'll be home! It'll be so exciting. Jim's never seen Darryl, you know." That was the baby's name.

The atomic bomb was dropped on my father's birthplace, Hiroshima, on August 6, 1945. Three days later, the bomb was dropped on Nagasaki. Japan surrendered on August 15, 1945. Horns sounded deep into the night in celebration of the end of the war.

Jim, my neighbor's husband, had served in the unit in Italy along with my uncles and had been recuperating from a wound at Walter Reed Hospital in Maryland. Three weeks later, Bernice and Darryl were gone.

★ ★ ★

Every Friday was payday, and Papa and Mama were paid in cash. The amount varied, because they often worked overtime. Papa would gather us around a leather suitcase, which he slid out from under the bed. When the war started, many people lost money they had in banks.

"You can't trust banks," Papa said. "This way we know exactly where our money is."

Our suitcase soon filled with cash. Each week, he separated the money by denomination and carefully counted the bills he and Mama had brought home.

"Brian, write what I count." Papa said. "That's eight twenties. You got that? Okay. Two fives, and six ones. What's that add up to?"

Then he gave me sixteen dollars for groceries and separated the rent and money for incidentals. He added what was left to the rapidly growing pile of bills that was leftover. The highlight of the evening was counting that stack. Papa had Brian keep track of it in a tablet.

"We're doing a great job saving," he would say. "We'll be able to buy a car and our own business in no time." When he finished the money-counting session, we would celebrate.

"Okay. It's time to go to the drugstore and buy our cokes and twinkies. Come on, let's go!"

We walked together as a family to the drugstore which was on the corner of 20th and Larimer. That was the highlight of our week. We would buy our treats and whatever else we needed at the drugstore and take them home to eat. When winter arrived, Brian would put his coke outside our window to chill it. Every now and then, it would freeze and break the bottle when he forgot to retrieve it.

* * *

Reiko Baba was a girl a couple of years younger than me. She wore bangs and pigtails always pulled to the front, and had droopy eyes like Ann Sothern, the movie actress. She not only resembled Ann Sothern in a Japanese sort of way, but spoke like her as well. She had a drawl and would often run out of breath before she finished a sentence. It made her sound as though she were playing a dramatic role in a movie.

She shared a bedroom with her parents in the tofu factory downstairs.

When she and her family stepped out of their bedroom they were in the middle of a factory with huge round vats and a kitchen area. The vats were used to make soy milk out of soybeans, which in turn was made into tofu. The smell of simmering soybeans didn't appeal to me, so I was glad I didn't live there.

Reiko's family used a small two-burner hotplate in their room for cooking. They used the factory's kitchen for water and washing whenever it was free. Although they had a toilet, there was no bath or shower. They bathed at the public bath house around the corner on 20th Street. Occasionally, Reiko used the community bath in our building. It was closer and, of course, free. I went over to Reiko's room fairly often, but we weren't allowed to play in the work area during the week. That was fine with me. On the weekend, the entire factory was our playground.

Sadly, Reiko moved away a few weeks after I met her. It was just before school started.

After Reiko left, I found a job at a wholesale produce store on 20th Street. It was "piece-work," as Papa would say. Instead of being paid according to how long I worked, I got paid for the amount of work I did. My job was to shell peas. One gunny-sackful, shelled, was worth two dollars. It took me the entire day to shell one gunnysack. Tall piles of empty gunnysacks grew next to the adults while I barely emptied one. It was hard work, hunched over, pulling pea pods out of the limp sack, cracking them open and scraping the peas into a bucket. By day's end, my hands were sore and my back ached.

But whatever I made was set aside for my allowance. I spent it on occasional expanded hot lunches when school started. A slice of white sandwich bread liberally slathered with gravy was seven cents. If a mound of mashed potatoes was added to that, it was ten cents. A piece of meat brought the price up to fifteen cents. It wasn't something I could eat every day. Mostly, I brought a sandwich from home.

Two doors down from our apartment was the Henry Hotel. Many families recently relocated from camps lived there. There was also a service alley that ran behind the buildings. A steep wooden staircase led from the covered porch of our apartment building down there to the garbage cans. The alley was also the gathering place for the kids on our block.

CHAPTER 19

"Sentimental Journey"
DORIS DAY

When school started, things changed. None of the other kids on our block on Lawrence Street were in junior high, so I went to a school where I knew no one. Not even Brian, since he was in high school. Furthermore, Cole Junior High was not a very friendly place. I was taking six classes and as far as I could tell, each class was made up of a different set of students. And as an eighth-grader, it was more difficult for me to make friends, because most friendships had been cemented in seventh grade. I managed to make one friend. She was also new to Cole. Her name was Martha, and her parents were from Armenia. She had dark curly hair and was rather heavy, with large blue eyes and a nose like Dick Tracy's. Only rounded. She was smart and had a great sense of humor. Unfortunately, she attracted the attention of a bully. She would tease Martha about her nose. At first Martha ignored her, Then, one day, Martha made the mistake of talking back to her. As Martha and I were leaving school, the bully walked up to her and hit her nose with the full force of her fist.

It was not uncommon for someone to get attacked at Cole. There always seemed to be an after-school fight, or some bully assaulting a weaker person like Martha. The following day, Martha transferred out of Cole.

After the Martha incident, I made a point of leaving school as fast as possible, afraid that I, too, might become a target. I ate lunch by myself and was always on the lookout for rowdy groups of girls. I kept my distance. I was totally alone. Now without Martha, there was no one I felt could talk to.

Every now and then, a school-wide assembly was called for a special program. On one particular occasion, a renowned magician was featured. The entire school was seated in the huge auditorium, and we all waited in the dark in eager anticipation. It was taking longer than usual for the performance to start. To ease the boredom, I began rummaging in my purse and found a matchstick I had soaked with cinnamon. These Diamond brand matchsticks were the mainstay for lighting gas stoves and were in ample supply in every household. I had found that matchsticks, because of their thickness, could hold more of the cinnamon flavor than toothpicks. I used matches that had never been lit.

I opened the wax paper wrapping and removed a matchstick. I sucked on it for a while. My wandering mind then settled on Mr. Nakano and the image of him igniting his match by sliding it across his pants. I wondered if it would light if I slid it across my skirt. I tried it, and it did.

No sooner had the match caught fire than no fewer than three teachers were grabbing my arm, collar, shoulder, and dragging me out of my seat. I never got to see the magic show and I almost got expelled.

★ ★ ★

Miss Mills, my homeroom teacher, bore a striking resemblance to George Washington, whose picture hung on the wall. Her hair was brown, rather than silver, but the hairstyle was the same. And, of course, she was a woman. But she seemed more like a man as she took long strides with her short stubby legs and swayed from side to side with shoulders hunched up when she walked down the aisle between our desks. She was stern and tried to keep firm control of the class. She always carried her pointer, a long tapered stick with a rubber tip at one end. Other teachers used it to point to something on the blackboard or map or something like that. In her hands, the pointer took on the personality of a weapon. Like a billy club, which the police carried. She never struck anyone with it to my knowledge, but no one doubted for a moment she would use it if she felt the need.

She had very strict rules about getting out of our seats. Some teachers would let us get up to sharpen our pencils without permission, but in her class, you had to raise your hand for any reason. It was a hard and fast rule. But sometimes, someone would raise their hand, and she would choose not to acknowledge it.

Miss Mills was also my math teacher. I had math immediately after lunch. One day I had the fifteen-cent lunch. That was the one with the slice of bread, mashed potato, thin slice of beef, and gravy. The beef had an unusual amount of fat on it that day. But it was delicious. Miss Mills had just passed out a short quiz, and we were given ten minutes to complete it. Suddenly, my stomach began to cramp, so I raised my hand. Miss Mills raised her hand, palm down, and lowered it. She pointed to the clock and lifted one finger as if to say, "One more minute to go. It can wait!" I dropped my hand and hoped that my stomach would calm down. It did. For one brief moment. Then the cramping returned with a vengeance. My stomach squeezed itself into a painful knot making it clear to me there was no room for its content. I was losing control. Everything was coming up. I bolted out of my seat and began to run down the aisle.

"Marie!" Miss Mills shouted as she blocked the aisle. "I didn't give you permission to get up! I want you to return to your seat immediately!" I hesitated for a moment. Then it was over. My lunch exploded out of my mouth. At her feet. She did a weird dance stepping tippy-toe from side to side with her shoulders hunched, skirt pulled up over her knees, trying to avoid the pile of semidigested meat, potatoes, bread, and gravy that was growing on the floor in front of her. When the heaving stopped, I pushed Miss Mills out of the way, stepped around the mess, and ran out the door.

In the restroom I stood over the basin, washing my face and rinsing my mouth, wondering what I was going to do next. I couldn't return to the class. I had totally humiliated myself. I imagined how repulsive and disgusting it must have been for those poor kids who sat on either side of the aisle. And Miss Mills must be furious with me, I thought. I'd probably be expelled. This, added to the lighted match in the auditorium incident, was surely enough to send me home for good. I raised my head to look at my pathetic self in the mirror, when I saw the reflection of a girl from my class enter the restroom. She was in my class, but I didn't know her name.

"Are you okay?" she asked, as she put her hand on my shoulder. I spoke to her reflection in the mirror.

"Yeah. I think my stomach has finally settled down."

"Miss Mills says it's all right. She wants you to return to class."

"Is she very angry?"

"No," she said. "But she's a bit flustered. She's been pacing back and forth and can't seem to get on with the class lesson. The janitor came in and sprinkled some stuff on your vomit and swept it up. It doesn't smell or anything."

"I can't believe that I did that!" I said.

"It's okay. It couldn't be helped," she said. "By the way, my name is Annie Hernandez. What's yours?"

We walked together back to the classroom, and from the doorway, all signs of my "accident" seemed to be gone. Everyone was very quiet and had solemn looks on their faces.

"I was just telling the class," Miss Mills said. "If you are feeling sick, you don't have to ask my permission to leave the room. Just go."

"You seem better, but I think you should go to the nurse's office now. I've written a note for you. Gather your things and Annie will accompany you."

Now I had to walk the path on which I had, just moments before, poured the foul contents of my stomach. As I walked with my head down, I could see little traces of it that remained on books stacked on the under-chair book shelves. A faint stench still lingered. Not quite enough to trigger another episode, but close. When I reached my seat, I quickly reached down to the shelf below it, scooped up my belongings, and once more, retraced my steps up the aisle. I ran out the door, with Annie on my heels.

The nurse had me lie down. I fell asleep immediately. I awoke refreshed, and she let me go home.

Home was an empty apartment. My parents were at work, of course, and there were no neighbors to visit—everyone was at work. And Brian was still at school.

When my parents finally did come home, Papa was in his usual nasty mood.

★ ★ ★

Papa was having problems at work. He had taken a job as a spotter, although he lacked the experience. It involved a lot of chemistry. But it paid $1.25 an hour, a twenty-five per-cent raise over his $1 an hour as a presser. Spotting was less physically demanding and more prestigious, so "he couldn't turn it down." It was much more difficult than he had expected, and he made mistakes. That meant that someone's garment didn't get cleaned well, or worse, it was ruined. He was on the verge of being fired. So there was no room for my problems at the dinner table or any other time. Brian was always doing homework and Mama was always upset by Papa's predicament. The only conversations at our house were very heated ones between Papa and Mama about Papa's future.

"You should be more sympathetic toward me at work!' Papa shouted at Mama. "They don't respect me. Everyone used to call me, 'Mr. Mitsui.' Now, everyone calls me 'Charlie!' I'm being insulted, and you pretend like nothing's wrong! You should be sticking up for me!"

"You want me to lose my job, too? It's your fault! You should be more honest! If you don't know how to do something, you should say so!"

"See that? You're on their side! . . ."

In camp, there was always *some*one for me to talk to. Here, there was no one. Lately, I had also been wetting my bed. I would dream that I was walking the cold dark hall to the bathroom and sitting on the toilet. It all seemed so real. I convinced myself that I wasn't dreaming. Then I would awaken when I felt myself lying in a warm puddle. It was disgusting. The situation at school, the situation at home, the situation in my bed . . . I was always on the verge of tears. The slightest thing would cause my eyes to well up. Watching kids walking to school together, or seeing clusters of kids at lunch would fill me with overwhelming loneliness, and I fought to keep my tears contained. When I walked around school, I would pull my books close to my chest and scurry down the halls with my head down, so I wouldn't have to look at anyone and hope that no one would recognize me as the "barfer" or the stupid girl that lit a match during assembly.

At lunch, I would find a spot that faced a wall and bury my face in a book, as I picked at my food.

I tried to be the first one out of class to avoid those who might want to hurt me. I had dealt with bullies before. But this was different. When I was younger it was name-calling or poking and tripping. Here, it was much more serious. Martha's nose had been broken. Another boy's face was slashed with a knife.

I had navigated rough waters before. But now I felt totally at sea with no help in sight. I was struggling to keep from drowning. Each day was a tremendous struggle. And it began when I awoke in the morning. I had a difficult time getting myself out of bed.

One morning was particularly awful.

"Hurry up, Marie. You're going to be late for school." Mama said. "You're getting to be a problem for me, lately. You must know that I have enough to do without having to worry about your getting up. I want you to take more responsibility for yourself! Now, get up!"

I wish she would leave me alone and let me lie here forever, I thought. I rolled over and pulled my pillow over my head. But she was relentless.

"Are you still in bed? I can't leave for work until I know you're up! Up! Up!" Her sharp voice penetrated my ears right through the pillow.

I dragged myself out of bed, pulled on my bathrobe, squeezed some toothpaste on my toothbrush, draped a towel around my neck, and slithered out the door. There was a long line to the toilet and sink. It was unusually slow this morning. The line wasn't moving at all! And I had to go! I finally turned the corner and was now on the porch. There were still three people ahead of me. My bladder was stretching to its limit. I could hold it no longer! I shifted out of the middle of the corridor to the edge as if to look out the window at something in the alley below. Then under the cover of my floor-length robe, I left a puddle, hoping no one would notice. I was so embarrassed. It was a carpeted area, much like our apartment, dark and intricately patterned. I stood firm protecting my puddle and continued to gaze out the window. I yielded my turn to those behind me until none were left. Then I moved from my spot to use the sink.

It was after this episode I realized that I didn't feel I had the energy to continue struggling with my problems. I began thinking about how life was so difficult, and that it wasn't worth the effort. I was tired of worrying about the problems at school and wetting the bed and other places. I was tired of being afraid of being attacked at school. I was tired of being alone all the time without friends or anyone to talk to.

Ideas about how I could leave this world began to invade my thoughts. I considered and eliminated the more painful methods and those that would be messy. These daydreams filled the spaces between mundane thoughts during the day and each night as I lay in bed.

In the movies, people took vast numbers of sleeping pills, but we didn't have anything like that at our house. I decided that I could go to the drugstore and see if I could buy some. I didn't know how much sleeping pills cost. Hopefully, my allowance would cover it.

So that was settled. Then I began to envision how everyone would react to the fact that I was gone. They would be so sorry they hadn't been friendly to me, I thought.

"Did you know Marie?" they would say. Those that remembered me, the very few, like Annie, would be able to brag that they did. Others would say, "I wish I had been more friendly toward her." But it would be too late

CHAPTER 20

"It Might As Well Be Spring"
JEANNE CRAIN

Saturday morning I lay in bed awake with my eyes closed. Something had awakened me. Perhaps it was the sound of Brian going out the door to baseball practice. I then realized that I was lying in a puddle again. I can't stand it! I felt so helpless. I'm going to the drugstore today to see about getting sleeping pills, I decided. In the meantime, I've got to get up and clean up the mess. Ugh. I'm going to lie here until it gets cold.

But something was amiss. I sensed that there was someone else in the room. A presence. A ghost? A robber? Was I still asleep? One way to find out is by opening my eyes, I thought. Suppose it's something I'd rather not see? I'd have to take that chance. I'll just take a small peek by opening my eyes a crack, I thought. So I opened them just a sliver and jerked with surprise at what I saw!

There *was* someone standing over my bed. A total stranger! A beautiful young woman, tall and slender, with large smiling eyes and clear complexion. I thought for a moment, I'm having one of those "I'm sure 'I'm not dreaming,' dreams," like the ones that fool me into thinking I'm on the toilet. I reached out and touched her.

"Hi, Marie. You sure are a sound sleeper. I've been standing here for at least five minutes! It's ten o'clock, you know."

"Who are you? How'd you get in? What're you doing here?" I said, rubbing my eyes. Why would anyone who looked like her be standing over my bed, I asked myself. Mature girls stuck together. They didn't bother with runts like me.

"It's me. Jean Okada. From Rohwer. Don't you remember me? Seventh grade? I knocked, but no one answered, and your door was unlocked, so I just walked in."

Our door was secured by a padlock on the outside. Papa and Mama had gone to work earlier, and Brian was off doing something with his friends. If they had locked the door, I wouldn't have been able to get out. Until now it didn't occur to me the door wasn't locked when any of us was left in the apartment.

"Is that really you, Jean?"

The last time I saw her she was about my size. Now she was tall and wore lipstick. She had large eyes with thick dark lashes that reached out toward the object of her gaze. She was missing one of her front teeth, but she was beautiful, nonetheless.

I was so happy to see Jean tears started to well in my eyes. Then I realized I had a problem. My bed and nightgown were wet. As long as I stayed on the wet spot, I was fine. The slightest shift resulted in cold discomfort.

"Jean. I can't believe it's you," I said, trying to lie as still as possible. "You've gotten so grown up. How'd you know I was here?"

"Don told me. My parents know his parents, and they were over for dinner last night. We were talking and his parents said that there was a family from Rohwer living in one of their apartments, and when they said it was you, I said, 'I know Marie. I'm going to have to go see her!' So, here I am!"

I rarely saw Don or his family, although they lived in the apartment next door. They were the owners. Their apartment had a real kitchen and bathroom. At least, that was what I heard. I had never seen it. They had no reason to be in the hall like the rest of us, because they had their own private bathroom and toilet

"By the way. Where's your brother?" Jean asked as she looked around the room. Then she noticed the door to the other room and peered in.

"I don't know. I think he's playing baseball with his friends or something. How'd you get into the building?" I asked. My door might have been unlocked, but the front door downstairs was always locked.

"I rang the bell and Don's mother opened it for me. She can open the door from inside their apartment."

"Oh, I didn't know that. I'm glad she did. And I'm so glad you're here. It's good to be able to talk to someone I know."

"What do you mean by that?"

"I don't know anybody at school. It's impossible to meet anyone, because we're constantly changing classes and everything, and everybody seems to have friends and doesn't seem interested in making new ones."

"I don't have many friends either, but I'd be happy to have you meet who I know," Jean said. "On one condition."

"What?"

"Help me meet some boys!"

"Help you meet boys? I don't know any myself."

"You have a brother! And he's in high school!" Jean said. Then she laughed, "I'm just kidding. . . ."

I wanted to get out of my bed and wet clothes, but couldn't as long as Jean was standing there. But I didn't want to say anything that would offend her and cause her to leave.

Finally, I reached a point where I had no choice. I threw caution to the winds and blurted. "Jean, do you mind waiting in the hall until I get dressed? It'll just take a minute."

"Hey, I can come back later. You haven't even gotten up yet. You probably have things to do." If she only knew, I thought to myself. Then she said, "I was thinking. If you aren't doing anything, you and I could go to the movies this afternoon."

"That would be great!" I said. "Can you come back around 11:30? Then we could get a ten-cent hamburger at Ken's."

"You know about that place? Aren't their hamburgers just out of this world?" Jean said. "I'll see you later." She then bounded out the door.

As soon as she was gone, I leaped out of bed and slipped out of my wet gown. I pulled on my robe, grabbed the soap and towels and headed for the shower. The last two times I wet the bed, I threw the sheets away. I didn't know what else to do with them. I guess I'd have to do the same with this one. Mama never said anything about missing sheets. I don't know if we had so many she didn't count, or she knew what was happening and was ignoring it. We slept in the same bed, but I never moved from the spot that I puddled, so she wouldn't have known about my accidents. She left for work before I woke up, giving me a chance to tear the bed apart after she was gone. In any case, the sheet inventory was going to be down one more sheet.

I took my wet nightgown to the sink which was used for laundry, dishwashing, food preparation, and handwashing after using the toilet. I scrubbed the gown on our washboard and hung it on the clothesline that ran the length of the enclosed porch. I would claim it before my parents came home from work.

Later, Jean came to pick me up as promised. I left a note

for Brian, and we went to the ten-cent hamburger place. It was a very narrow shop with just enough room for customers to stand opposite a counter from the cook. There were no tables. A customer would order her hamburger, and the cook would turn his back while he placed a pre-formed patty on the griddle before him. The secret of the tastiness of the burger was in the way he salted it, we all concluded. He would flip the patty just as little beads of red began to break through the raw surface. Then he would give two quick flicks of the oversized, dented aluminum salt shaker, depositing just the right amount of the tiny granules on the raw side. When little red beads formed on the cooked side, it, too, received a couple of shakes of salt. The cooked patty was then scooped up and placed on a bun that had been toasted on the griddle. This he wrapped in waxed paper. There was no need to add any condiments to this sandwich. It was perfect just the way it was. We took our hamburgers outside and ate as we walked down Arapahoe Street to the theater.

We went to see *State Fair*, starring Jeanne Crain, Dick Haymes, and Dana Andrews. It was a musical about a fair and the adventures of a family who attends it. Jeanne Crain and Dick Haymes played siblings, and they find romance there.

"Do you want to come by my place?" I asked Jean as we walked home after the movie.

"Well, I probably should be getting home."

"We can take the alley. Brian and his friends might be playing catch."

Jean's face lit up. "On second thought, I guess I could be a little late."

As we approached the alley, I could hear voices. I guessed right. Brian shouted as soon as he spotted me, "Hey, Marie, how was the movie? Who's your friend?

"Jean was in my class in Rohwer. She knows Don's family. That's how she found where we lived."

Brian introduced her to his friends and I watched as she flirted with them. I tried to slip away to retrieve my nightgown off the clothesline before I went shopping for dinner. As I started up the steps, Jean called to me.

"Do you want to go to church with me tomorrow?"

"I have to ask my parents. I think it should be all right. We never do anything else on Sundays."

"I'll come by to pick you up around 9:30 tomorrow morning. If you can go, fine. If not, not a big deal."

"Okay. And thanks for everything, Jean. Bye . . ."

The Buddhist Church was a block away on Larimer Street. Mama was happy to hear that I was going.

"Thank you for taking her," Mama told Jean when she came by the following day. "Going to church is a good thing."

"Church is a really great place to meet boys," Jean giggled as we left the building.

The church was a little cottage nestled among shops and restaurants on the busy street. It had a gabled roof, clapboard walls, and a small covered porch. The front door opened into the living room, which was the sanctuary. There was a shrine on a table in the front of the room and folding chairs arranged in two sections in front of it. A curl of sweet incense smoke drifted up from an urn and managed to reach my nostrils, though I sat in the back of the room. The service was conducted in Japanese by a very nice minister, who made a point of speaking to me afterward. I understood very little of his spoken words, but his warm and friendly manner was very easy to understand.

One of the rooms of the house was the social hall where cookies and punch were served after the service. There I met Masako, who lived on 21st and Curtis, just a couple of blocks from me. She was also an eighth-grader and was in my science class, but I had never noticed her. I concluded that was because Mr. Ward, our science teacher, didn't call roll. He used a seating chart. And I sat up front.

Masako and I talked about how weird our science teacher was. He had pale blue eyes that constantly darted around the room, as if daring anyone to get out of line.

"Remember how on the first day of school he said he had an atomic bomb in one of his drawers, which he would use if necessary? That was supposed to be funny. Weird, weird, weird." I said.

"He's also very tough. How far along are you on your science project," Masako asked.

"I haven't even started. It's not due until next spring, is it?"

"Yeah, but kids who took from him last year say you have to keep up with his assignments. If you leave it to the last minute, it's too much to do. You want me to help you?"

"Could you? That would be so great," I said.

"Bring what you have over to my house after school, and I'll see what you've got," said Masako. "And how about walking to school together? You can pick me up around eight. Then we'll pick up Mary, who lives on 23rd. And then there's Jean. . . . By the time we get to school, it's pretty much of a crowd. It's fun. And it feels safer."

I have died and gone to heaven, I thought. At last I have some friends! I couldn't wait to return to school.

I saw Jean only occasionally after that. She was more interested in boys than girls. But I feel she saved my life. If she hadn't come by that Saturday morning, I might not be here telling you this story. The need to throw away sheets disappeared, too. I no longer had those misleading dreams. Best of all, I looked forward to going to school.

Things settled down for Papa, too. At work, he was transferred to the benzene room. The benzene machine was like a washing machine but used benzene rather than soap and water. He was much more relaxed when he got home at the end of the day.

A few weeks later, Papa said he had a surprise for us. He had just returned home from work.

"Look out the window," he said.

"What are we supposed to look at," asked Brian.

"Look down at the street right below our window."

"At that old brown car?"

"Yes, the car!" Papa shouted. His excitement was turning to impatience.

That was the surprise. It was brown and boxy with a square of black canvas for the roof and a spare tire fastened on the back. It was one of the ugliest, old-fashioned cars I had ever seen. I remembered the sleek "torpedo body" 1940 Dodge that we had before the war. What a contrast. But I knew I had to act pleased.

"What a nice . . . big car!" I said with a forced smile.

"It's a 1934 Oldsmobile. And I bought it for just two hundred dollars! It's a real bargain. The only problem is that it has a cracked block. It's just a small crack. All we have to do is make sure the radiator is always full of water. The tires are also odd-sized. And they're recaps. They don't make tires this size anymore, but we should always be able to find recaps, if these wear out."

It was clear that he was proud of his new purchase. No one dared tell him what they really thought.

"That's great, Papa. Can I go down and look at it now?" Brian said.

"Why don't we eat dinner first. Then we can all go out for a drive," he said.

We all hurried through our dinner of raw squid (five cents a pound), ground ginger, lettuce, rice, and miso soup, left the dishes in the dishpan to wash later in the community sink, and hurried downstairs.

It was a four-door sedan. Brian wanted to sit up front, so Mama and I would have to sit in the back. I was taken by surprise when I opened the rear door. The seats were identical to the ones in the playground director's car at Helen Wills in San Francisco. They were a light, plush mohair, with soft bristles that stood straight up and stitching evenly spaced about six inches apart. In my mind's eye I saw a mound of jellyfish in the middle of it. After I recovered from the shock of the seats, I looked around and noticed there was a shade for the rear window. Just like the shades on the train that took us to the camp. I tried to put all of that aside, slid over next to the far door, and settled into the soft, comfortable seat.

"Hey, Marie," said Brian as he turned around, "these seats look exactly like the playground director's. Remember that thing with the jellyfish?" said Brian.

"Yeah," I said, "Don't remind me."

The car ran amazingly well, considering it was ugly, had a cracked block and recapped tires, and was filled with reminders of a past I would have liked to have forgotten.

★ ★ ★

In the spring, there was an all-school musical, and our home economics class was selected to participate. We had made aprons to wear in a dance number. When I discovered that "It Might As Well Be Spring" was to be the song we would be dancing to, I was determined to be in it. It was one of the songs featured in *State Fair*, the movie Jean and I had seen together. The dance was done with brooms as props. We were supposed to be maids or something doing spring cleaning. It was sort of silly, but fun. The musical was a major school event on a Saturday afternoon at the Civic Center Auditorium. I must have been one of the more confident dancers, because I was placed in the front row. Or maybe it was because I was short. In any case I had an excellent view of the huge audience, made up of a mixture of adults and children. Families of the performers. Unfortunately, my parents were working that day and Brian had a baseball game. I think I was the only one whose family members weren't there. But I enjoyed myself nonetheless.

Soon after, we moved from Lawrence Street to 21st Avenue, about a mile away. The former occupants were Papa's friends who had found a larger place. We would now have a real stove and oven, a sink with a drain attached, and an icebox. Something to keep food cold. It wasn't a refrigerator, but now we could give up our daily shopping. The ice box was made of wood with a compartment on top for a block of ice. Below that was the space for food. The last layer of the box was space for a pan. The melting ice dripped into it. Once again, something to be emptied. But this time, the traveling distance from the bucket to the sink was just a few feet. The pan rarely overflowed. That was not the problem.

Our box used a twenty-five pound block of ice, which was delivered by the ice company. They gave us a card that had the various sizes of ice blocks written at the corners, with the bottom of each number toward a different corner of the card: 25, 50, 75, 100. If the card was in the window, the ice man would deliver ice according to which number was right side up. If we didn't need ice, we were supposed to remove the card. Saturday morning was our delivery day. If we forgot to remove the card from the window, the ice man would be at our door with a block on his shoulder.

Our assigned ice deliverer happened to be one of my classmates, Dan. I'm sure he thought that I wanted an excuse to see him, because I kept forgetting to remove the card when we didn't need ice. I would bolt up on Saturday morning. It was probably the sound of the heavy truck rumbling down the street. I would suddenly realize I had forgotten to remove the card. By that time, it was too late. Dan was at the door with the heavy block balanced on his shoulder. Fortunately, Dan was a sweet guy and didn't complain.

"She's just unconscious," Brian would say. At dinner, Brian would share my unconsciousness with the folks.

We also had half a bathroom. That is, we shared it with our neighbors next door. It was a bathroom with two doors. One leading to their apartment and the other to ours. The trick was to remember to unlock our neighbor's door after we finished. Our neighbor rarely left our door locked, but they were constantly pounding on our common wall reminding us to unlock theirs. I was usually the guilty party. And it really caused a commotion when that happened. For some reason, I would have lapses of memory. As I turned the lock on the neighbor's door, I would repeat to myself, "Don't forget to unlock the door. Don't forget to unlock the door . . ." By the time I was done with my business, other thoughts would totally obscure "Don't forget to unlock the door." If one of the others of my family went in after me, they made certain it was unlocked. That happened most of the time. Again, it was because I was "unconscious."

Between our ice delivery and the bathroom, I was in perpetual trouble.

CHAPTER 21

"To Each His Own"
THE INKSPOTS

A few days before the end of the school year, Miss Mills asked me to stay after class.

"Most of your former internee classmates are returning to California. . . ." she announced.

"What? Who's leaving?" I interrupted.

"Masako, Violet, Janet, Jean, and others. Promise me, Marie, that you won't leave, too. . . ."

As she spoke, memories of those first miserable weeks at Cole bubbled up. All my friends who have since made life at Cole bearable would be leaving! Everyone will be gone, I thought. How will I survive? Why hasn't anyone told me?

"Marie?"

"Yes?"

"Promise me you won't leave, too."

"Sure. Okay. I promise," I said without looking up.

"Good. You're one of our best students. I don't want to lose you, too." Sure, I thought. One of your best students. One of your favorites, too, who ruined your shoes.

I rushed to science hoping to catch Masako before class started.

"Masako! Why didn't you tell me you were moving to California!"

"I don't like talking about it. . . . But how'd you know? I just found out myself."

"Miss Mills told me," I said. "Did you know that a whole bunch of other kids are leaving, too?"

"You're kidding!. I don't need to feel so bad then. If everyone else is leaving, I guess it won't be so bad. What about you, Marie?"

"I don't know. I hope so. This place would be unbearable without all of you. I don't want to be the only one left."

When I got home that day I told Brian.

"The same thing is happening at Manual High," said Brian. "We've got to convince the folks that we should leave, too."

* * *

But when Papa got home that night, he greeted us with a surprise.

"I've found a house! It's over on 23rd and Arapahoe. I've made an appointment for us to look at it after dinner," he said, his voice ringing with excitement.

"We're going to buy a house?" I asked, "Here in Denver?" This was the first we were hearing of it. I had no idea Papa was looking for a house. So much for returning to California, I thought.

"Yes," Papa replied, "not too far from here. Mr. Yamanaka at the cleaning plant is returning to California and is selling his house. He never went to camp. Instead, he came directly from Los Angeles."

We were never able to buy a house in San Francisco. We couldn't even rent one in the Sunset. But here we could buy a house? Just like that? Wow.

"We'll go take a look at it after dinner. I have the key," said Papa.

It was a two-story beige stucco house. It had a Spanish look to it. A staircase curved up to the second story built over the garage. The front door opened to a large entry area.

"In Colorado, they will let me buy a house. Not like California. I feel like a real man!"

"Look over here," he said pointing to living room. A handsome fireplace with an arched opening stood on the opposite wall. His gestures brought back memories of Lawton Street when he showed us the empty store. There he was trying to convince us of his cleverness and his vision of converting a bleak space into something livable. But this required no imagination. It was the most livable place we had ever seen. "It even has a dining room. And a place to eat in the kitchen, as well," he said as he continued to lead us through the house.

"Take a look. It's a real kitchen with a stove that has an oven, and look at this refrigerator." Mama peered into it as Papa spoke.

"It's not as nice as the one we had on Lawton Street. But it's a refrigerator."

"You won't have to worry about the ice man anymore, Marie," said Mama.

"And you two can each have your own rooms," Papa interrupted. "We'll have our own bathroom. No more worrying about locked doors."

"Can we afford it?" Mama asked.

"They want $2,000 for it. We have at least that much saved up."

It was the perfect house. It was the kind of place where normal people lived. It was beautiful from the outside, beautiful on the inside . . . it was perfect! It was a dream come true. This was terrible.

"Brian," I whispered. "What are we going to do? It's

such a beautiful house. It would be so nice to live here. And Papa and Mama are so excited. This is a revolting situation. But if we decide to live here, we won't be returning to California. All our friends will be gone. Brian, what are we going to do?!?"

"I'll just have to talk to Papa. Explain how we feel."

"What's the matter? You two. What're you whispering about? You don't look happy. What part of this house don't you like?" Papa shouted. "Do you know how hard I tried to get this house? When I found out that the Yamanakas were moving, I took him out for drinks to persuade him to sell it to us."

"It's a really beautiful house, Papa," Brian said. "It's not that we don't like it. For the first time in our lives, we would be able to live in a real house. It's perfect. The only thing is, all our friends are returning to California. Marie and I want to return to California, too. If we buy this house, that would mean we would have to stay here forever."

Papa was quiet for a moment. Then he said, "The most important thing for me is that you two are happy. I am sorry that you have had to live in the kind of places that you have. I just wanted you to be able to live in a decent place. But to be honest, I'd like to return to California, too. Everyone in our family has returned now. I especially miss Uncle Ray." He paused as he gazed out the window.

"But I know you have made friends here, so I didn't think you'd want to move again," he continued. He turned to look at us. "We've made so much progress here. If we go back to San Francisco, it'll be like starting all over again. Housing is very scarce. People are living in the Buddhist churches."

"I think we should go back anyway," I said. "If we stay here it'll be like starting all over again, anyway, since all my friends will be gone. At least we have relatives in California. And we'll be back in San Francisco, where we belong."

"What about you, Mama, what do you want to do?" Papa said.

"Of course, I want to return to California. I'd like to be able to visit Grandma. She's almost seventy. She probably doesn't have many more years left. "

"So, we're returning to California?" Brian asked.

"Papa," I asked, "is it decided we're going home?"

He nodded. "But before we celebrate, we have to find out if we can get work there. "I'll write to Ray and see if he can find me a job."

* * *

Two long weeks passed before we heard from Uncle Ray. Finally, a letter from San Francisco! Brian was the first to see it. He would have opened it and read it, had it not been written in Japanese.

"He says there are three job openings available to us!" Papa said as his eyes scrolled down and up the page. "They're crying for pressers and silk finishers. We can take our pick of jobs! Okay! We're really returning to San Francisco! Before we all go back, Uncle Ray wants me to check the jobs out for myself and find a place to live."

Then he turned to Mama.

"You'll have to tell my boss that I'm sick and can't work. It's important that you keep working while I go to San Francisco, just in case things don't work out."

"How're you going to get to San Francisco?" Brian asked.

"By car. You'll have to come with me to help with the driving."

"Wow, I'd hoped you would say that! That'll be great!" said Brian. "I get to do some serious driving!"

The next couple of days the entire family was busy

making plans for Papa and Brian's trip to San Francisco. The car had to be checked by the mechanic, clothes packed, and snacks assembled. I peeked over Papa's shoulder as he and Brian planned the route they would take to San Francisco.

Early Monday, August 3, 1946, Mama and I stood at the curb and waved to Papa and Brian as they drove off to San Francisco. For a brief moment, I was Alice, waving to me as I left San Francisco, four years earlier.

That evening Mama and I were trying to imagine how much progress they had made.

"They're probably approaching the Wyoming/Utah border by now," I said. "At least that was their goal for the first day."

Just then, there was a commotion in front of the house.

"I think we have visitors, Mama," I said. "But who'd be dropping by at this hour?"

Mama peered out the front window and gasped, "Papa and Brian are back!"

We rushed out to greet them as the cab drove off.

"What happened? Where's the car?" I shouted.

"It broke down in Cheyenne, Wyoming, and it's being fixed. We came back by bus."

"So, the car can be fixed?" asked Mama.

"It'll take a few days, but it's fixable."

The following week, Papa and Brian were off again. This time they rode the city bus to the Greyhound terminal. We didn't see them again for two weeks.

When they returned, they were brimming with news about who they saw, what they saw, and, most importantly for me, a description of the place they found for us to rent.

"It's in the middle of Japanese Town," Brian said. "We have two rooms. One at either end of a flat. The front room is really large, so you and I can share that one. It has bay windows and a fireplace. The smaller one is at the other end of the flat and the folks will use that one. We won't have our own kitchen or bathroom. We have to share them with another family. They're the owners. It's a couple, two teen-aged children, a grown daughter, and one grandchild. But the folks' room has a sink, hotplates, and eating area, so we could eat there, if we don't want to use a full-size kitchen."

"That's the best we could do," Papa said. "There is a housing shortage in San Francisco, just as I suspected. The jobs are at great cleaning shops, so I'm looking forward to working. But Uncle Ray says we should look toward buying our own business. That's what he's done already. Since we didn't buy that house, we have enough cash to do that."

"What's a bay window?" I asked.

"You explain it to her, Brian," Papa said, shaking his head. "In the meantime, we have lots to do. Let's get busy."

Papa purchased a one-wheel trailer, which he attached to the rear of our car. All our earthly belongings had to be packed on it. We also had to leave space for four recapped 550 x 17 tires, since no one made tires this size anymore. Old ones were salvaged by some garages and new treads attached. We were grateful for that. We were warned that they were not easily found outside of large cities; hence, our stockpile.

Our old car's other special need was water because of its cracked block. We filled jugs with water for the leaky block's unquenchable thirst. By the time we finished loading our car's necessities, there was little space for ours. Much like we did when we left San Francisco, we pared our things down to the bare essentials. Even so, the result was a tall, precarious heap of suitcases, bundles, tires, and water jugs that reached above the level of the roof of the car. It was evening by the time we finished arranging and packing the trailer into an acceptable mound.

The following morning, in the middle of August 1946, we left Denver and headed toward San Francisco. Foremost in everyone's mind was the hope that the aging, ailing car would safely deliver us home to California.

We headed north toward Wyoming. It was a magnificent drive. The majestic rocky crags of Colorado yielded to the soft rolling hills and meadows of Wyoming. Little streams and brooks meandered alongside the roads. After a couple of hours we pulled over to eat lunch. We parked next to a gently babbling brook that ran alongside the road and gazed in amazement at the quiet beauty of the area. We munched the rice balls and pickled vegetables Mama had prepared before dawn that morning. Ahead toward the horizon a huge wall of dark clouds appeared to be creeping toward us like a dense, dark fog. We were soon to learn that these clouds would appear in waves and become our constant companion across the entire state of Wyoming. When at last we met the clouds, we were greeted with sudden intense showers. The clouds poured on our windshield in torrents as if someone were throwing buckets of water at us. Then the rain would stop as suddenly as it started. Dark clouds would reappear in the distance, then drench us once again when we met.

Although water poured from the heavens, blurring our windshield and creating rivulets on our path, it could not satisfy the thirst of our engine's cracked block. We soon ran out of our water jug reservoir. During the breaks in the rain, we searched for sources to replenish it. We discovered that we had to be on the lookout for livestock. Livestock meant water troughs. We raided the supply of water ranchers created for horses and cows.

The first night, we didn't eat at a restaurant in the small town we passed through, for fear we wouldn't be served. Papa and Brian had had that experience on their earlier trip through the area. We stopped at a grocery store instead, and Mama bought makings for sandwiches, which we ate in the car. At nightfall, we pulled over on the side of the road and slept the best we could in the car. Hotels and motels were out of the question. They had even stricter rules about who they would and would not serve, Papa said.

From Wyoming we entered Utah. The most memorable event of that part of our trip was Salt Lake City. We were able to eat at the Chinese restaurant that Papa and Brian had found on their earlier trip.

We sat in a secluded room enclosed by a curtain. It was set up just like the Chinese restaurants in San Francisco. I felt transported to those days before the war. My excitement about returning home grew.

But most of our energy was focused on the journey, without much thought beyond that. Our trip was broken up by a series of stops for water or flat tires. Anxiety ran high that we would eventually find ourselves totally dry, or totally tire-less.

About twenty-five miles out of Winnemucca, it happened. Our last tire blew. We had no replacement. It was on a road with little traffic, in the midst of miles and miles of low shrubs and no trees. Papa shifted the weight on the trailer and unhitched it. One end sloped up to provide shade for us. We pondered our plight.

It was decided that Mama should represent our family to strangers, because she spoke better English and was a woman. Papa felt that people would be more sympathetic and less likely to be prejudiced against a woman. Tipping the scales in Mama's favor was also the fact that Papa resembled the emperor of Japan.

Mama tried to flag down the intermittent cars that passed, but no one stopped. Then Papa spotted a train in the distance running parallel to the road.

"Maybe you can stop one of those trains and ride back into Winnemucca," he said to Mama.

I tried to envision that. Mama would walk across the

desert in her cuban-heeled shoes and flag down a freight train. The engineer would stop, let her climb into the cab? Or she would run astride of the train as the engineer decelerated and she would hop on one of the cars, like they do in the movies?

Just then a pickup pulled up in front of us.

"What seems to be the trouble?" the driver asked.

Mama told him what had happened.

"I can take you back to town to a garage I think can help you," he said.

To my surprise, Papa led Mama to the pickup and opened the door for her. I couldn't believe what was happening. Papa put Mama in a total stranger's car!

"You go with him and I'll stay," Papa told Mama as he helped her climb into the cab. "Someone has to stay with the children," Papa said. With that he slammed the door shut and told us to stand back.

The pickup kicked up dust as it moved off the shoulder and swung a U-turn onto the road. I watched as the truck faded in the distance. Will I ever see Mama again, I wondered.

After what seemed like hours, a garage truck pulled up behind our stranded car with Mama sitting at the driver's side.

"I'm so glad you're safe," I said and threw my arms around her.

"Of course, she's safe!" said the driver, "and we have a couple of tires for you. Hopefully, these should take care of the rest of your trip. You'll be out of the desert soon, so your tires won't heat up so much. That's what makes them come apart."

I was so grateful to the men who came to our aid. It gave me hope to know that there was also kindness and generosity in the world. Papa was in tears and wanted to give the garage man extra money.

"You folks have been through a lot. I'm glad to be of help," he said as he took Papa's hand and closed it around the money Papa offered him.

That evening, we had dinner at a Chinese restaurant in Reno and spent our last night in the car. We were near the Nevada/California border.

The following day, Brian drove as our car labored up the mountain into California. We stopped twice to quench the car's thirst. Brian was so relieved when we finally reached the summit.

"Boy! I didn't think this car was going to make it up that grade!" he said. "It's a lot harder this second time with the car so loaded and pulling a trailer. Going down should be easy. We can just coast."

As we made the descent toward Lake Tahoe, the car began to pick up speed.

"Slow down, Brian," Papa said, "you're going too fast."

"Did you hear me? I said SLOW DOWN! You're not going to be able to make the turns! YOU'RE GOING TOO FAST!!"

"SLOW DOWN!!!"

"I can't!" said Brian, finally. "Pop, We don't have any brakes. . . . The brakes don't work anymore!"

"You were riding the brakes! You should have been pumping them!"

"I know, but they don't work anymore . . ."

"Pump them! PUMP THEM!"

The trailer whipped the car in delayed action to the curves in the road. The front and back of the car jerked in opposite directions. And cars were coming up the hill.

"Keep a good grip on the wheel! Don't oversteer!" Papa yelled.

"I'm trying my best!"

So there were curves, a "fishtailing" trailer pushing us,

and oncoming traffic. I was being thrown back and forth between the door and Mama.

"Get down on the floor, Marie! You're going to get hurt!" Mama yelled. I slid down into the well in the floor formed by the middle hump and door. I pulled my knees to my chest and curled up into a ball. We came this far and now that we've finally reached California, we're going to crash and die, I thought.

After what seemed like forever, the car stopped its jerky movements and settled into a peaceful, straight course. I crawled out of my niche back onto the seat. We were now on flat land. Miraculously, we had managed to survive. Brian pulled off the road and Papa took the wheel. He drove the grade up through Donner Pass and down into the Sacramento Valley.

In Sacramento, we stopped at a grocery store and we all went in without fear of rejection. It was a store that Papa and Brian discovered earlier. It was run by Japanese Americans. We helped Mama gather items for our lunch. Although it was very hot, we had a picnic in the shade of a huge elm tree in a nearby city park. It was the best lunch ever.

We made a detour in Richmond in the East Bay to visit my adult cousin, Brent, who was living in temporary housing the government had built during the war for shipyard workers. They lived in a real apartment with indoor plumbing and everything.

"Why don't you stay here?" Brent asked. "You won't have to share your bathroom and kitchen. It's a nice friendly little community with lots of Japanese Americans."

It would have been nice not to have to share parts of our living space, but Papa decided it was too long a commute to San Francisco. Finally, we started the last leg of our journey. We were almost home.

As we approached San Francisco Bay, a cool breeze blew

in through the open windows. The towers of the Golden Gate Bridge peeked through the fluffy white shroud that surrounded its base and most of the water. As we passed the Emeryville mudflats, the familiar odor of the black muck that carpeted its shoreline wafted into the car.

Misty puffs separated from the fogbank across the bay floated toward us. Foghorns groaned in the distance. They all seemed to be saying, "Welcome home. Marie. Welcome home!"

AFTERWORD

AN EPILOGUE OF SORTS

In commemoration of the fiftieth anniversary of Japan's attack on Pearl Harbor, a gathering of a civic organization in a neighboring town was planning a special program. Speakers were to be selected to share their recollections of that day. I was asked to speak. I was reluctant at first, but the chair of the event was someone I had known for many years and was very persuasive.

"You must share your story, Jeanette," she said. "It's an important part of our shared experience. Today with the gift of wisdom the passing years have given us, we can come together as a family to reflect and bond."

This was true. Postwar, the ban on interracial marriages was removed; racial covenants were outlawed; the McCarran-Walter Act permitted my parents to become naturalized citizens; and in 1988 we received a formal letter of apology from our government for wrongfully imprisoning us during World War II.

I was watching my mother shorten my coat that December 7th morning. I could share that and my parents' reaction to the attack. Folks could see the commonality in our diverse experiences. We were all Americans experiencing the horror of having been attacked by a common enemy. I agreed to participate.

"Great, Jeanette. I am so pleased!"

★ ★ ★

It was a Sunday afternoon. I was early, but the door was open, so I walked in to find a crowd of tall people scurrying about tending to last-minute details. It was as though I had entered a forest of moving trees. No one seemed to take note of my arrival. At other functions, there would usually be a greeter. Being that I was waist high to most of these people, they probably didn't see me. A manzanita among sequoias, I thought. This happens to me often. In restaurants, for example, a host will look past me to seat the person at his eye level. It wasn't too long ago, though, that I would interpret seeming slights as racially motivated. But I had since outgrown such paranoia. My friend was nowhere in sight. As the chair of the event, it was understandable that she would be occupied elsewhere.

No matter. I'll just look around on my own. To my right was a table with neatly arranged handouts. Mostly recruitment material for the organization. There were about fifty chairs set up in the middle of the room. I decided to take a seat toward the front. As I turned to my left, I was startled at what greeted me. "JAPS BOMB PEARL HARBOR," screamed one poster. Similar headlines on several other newspapers were mounted on poster board supported by easels.

I shouldn't have been surprised by the display. After all, this was an event to commemorate the day. But the headlines aroused a deep feeling of distress and humiliation that I thought was gone. I felt like I was caught naked in the spotlight of shame. The rush of childhood memories was released into my consciousness with a feeling of overwhelming degradation. I was transported back to December 7, 1941 and filled with the emotions of that time. I was the nine-year-old, once again. I quickly took a seat and hoped no one noticed me. I wanted to hide. Actually, I wanted to leave. I felt like an intruder at a family gathering. Like the murderer at the wake of the victim. I definitely didn't feel like a member of "the family."

On the other hand, I was an invited guest who had accepted an invitation. My deep-rooted sense of obligation, no matter how misguided, tugged against my impulse to remove myself from what I now perceived, a hostile environment.

My impulse to leave began to prevail. I decided on an escape route and was about to get up, when a young woman approached me. They aren't ignoring me, I thought. I was wrong. A "welcomer," at last!

"Is this seat taken?" she asked. I was sitting in an empty row.
"No, it isn't."
"Do you mind if I sit here?"
"Of course not."
"Are you a member here?"
"No, I'm not. Are you?"

My heart sank. She was not a member, either. But as she spoke, her warmth and kindness helped me to relax. She obviously had chosen to sit next to me because I was alone and perhaps because I was the only person in the room with a Japanese face.

She had heard about the program from a friend. She lived in the neighborhood and had young children. We found that we had each sent our children to the same pre-school, though, of course, not at the same time. We became engrossed in easy conversation.

The person in charge of the event, my friend, eventually took her place in the front of the room. It was fifteen minutes after the appointed time.

"I apologize for the delay," she began. "One of our invited speakers has not yet arrived. . . . Oh, there you are!" she said as she looked toward the door. She was just walking in. "I was worried you might not make it! I guess we can start now that everyone is here."

Well, I guess she knows I'm here, too, I thought. And she chose not to acknowledge me. My paranoia returned and was now firmly in place. I concluded that she had deliberately ignored me.

"I'd like to begin by welcoming all of you, and thank you for giving up your Sunday afternoon to attend this gathering. I'd like particularly to express my appreciation to our speakers," she said.

"The format will be rather informal. I'd like to have you speak from your seats and tell us what you were doing when Pearl Harbor was bombed."

The first speaker was a navy veteran who was in the Pacific at the time, though not at Pearl Harbor. He spoke of the anxiety he felt

243

having been at sea at the time, not certain if they would be attacked as well. It was a moving account of a sailor awaiting his inevitable duty to engage in battle.

The second speaker was an American who was in China with her parents at the time of Japan's attack. She related how her father was arrested by the Japanese who were occupying China at the time. Their family was detained as well.

The third speaker, an American whose family was visiting Japan, told how they, too, were detained by the Japanese.

Now I felt I was being held responsible for Japan's treatment of these people as well.

A voice interrupted my thoughts. "Jeanette? Jeanette? We'd like to hear your story now."

"Jeanette has a special story to tell." I felt a hand on my shoulder. I looked up and it was "my friend."

I rose from my seat and turned to face the audience

"My name is Jeanette Arakawa," I heard myself say, "and I was personally responsible for Japan's attack on Pearl Harbor. I was nine years old at the time."

"At least that's how I've felt all my life."

Then I found myself enveloped in an amazing calm. It was as though I had finally confronted a monster long embedded in me and expelled it. I felt ready to go on.

★ ★ ★

An article appeared on the editorial page of the local paper the following day. The headline read, "I WAS RESPONSIBLE FOR THE ATTACK ON PEARL HARBOR—I was 9 years old at the time."

When I told my mother, she said:

"I wouldn't say things like that, Jeanette. People might believe you."

I began writing narratives late in life. Although my early adult years were dedicated to multicultural issues and education, it was not until retirement that my writing shifted from essays to personal stories. I began keeping logs of my travels and wove them into narratives to share with friends. To my surprise, they found the stories entertaining. This prompted me to take a creative writing course through the Stanford Continuing Education Program. I was in my sixties at the time.

My first teacher, a Wallace Stegner Fellow, asked to speak to me after class one day. I had submitted two short stories. The first was about a bank robbery in which I am shot and have a near-death experience. The second was based on my World War II experience.

"Did this really happen?" the teacher asked as he threw his hand in the direction of my assignments.

"Are you asking if I've ever been shot during a bank robbery?"

He was in his thirties and had been raised on the East Coast. He was totally unaware that Japanese Americans living on the West Coast were incarcerated during World War II! He persuaded me to further elaborate and develop the story into a book for others like himself. Not insurmountable. During my years of volunteering in schools and other venues, I had assembled anecdotes that I had shared from which I could draw. He offered assistance. Unfortunately he left to study in France.

The following year, it was my good fortune to have another great teacher. Under his guidance, I continued to add to my story. That semester, there were a number of creative writing classes, and instructors were permitted to select two of their students to do readings at Stanford's Pigott Hall. My instructor selected me to be one of the speakers! In my wildest dreams, I would not have imagined that my humble attempt would be chosen. Whatever the reason, this little old lady was given the encouragement needed to continue her project.

Many years have passed since those days at Stanford. In the period that followed, my husband Kiyoto, son Doug, granddaughter Skylar, my brother George, Kiyoto's sister Yasuko, and editors

Christopher White, then Sally Barlow-Perez were inspirations to me to sustain the flow of my creative juices.

ACKNOWLEDGMENTS

I'd like to begin by thanking you for your interest in my story. I hope you were able to find some shared threads in it. I am also grateful to all others whom I have encountered during these eighty-four years of my life including my parents, brother, and extended family of my youth, as well as my husband, two sons, granddaughter, and extended families of my adulthood. My gratitude also extends to all the communities, groups, and individuals who have been my source of encouragement, strength, and support at various periods in my life.

Among the many groups and communities who helped me regain my self-confidence after WWII are the following: the Shin Buddhist temples, the Palo Alto Unified School District and PTAs; the Sequoia JACL; Asian Americans for Community Involvement; Parents' Nursery School; the Nueva Learning Center; Medaka no Gakko; Stanford Hospital Spiritual Care Volunteers; the Japanese American Museum of San Jose: and the 2019 World Buddhist Women's Convention Committee.

Also, I would be remiss not to take advantage of this unique opportunity to thank those individuals whose names happen to remain in sharp focus against the misty collage of faces in my memory, serving as surrogates for my countless mentors . . . to name a few: my incredibly faithful and tolerant friends of over fifty years, Eimi Okano, Margaret Abe, and Cyd Hatasaka (fellow Rohwer internee), the Hiura family, Rebecca Morgan, Jean Ames, John Martin, Ruth Lundy, Tsukasa Matsueda, June Matsueda, Yutaka Kawazoye, Marie Bryant, Barbara Holman, Liz Mallory, Kay Phillips, Ami Doi, Kiyo Nishiura, Charles Kubokawa, Dr. Harry Hatasaka, Floyd Kumagai, Rev. Keisho Motoyama, Evelyn Motoyama, Glenn Kameda, Joyce Miyamoto, Marjorie Nakaji, Patti Tomita, Rev. Kakuyei Tada, Mrs. Tamiko Tada, Yaeko Hirotsuka, Agnes Kuwano, Linda Kameda, Rev. Hiroshi Abiko, Misaye

Abiko, Alice Fukushima, Amy Yoshida, Dr. Allan Seid, Mari Seid, Paul Sakamoto, Ed Kawazoe, Helen Tao, Mike Honda, Virginia Debs, Annabel Jensen, Linda Stoney, Mary Laycock, Janice Carr, Dr. Taitetsu Unno, Alice Unno, Reiko Kameda, Janet Kameda, Laurie Mann, Otis Haschemeyer, Doug Dorst, Rev. Will Masuda, Kiyo Masuda, Ann Okamura, Father John Hestor, Don Gee, Meg Suzuki, Sherri Kawazoye, Dr. Nobuo Haneda, Tomoko Haneda, Steve Kaufman, Christine Blaine, Don Bender, Michael Rimkus, Noor Karr, Rev. Masako Sugimoto, Kazy Taga, Lois Takaoka, Terrie Masuda, Mike Kaku, Jimi Yamaichi, Aggie Idemoto, Leila Meyerrhatkin, Grace Ikeda, Bishop Kodo Umezu, Rev. Ron Kobata, Rev. Michael Endo, Carol Tao, Hiroko Tsuda, Janice Doi, Sumi Tanabe, Janet Umezu, Susan Bottari, Karen Suyama, Denise Montgomery, JoAnn McClennan, Jin Kaku, Peggy Okabayashi, Lois Kashiawase, Fusako Takahashi, Yumi Hatta, and Rev. Dean Koyama.

Presently, Teresa Chan, Gary Sakamoto, Rhonda Pierce, Celine Wong, Lisa Choy, Sharon Espar, Joy Chrisis, Linda Koyama, Yoko Yanari, Pamela Tom Swarts, and Mae Chen uplift the spirit and confidence of this aged person in their midst.

To you the reviewers of my book, I am deeply grateful for devoting very precious time from your busy schedules to read and evaluate this humble work.

But were it not for the ultimate encouragement and persuasion of Dr. Satsuki Ina (producer of the PBS documentary "Children of the Camps") my story would have remained a dead file in my computer. Without my Stanford Continuing Education Wallace Stegner Fellow teachers, the file would not have been conceived. And thanks to Peter Goodman, Michael Palmer, and Linda Ronan of Stone Bridge Press, The Little Exile *lives.*

In gratitude,
Jeanette S. Arakawa

JEANETTE S. ARAKAWA was born in San Francisco, California to Japanese immigrants. Between 1942 and 1945, during World War II, she was part of a diaspora that took her to Stockton, California, Rohwer, Arkansas, and Denver, Colorado. She returned to San Francisco in 1946. Jeanette and her husband, Kiyoto, have two sons and a granddaughter. Over the years Jeanette's devotion to educational issues has permitted her to share her experiences in the classroom as well as other forums. She continues to be an active member of her temple. Writing, line dancing, taiko (Japanese drumming), and singing occupy the spaces available in her busy life. She lives in the San Francisco Bay Area.